THE GIRL BETWEEN
TWO WORLDS

The *Girl* between *Two Worlds*

K.M. LEVIS

ANVIL
TEENS

THE GIRL BETWEEN TWO WORLDS
by Kristyn Maslog-Levis

Copyright © 2016
Kristyn Maslog-Levis

Published and exclusively distributed by
ANVIL PUBLISHING, INC.
7th Floor Quad Alpha Centrum Building
125 Pioneer Street, Mandaluyong City 1550 Philippines
Telephones: (+632) 477-4752, 477-4755 to 57
Fax: (+632) 747-1622
anvilsalesonline@anvilpublishing.com
marketing@anvilpublishing.com
www.anvilpublishing.com

Book design by Dani Hernandez (cover) and Joshene Bersales (interior)
Illustrations by Marrow Jerry Cabodel

First printing, 2016
Second printing, 2018

The National Library of the Philippines CIP Data

Recommended entry:

Levis, Kristyn-Maslog-.
    The girl between two worlds / Kristyn
Maslog-Levis. -- Mandaluyong City : Anvil
Publishing, Inc., (2016), 2016.
 pages ; cm

ISBN 978-971-27-3360-4

1. Spiritualism. 2. Spiritual warfare. I. Title

133.9   BF1261.2   2016   P620160178

Printed in the Philippines

For Inara,
when she is old enough

Engkantos are forest spirits that appear in human form. People have believed in their existence for centuries.

When you walk in the forest, say "tabi po" (excuse me) lest you kick an Engkanto sitting on the path.

Offer something to the Engkanto before you cut a tree so you do not get slapped.

When you cannot find your way home and the road seems to change, wear your shirt inside out to appease the Engkanto.

Never fall in love with an Engkanto. It will take you to their kingdom and you can never return.

Chapter One

The creature was outside the house, flapping batlike wings and trying to find a way in. I dropped to the floor and started crawling to the window, hoping it wouldn't spot me. If it was a dangerous thing that I had managed to attract, then I needed to do something to stop it.

It was so close to the window that I inhaled a whiff of rotting meat. The full moon illuminated the creature as it flew past. I froze and looked up in time to see a pair of red eyes staring at me from the other side of the window. There was a collective gasp from my friends. It was definitely not a bat. There was a faint trace of a human figure—no, the upper half of a human figure with bat wings the size of a sail.

It defied all rational explanation. Despite being cut in half, the monstrous creature was flying in the middle of suburban San Francisco. Its entrails were hanging out of its body. There was nothing where its lower half should be.

There were books I had read about scary folklore when I was a little girl in the Philippines. Creatures that could split their bodies into two. The upper half—head, torso, and arms—would fly across the night sky and hunt for babies to eat, while the lower half remained on the ground. Right now, I desperately wanted to believe those stories were just products of eccentric writers trying to scare little girls and boys. But it looked like they were true sightings.

The creature looked female with long dark hair and pale skin, but what scared me the most was its face. The red eyes bulged and glowed in the dark, like a crocodile sneering at its prey. Its face was like a wolf's snout skinned down and dripping with blood. Its teeth were like broken glass and its tongue was a meter long and several inches wide. It was wearing a white blouse covered in blood. Was the blouse a part of its disguise during the day so it could blend in with the humans?

I could not move from my spot. None of us said anything, afraid to breathe, shaking in fear. I knew immediately I was in big trouble because I had no idea how to overpower this creature. I was not even sure if it was what I thought it was. I was warned that dark beings would try to kill me, but this monstrosity was more grotesque than what I had imagined.

There was nothing in the room that could be used as a weapon. The creature outside was becoming more aggressive. It was trailing its claws on the walls. We could hear the screech of its nails against the bricks. It was taunting us.

A whip slammed through the windows, pushing it open. We staggered away, half crawling, half stumbling to the other end of the room. The whip sliced through the blinds, except that it was not really a whip. It was the thing's tongue, stretching longer and longer, trying to reach us.

A thought entered my head, as clear as daylight: I was going to die tonight.

Chapter Two

San Francisco Tribune, May 2012
New Migrant Goes Missing

The disappearance of new migrant from the Philippines, Marie Harris, from her home in San Jose has left authorities baffled.

Initial investigation has revealed no evidence of forced entry to the home she shares with her Australian husband and daughter. According to a police spokesperson, Harris arrived in her home on the May 24 and had dinner with the family before heading off to bed. When her husband woke up, Harris was not in the bed or in the house. Her wallet, phone, car and house keys, and clothes were all found in the same place she left them the night before. All the windows and doors were still locked and there was no sign of footprints surrounding the house.

Sniffer dogs were used to track her down but without success. The family's neighbors say they didn't hear or see anything that night. Harris arrived in California only weeks before her disappearance. The police are asking anyone with information to come forward by calling the Crime Stoppers hotline 1300-333-000.

June 2015

My name is Karina Harris and I had the worst couple of months of my life.

I lived a quiet life. No monsters with batlike wings ever followed me around. I didn't even have a pet.

That creature with the wide tongue and half body was never part of my life. No creatures were ever part of my life.

Let me start from the beginning—the night before my sixteenth birthday.

I dreamt of Mama. I knew it was a dream because Mama was with me. Not missing nor dead, like the police believed.

In the dream, she was with other people in a place I had never seen before. It was hazy but I could make out the gray concrete floor and chipped bricks surrounding them. I couldn't see much of anything else. I was shaking. It felt like I had just seen something I wasn't supposed to see. Mama looked at me. Suddenly, we were back in the house.

She was telling me they had decided to give me a car. I was jumping and hugging them, so ecstatic to have both my parents there. But Mama started fading—her feet turned into dust, blown away by an invisible wind. Her legs disappeared, then her arms, until nothing was left of her. I tried to scream for her to come back, but I couldn't speak. I woke up, sweat trickling down my face, my heart pumping so hard it felt like my chest was going to explode.

I clutched my necklace in the dark. It was a simple leather string with a small red rock pendant. It was the last thing Mama gave me before she disappeared.

"No matter what happens, never take this off. Ever. Do you understand me?" Mama instructed, wearing the most serious look I had ever seen on her face.

"I promise, Mama. But you're scaring me," I answered.

"I'm sorry, Karina. Don't be scared. It's just important for me to know that you will carry this with you always."

She kissed me goodnight then left the room. It was the last time I saw her. I had never taken the necklace off, not even once.

Looking in the mirror that morning, I saw myself as the splitting image of Mama. The same brown hair and light brown eyes that turned hazel when light hit it. When I smiled, it was Mama's smile that stared back at me. Dad even said that sometimes when I get annoyed and raise my eyebrow, I looked exactly like Mama.

I was heading for the shower when my window opened with a bang, making me jump. And then I heard it, the faint sound of her voice.

"You look beautiful, Karina." I looked in the mirror and saw Mama in her nightdress. It was the same one she wore the night she disappeared. I turned but there was no one there. I looked in the mirror again but she was gone.

I thought I had gone crazy that my mind was playing tricks on me. It had been three years since we migrated to the United States. It had also been three years since Mama vanished into thin air. The police had given up hope finding her. Their investigation ended nowhere. They tried pinning it on Dad for a while. They made it seem like he was some weird Australian guy who impregnated an Asian woman just for the heck of it. But with no evidence to back their allegations, they had to let him go.

Dad insisted I throw a party for my birthday. Maybe he thought a party would distance me from the infamy of Mama's case. I knew he did not want me to know about it but I had seen him on the computer every night. His browsers were opened to missing persons' websites and forums. He had hired a private investigator recommended by some of the people he met online. He had not given up hope and that gave me some comfort.

Where was I? Oh yes, the monster. I really thought I was a goner then. You would, too, if you saw and smelled that disgusting tongue inches from your face.

Before it could reach us, a bright light shone from outside. The thing turned around and let out a screech. I could smell its burning flesh as it quickly flew away, smacking against a few branches.

My best friends, Mark and Alyssa, let out a huge sigh of relief. We quickly looked out the window to see where the light came from. I caught a glimpse of my grandfather disappearing into the night like a true superhero.

It was funny how only a couple of weeks ago I did not even know my grandfather was alive. Lolo saved us but he might as well be a stranger. I only met him after I turned sixteen. He showed up at my door the same day my powers emerged.

It was the morning after my birthday party. I was happy to have just my best friends there. I didn't want a big party. It wasn't like I didn't have any friends or I hated everyone. It was just that Mama's case had followed me everywhere, especially at school. I had only been going to Rose Garden Private for a couple of weeks when Mama disappeared. They treated me differently after that, like I was a leper, like my sorrow was contagious. I knew what they said behind my back. Stories had circulated and changed over the years mainly because of the lack of conclusive evidence as to what really happened.

Some kids said she was a prostitute in the Philippines and that she ran off with a rich Australian businessman. Some stories said she had psychological problems and was kicked out of the country. Others believed my father killed her and buried her in our yard while I was sleeping. Hanging out with those kids was not my idea of fun on my birthday.

The house was quiet the morning after the party. No parents with their coffees and Sunday papers. I heard a beep and looked at my phone. It continued to buzz but it was an unfamiliar number.

"Hello, Karina speaking."

I heard a buzzing sound at the other end, and nothing else. For a moment, I thought it was a wrong number. But then a man's voice came through, solid and authoritative, like the voice of a commanding officer in one of those war shows on TV.

"Karina? Is that you?"

"Yes. Who is this, please?"

"This is your grandfather."

"Knoppy?" I asked, thinking it was a long-distance phone call from my father's dad in Australia.

"No. This is your Lolo, your mama's father."

I froze. Mama always said my Lolo died a long time ago. Was I getting a call from the grave? My heart raced as fear gripped my body. I sat down, not trusting my feet to hold my body up.

"It can't be. Mama said you died a long time ago. Are you . . . dead?" It was a ridiculous thing to ask, but I had to. Could ghosts use mobile phones?

"No, I'm not, little one. I just arrived from a long journey and now I'm here. I will see you very soon."

The line went dead. I had always wondered why Mama never talked about her family. I had never met a single relative on my mother's side and I never questioned that.

She said she ran away from home after her parents died and that she didn't have many relatives growing up. Mama said there was a huge fight and she was afraid something bad would happen to her so she ran away. Every time she told me the story, she would make them all sound so horrible that I used to pray as a kid that they never find us. Sometimes I imagined my grandparents were spies and Mama had to run away to protect their identities.

I had all these thoughts swirling in my head when I saw the yellow flowers Dad bought for my birthday. Yellow flowers always cheered me up. It was a shame that some of them were already wilting.

I touched a yellow rose that had started to go brown. Slowly, the brown parts changed color, firming up to my touch and becoming golden yellow again. I pulled my hand away and quickly stood, knocking the chair down in the process.

The healthy yellow rose was wilting just a minute ago. Now it stood straight in the center of the vase, fresh and vibrant. I touched another flower that was starting to go brown in the edges but nothing happened. I started touching all of the flowers—still nothing.

But I knew it happened.

That was how it all began. I turned sixteen, Lolo called, and then the yellow flower came back to life.

That was how I got myself into trouble.

I was instructed not to use my new abilities outside of our home because of the possibility that our enemies would sense me. I didn't listen. Whoever they were, they tracked down where Alyssa lived. I shuddered at the thought of what the monster could have done to us had Lolo not arrived in time. I knew Lolo would tell Dad what happened. No amount of grounding would make me feel as bad as I felt.

After the attack, we locked the windows and drew the curtains, seeing the traces of claws against the wall outside. I walked back to the bed where Mark and Alyssa huddled under the blanket, staring at me with wide eyes.

"What was that?" Alyssa whispered in the dark.

"I'm not too sure, but I have a feeling I'm going to be getting some really bad news when I get home tomorrow," I said, still whispering.

"That looked like the ugliest vampire I've ever seen," Mark said, moving closer to us.

We all tried to go back to sleep. No one talked after that. We were all frightened by the vision we saw outside the window. Minutes later, Mark moved his sleeping bag closer to our bed. We continued to stare at the ceiling, waiting for the sun to come out. We drifted in and out of sleep. We woke up every time one of us moved, scared that the monster was outside the window again.

Life just got more dangerous. I had to be more careful, more responsible. That incident had made it clear that I would be responsible for more than just myself.

17

Chapter Three

San Francisco Tribune, June 2012
Husband of Missing Migrant Arrested

The police have arrested the husband of the Filipino migrant who went missing last month, shortly after arriving in California.

Marie Harris left no clues behind when she suddenly disappeared from her San Jose home. Her husband has been taken into custody as the primary suspect.

The police are refusing to comment whether they have evidence against Harris's Australian husband. Last month, the case baffled authorities as they found no trace of Harris leaving the house the night she disappeared. They are asking anyone with information to come forward by contacting the Crime Stoppers hotline.

June 2015

The first time I realized I had abilities, I tried making it happen again. I remembered what I was thinking before I touched the flower. I was thinking that it was sad that such a pretty flower was dying so soon. I felt an intense desire to make it pretty again but at the same time I felt sad I couldn't do anything to bring it back to life.

I leaned closer to the vase. I looked for the sorriest flower in the bunch and saw a limping yellow gerbera. I took a deep breath and thought about how much I wanted the flower to be pretty again. I pictured how I wanted it to look in my head and slowly touched its bowing stem. The flower started to lift, the stem turning greener and slowly firming up. Fresh color spread to the petals, like ink spilled on paper.

I took the flower out of the vase and stared at it. The yellow gerbera looked like it had been freshly picked from the ground.

At the back of my mind, I knew it was just the beginning of something bigger. The first thing I did was go to Mark's place with Alyssa to figure things out.

"This better be good," said a very cranky Mark when I called him.

"Alyssa and I are outside. We have pancakes. Come down and let us in." I heard Mark grunt before the line went dead. He loved sleeping in.

I heard footsteps from inside the house, and Mark opened the door. He was still in his pajamas, his hair sticking up on one side and flat on the other. Despite my nervous post-birthday morning, I couldn't help but laugh. Alyssa also bursted out laughing as we entered the hallway leading to his room.

"Shut up, Mom's still sleeping," he whispered.

Mark's mom was so used to having us in the house that she didn't really care how often we dropped by, even when it was unannounced. I think she was hoping one of us would end up as her son's girlfriend. But the thought of Mark having romantic feelings for me or Alyssa sent chills down my spine. It wasn't like he's ugly. As a matter of fact, I knew some of the girls at school had a crush on him. But Mark was like my long lost brother, and that was how I'd always see him. He'd been my sidekick ever since I arrived in San Jose.

Mark was a dorky version of the nasty brother in *The Vampire Diaries*. He had the potential of becoming a hunk, but somehow he was missing an ingredient—coordination. He was a big klutz and totally hopeless at sports or anything close to physical movement. His superpower was his brain. Mark was a genius, although not a lot of people knew about it. I liked him because he was the only one I knew who could top my addiction to books. He was someone who understood why hanging out in secondhand bookstores was better than going to the mall.

I met Mark a couple of weeks after we moved to Rose Garden. I was still very new to the country and didn't have any friends. He didn't seem to be the type who talked to random people, but something must have compelled him to open his mouth. I was in the library, holding a copy of a very old Nancy Drew novel. There were other books piled on the floor. We sat on the floor in silence, going through book after book. We compared our own collections and criticized each other's favorites. We did not even realize the library was already closing.

After that, we hung out a lot more, reading books, buying books, reviewing new ones that came out. Alyssa joined our group shortly after, and although she wasn't into books as much as Mark and I, she ended up being a good part of our trio.

I first met Alyssa on my way home from school. She was trying to get gum off of her long blonde hair with no luck. I could see she was close to tears so I went up to her to help, but I was too late. She had already managed to spread the gum so that it had become a huge clump of monstrous tangled hair.

I offered to help her. We walked to my place from school without talking. I didn't really know what to say to her and she was still obviously distressed about the gum-in-the-hair situation. When we got home, Mama looked at the mess and made us a cup of rich hot chocolate. Mama brought out her bag of hairstyling tools and started working on Alyssa's hair. She talked to Alyssa about little things and cracked a joke or two that made us laugh.

Finally, Mama finished cutting Alyssa's hair. When Alyssa saw the pile of hair on the floor, her eyes widened and she looked like she was about to cry again. But before she could open her mouth, Mama handed her the mirror. Alyssa smiled when she saw her reflection.

Mama may not be good at a lot of things, but she had great skill in hairstyling. Alyssa's long hair had been replaced with a very fancy-looking bob that framed her face perfectly, though in reality, she'd still look great even with a shaved head.

Of course, that was three years ago and the dynamics had changed a bit. Alyssa was currently the most popular girl in school but she never became snobby. I'd like to think I had something to do with that.

"Okay, so what's going on? It's Sunday morning. We are supposed to be sleeping in," Mark's comment brought me back to my predicament.

"I have no idea. She wouldn't tell me anything until we got here."

"Move," I grabbed the pillow Mark was using to cover his head. He was still desperately hoping to get more sleep. His room was small but very tidy, much tidier than mine, in fact. 21 His bed was pushed to one corner to make room for a giant desk covered with computers, cables, and various contraptions he'd been working on. His extensive book collection was neatly stacked in a makeshift bookcase that covered one of the walls from floor to ceiling. I helped him build it one afternoon, and by help, I meant I handed him the nails.

After Mark's dad died, his mom had to juggle several jobs to keep things afloat. Mark had three part-time jobs to help her out. At night, he moonlighted as a cheap "web designer." I knew he did other computer things, some not so legal, but I didn't meddle in his business. I knew how much they needed the money.

"I want to show you guys something I did this morning. You're not going to believe it." I pulled out the bouquet from the bag and placed it on the bed.

"Your birthday bouquet? We saw that yesterday," Mark said.

"Yes you did, but you didn't see this," I said, pulling out a yellow rose from the bunch. I placed it on the bed where we could all see it, then I touched one of the brown petals.

"What are we supposed to . . . " Mark started to say but I immediately shushed him.

I closed my eyes and touched the flower again. Everyone was silent for several minutes, staring at my hand on the petal. Just as Mark started to speak again, the flower began to change. The wilting petal turned from brown to bright yellow, then the rest of the flower followed suit. The other petals were restored to a bright yellow, and the stem's color turned green. A quiet gasp escaped from both Mark and Alyssa as the leaves and thorns that had been removed from the stem started to grow back. I pulled my hand away, surprised at the transformation.

"Wow!" I looked at Alyssa, her mouth hanging open. I stared at the flower, just as perplexed as they were.

"How did you . . . " Alyssa asked.

"I don't know. I woke up this morning and it seemed like nothing had changed, but when I touched one of the flowers, it just happened."

"This is scientifically impossible," Mark said, scratching his head, turning the flower in his hand.

"I pictured what I wanted to happen in my head and just kind of felt it. When I touched the flower, that's what happened. I am scared and I can't talk to my dad."

"Why not?" Alyssa asked.

"Someone called me this morning. I got a call from my grandfather. You know, the one who was supposed to be dead?"

"Holy crap! Seriously? Fantastic! You should document this and investigate it. A real paranormal activity. How amazing is that?!" Mark sat up on the bed, fully awake, absolutely excited by the news.

"He's not really dead, you dufus. Mama lied to me." Even before the words escaped my mouth, I regretted saying it.

Mama was not one to lie, but it seemed that she had kept a giant secret from us for a very long time.

"Why is it that the really cool things only happen to other people and not to me?" Mark ducked as Alyssa tried to hit his head with a pillow.

"He said he'll see me very soon. I'm scared but also curious. What if he knows where Mama is? Mama was never comfortable talking about her past. She always gave me vague answers."

"If your grandfather knows anything, I don't think he has any choice but to tell you the truth after what you just did. This is not an ordinary thing to keep from you," Alyssa said.

"Will you show your dad this new magic trick?" Mark asked.

"I'm not sure. I think I need to find answers first before showing him. Will you guys come with me?"

"Sure. It's not like we have anything bigger to attend to today anyway."

We walked to my house and the two of them walked in like it was their own home. I stood there for a moment, watching them. It had been over a year since we decided to move out of the house we shared with Mama. It became too much for us to wake up in that house, wondering every day if she might be back in the kitchen making us breakfast.

In the end, Dad decided to rent it out while we moved to a smaller place just a couple of blocks away. Every now and then, when I was deep in thought, I'd find myself walking home from school to the old house, like my feet had a mind of their own. I think a part of me was hoping that Mama would be waiting there, wondering why strangers were living in her house.

I remember the first time we moved in that house. Mama was glowing. She was as bouncy as a little girl in Disneyland. There were a lot of boxes to unpack but she loved unpacking them. She loved settling in the house, decorating it and turning it into a home. She loved the promise of a fresh start. She pulled me close one day to tell me something.

"We are very lucky to have this place, but you must never forget where you came from," she told me. "You must always remember that there are others who don't have what we have. Be thankful for the blessings you have now."

A tear ran down my cheek and I quickly wiped it away before anyone saw it.

Chapter Four

San Francisco Tribune, August 2012
Still No Clue on Missing Migrant

The police are continuing their search for Marie Harris, the Filipino migrant who disappeared from her home in May shortly after arriving in the country.

After three months of investigation, authorities have not found any new evidence to explain the disappearance of Harris. Her husband was cleared of any wrongdoing after authorities failed to secure evidence against him.

The case is gaining interest from various immigration bodies asking for a more thorough assessment of migrants given a visa to live in America.

"This is a clear case of failure on the part of the immigration department. There is very little support for migrants after entering the country. We don't know what these people are going through psychologically and emotionally," says Susan Boyd from the Fil-Am Migrants Association.

The Philippine government has also urged American authorities to continue their search for Harris. The case has gained interest in Harris's home country where politicians are now calling for changes in legislation related to citizens migrating overseas, as well as for overseas workers.

June 2015

Mama used to say the stars had to align just the right way to create me—like the stars somehow had something to do with my conception. It was a good fantasy. It made me feel extra special, and not mind that I looked different from other Filipinos. I was referred to as mestiza, a term coined during the Spanish era and used specifically for people of Filipino and Caucasian racial mix.

Being different from everyone else elicited a lot of gawking from people. I wanted to be alone so much, to find a place where no one could watch me. Everything changed after I found the public library—a quiet old building rarely used by people. It was there that I read my first non-children's Filipino folklore tales.

More and more I explored the library, borrowing books by the bulk and reading as much as I could. I found myself getting pulled into the fantasy genre when I was ten years old. I became fascinated with stories about mythical creatures like the *engkanto*—said to be beautiful creations living in a mystical kingdom that couldn't be seen by humans. Many of the stories said that once a human was invited into their kingdom, he could never get out. Sometimes, I fantasized about being invited to this magical kingdom. I would stare outside my window for a long time, pretending to see little men living under a tree, or a fairy floating around a new bloom.

The first and only time I mentioned this to Mama was when I took one of my favorite books about the *engkanto* kingdom with me to bed, expecting her to read it to me. But when she saw it, she went pale and told me not to waste my efforts on reading about such fictional kingdoms and creatures. She didn't seem angry with me. It was more like she saw a ghost.

Mama had always been reasonable with me, so when she asked this one favor, I agreed. But weeks later, I couldn't help myself. Something compelled me to go to that section of the library, so instead of taking these books home, I went somewhere else where Mama wouldn't see me reading them.

That was why I was quite surprised when I found an old book stashed behind the wardrobe after Mama disappeared. Had we not moved houses, I wouldn't have found it. It was an old children's book naming all the creatures of Filipino mythology. The only difference was that this one was heavily edited in Mama's handwriting. She took out sentences that described the creatures and wrote the descriptions herself. It was like she was creating a new folklore or correcting the one commonly known to Filipinos.

Not just that, she also added details to the simple drawings of the book. There were claws, fangs, and fur in places that the book didn't have. Sometimes the drawings were totally crossed out that you couldn't see it. And in the margins were very detailed charcoal pencil drawings of the monsters. I never told Dad about the book. I hid it in my room. Every now and then, I would pick it up and touch Mama's handwriting, like it would bring her back to me.

I dreaded the thought of facing Dad and asking him about Lolo. If he didn't know about my grandfather, too, he'd feel just as betrayed, and I didn't want to add more pain to my dad's pile of sorrows.

We sat in the living room, quietly waiting for one of us to make the first move. I stood up to find Dad when I heard a knock on the door. My heart beat a bit faster. No one visited us aside from Mark and Alyssa, and they never knocked. I opened the door and gasped. Standing in front of me was an old man who was the splitting image of Mama.

"Good morning, Karina. I am your grandfather, Lolo Magatu," the man said, extending a tanned hand. His grip was firm but reassuring, and a feeling of calm unexpectedly washed over me. I had learned about stranger danger my whole life, more so after Mama disappeared. But there was a familiarity with this man I could not describe, like we had known each other for a long time.

"Lolo?" I said, the words foreign on my lips.

"Yes mija, I am your Lolo."

Mija, he called me by the pet name that Mama has for me.

He continued, "My apologies for giving you a fright this morning, but I think it's time you know about your mother's real life."

I could feel the tension rising in the room. No one moved, afraid to break the silence.

"I know this is a shock for you but it is extremely necessary that you find out. I know your power has already revealed itself this morning. You need to be able to control your abilities, and fast."

My mind was a jumble of thoughts and questions. It was difficult for me to come up with a reply. When I heard Dad come in the living room, my heart raced even faster.

"Hey, I thought you were out . . . " Dad stopped when he saw Lolo. I knew he could see the uncanny resemblance to Mama, like they were cast from the same mold.

"You're Marie's father," he said, walking toward us. Lolo nodded and extended his hand. "But how . . . "

"And you must be Patrick. It is a pleasure to finally meet you."

Dad gestured for Lolo to come in, unable to say anything else. Mark and Alyssa made room for everyone in the living room. They have been so quiet, I almost forgot they were there.

"I'm sorry to tell you this," Dad said, trying to steady his voice, "but Marie has been missing for several years now and we don't know where she is."

Lolo only nodded to Dad, not surprised at all by the revelation. "I know. That's why I'm here."

"I don't understand," Dad said. Lolo turned to me, looking at my hands clenching and unclenching.

"Your mother only ever wanted for you to have a normal life. But I knew that was never going to be possible. I need you to know that she did everything she could to delay this. But all this is inevitable."

"What is inevitable? What are you talking about? Karina, what's going on?" Dad said, his voice rising.

"Should your friends be here for this?" Lolo said, ignoring Dad's questions.

"I trust them, and they already know about what I can do. I'd rather have them here."

"Then you better sit down, all of you. I am Hari Magatu," he said to Mark and Alyssa.

"Harry?" Mark whispered to Alyssa. Lolo looked at him and I swear I could see Mark shrivel up.

"Hari is Filipino for King," I said to Mark. "Hold on. King? Like royalty? How can you be royalty?" I tried to calm myself so I could hear what he had to say over the rapid beating of my heart.

"Your mother ran away from home when she was sixteen. She is the princess of our world."

"World?"

"My world is called Engkantasia and I am the king. We are not humans, but we look like one. Your mother was raised to be the next ruler of Engkantasia, but she did not want the responsibility, so she ran away."

I looked at the family photo near Lolo. It was taken the day before we moved to San Jose. We were all smiles, excited about the new life we were going to live. It seemed so long ago that sometimes I think it never really happened.

"Isn't that like in your old books, Karina?" Mark asked.

"Yes, the *engkanto*. Engkantasia. They're just stories from books. Like deities of the forest that play tricks on humans. Just children's stories," I replied, my voice breaking a bit.

"Our world is surrounded by areas with heavy rainforests. It is invisible to humans, but we have the ability to see the human world. When your Mama ran away, she lived in heavily populated areas, far from any traces of the rainforest. Have you noticed that she never wanted to go camping or spend holidays in the mountains?"

I remembered how Mama insisted we go somewhere else when I said I wanted to see the rice terraces of Banaue before we migrated. I never really understood her desire to stay in the city all the time.

"I'm sorry but this is all too much to take in. If you were me, you wouldn't believe any of this. It's crazy . . . "

But before I finished my sentence, Lolo held up his arm. Instead of a hand, I saw green vines with flowers surrounded by a light yellow glow. He placed his arm on the coffee table and leaves and various plants I had never seen before sprouted from it. I heard a collective gasp and I realized I had been holding my breath. He spoke again, unperturbed by our reactions, like what he was doing was the most natural thing in the world.

"Your mother never expected to have a family. She feared for you. She knew you would become our world's ruler one day, and she didn't want that life for you."

"Ruler?" I searched his face, still reeling from the vision in front of me. "What do you mean ruler? Am I supposed to live in Engkantasia?"

Lolo hesitated. The vines, leaves and flowers slithered back into his arm, changing our surroundings back into a normal living room.

"Our world is in danger. After your mother ran away, there was a battle for the throne. She was supposed to rule the land when I passed on, but . . . " Lolo paused, staring at the family photo. "We managed to stop the threat but it's gotten stronger over the years. When I found out about Marie's disappearance from your world, I sent out my best soldiers to find her."

"And?" Dad said, hanging on to Lolo's every word. Lolo shook his head and let out a deep sigh.

"Even all my powers were of no help in locating Marie. No one can sense any trace of her, which is unusual. This tells me your mother's disappearance was not of this world. I traveled here to be with you when you turned sixteen because it is after this birthday that your heritage manifests."

"Heritage?" Dad said, looking at me.

"This morning, I touched a dying flower and brought it back to life. I wanted to tell you but I didn't want to believe it was really happening," I told him. I felt guilty that I hid it from him, no matter how brief.

Dad squeezed my shoulder and kissed my head, like he always does when he's comforting me. "Was it painful? Were you in pain?"

"No, Dad, I'm okay. It wasn't like that," I smiled, hoping it would make him feel better. Then I remembered what I saw in the mirror. "Lolo, when I woke up this morning, I heard Mama say something to me, and when I looked in the mirror, she was there but then she disappeared. I thought I was just going crazy but now I'm not so sure."

"What did she say? What did she look like?" Dad said.

"She said I look beautiful," I whispered, holding back tears as I remembered her image in the mirror. "She was wearing the same dress she wore the night she disappeared."

I looked at Lolo and caught him looking at my necklace. I instinctively touched it, like I would when I felt nervous, caressing its smooth surface and willing it to give me strength.

"Who gave you that necklace?"

"Mama did. She gave it to me the night before she disappeared," I said, still holding on to the stone.

"May I?"

I nodded and moved closer to him. Lolo held the stone and I saw light coming from it, getting brighter and brighter. A burst of air escaped Lolo's hand, making me close my eyes. When I opened them, I saw images of Mama everywhere in the house—as a child, growing up in unfamiliar surroundings and even more unfamiliar creatures. It looked like we were staring at memories of Mama.

"Is that your mom?" Alyssa asked, which startled me a bit as she hadn't said anything for a while.

"I think so," I said, also uncertain at what I was actually seeing. "Lolo, are these Mama's memories?"

Lolo released the stone and all the images were sucked back into it. There was deep sadness in Lolo's eyes, so familiar because I had seen it in my dad's every single day. It must be hard for Lolo especially since he hadn't seen Mama for a very long time. Although I had only met him, I felt like we had shared a lifetime together. I reached out and touched his hand, surprising him with my gesture.

"What you just saw were your mother's memories and mine. When she gave you that stone, she gave you everything she had. Her powers, her memories, her secrets. She did it to protect you."

"Why would Karina need protection?" Mark said. He looked nervous.

"There are creatures from Engkantasia, dark ones, who are determined to take over the throne. This means destroying any possible heirs."

"Including Karina," Dad said, gripping my hand. "But she's only sixteen. What are we supposed to do about all this?" Dad was starting to panic. Who could blame him? The life we knew was unravelling fast yet again.

"No one can force Karina to do anything. She has to want to become the ruler of Engkantasia. If she does, she has a lot of training to go through in so little time. She needs to get stronger so she can defend herself."

"You must understand that her powers will keep manifesting if she doesn't take control of it," Lolo continued. "She is not only in danger, but she could also be a danger to everyone around her. This mix of human and *engkanto* has been forbidden for thousands of years. It brings complications to our existence. The last time this happened, it almost destroyed both worlds."

"If that is the case, then why come for Karina? Why ask her to take the throne? She is human. She doesn't belong in your world," Dad said. His hand gripped mine tightly.

"We are running out of options. I agree that this is unprecedented but it's for the greater good," Lolo sighed.

Just when I thought we were slowly getting our lives back, something tore it to pieces again. Fear and uncertainty never seemed to leave our lives.

"What can we do to protect ourselves? What can I do to protect Karina?" Dad asked, gripping my hand so hard it started to hurt.

"Marie was supposed to help Karina hone her abilities, but I think she already knew something was going to happen to her. Otherwise, she wouldn't have left herself vulnerable and given all her powers to Karina," Lolo answered.

He looked at the necklace again, touching it lightly. "This stone has been protecting you since your mother disappeared. But now you need more than that to overcome what is about to happen. That is why I'm here, to train you like I trained your mother."

I still had a million questions but I could not say anything. I felt like all the energy had been sucked out of me and I just wanted to sleep forever. I looked around the room and it seemed like everyone was feeling the same way. I excused myself and headed upstairs, crashed on my bed and closed my eyes. I wished that when I woke up, it would all be nothing but a dream.

Chapter Five

San Francisco Tribune, October 2012
Missing Migrant Feared Dead

After months without progress, authorities have resigned the case of the missing Filipino migrant as a recovery effort.

Marie Harris, the Filipino migrant who disappeared from her house without a trace shortly after she migrated to America with her family, is feared to be dead.

However, her family remains optimistic that they will find her, organizing their own search operations outside of the police investigation.

34

June 2015

Did you ever get that feeling that something was nearby but you couldn't see anything? You'd hear tiny sounds of scampering or the frantic wings of an insect but you coudn't quite figure out where it was coming from.

It was like that time when we were still living in the Philippines and I slept under a mosquito net. I woke up in the middle of the night after hearing the buzz of cockroach wings. People always thought I was crazy to say that I knew the sound of cockroach wings, but I did. I knew the sound that my worst fear made. I opened my eyes in a panic, adjusting in the dark. I saw the little bugger crawling on top of the mosquito net. I kept telling myself that it was outside the net—that it couldn't possibly crawl inside. But at the back of my mind I knew it wasn't true. Sure enough, the giant cockroach dropped on my face.

That was how I felt when I woke up in my dark bedroom. A sense that there was something close, something dangerous. Something I should fear. But I couldn't quite figure out what it was. Did I hear something that woke me up? Did I see a glimpse of a shadow in the corner of my room? Of course, that was before the monster ever came to slice me with its tongue so I was adamant that I had nothing to worry about.

I was not sure how long I dozed off after that dramatic exit from my meeting with Lolo. My hair was sticking to my face and I was sweating under the comforter. The house was quiet and I almost convinced myself it was all a dream. But then I heard voices coming from the living room. I sat up, contemplating on whether I should join them or not. Maybe I could just stay in the room forever and bury my head under the pillow.

I took a deep breath and headed outside my room to find Dad. I found him in the living room, staring at the TV, a can of beer in his hand.

"Hey Dad, where is everyone?"

He turned around and smiled, already a bit tipsy. "Mark and Alyssa left after you went to sleep. They said they'll see you tomorrow at school."

"And Lolo?" I asked hesitantly, a part of me hoping he was just a figment of my imagination. I heard Dad sigh.

"He's in the guest bedroom," he said so quietly I almost didn't hear him.

"Oh." I guess that was that. "Is he staying with us then?"

Dad nodded, and continued to drink his beer. I was hoping to talk to Dad about everything but it didn't seem like the right time.

Instead I went to the spare room to find Lolo. There were more questions I needed to ask him. I raised my hand to knock on the door when I heard him.

"Come in, Karina."

I turned the knob and peeked inside the room. It was dark and quiet. The bedside lamp was off but there was a luminescent glow in the corner of the room. I blinked to adjust my eyes to the darkness and walked inside.

"Lolo? Where are you?"

I saw the glowing thing move toward me and I realized he was holding it in his hand. It was ball of light floating around like a torch, except this one didn't need batteries.

"I thought this might be a more sustainable source of light than that," he said, pointing to the lamp. He took my hand and placed the light on my palm. It should feel warm, but I sensed nothing. I waved my hand around and it just sat there, following my palm. I moved to the bedside table and turned on the lamp, filling the room with more light. I handed the ball of light back to Lolo, and he closed his hand, extinguishing it. He sat beside me, and for a while, we just stayed like that, in uncomfortable silence.

"You can ask me anything, mija," he said, finally breaking the silence. Again, my heart tugged at the pet name, the same one Mama used to call me.

"Tell me more about Mama. What was she like? How did she run away? How come you never looked for her?"

I could see it pained him to talk about Mama, but he sighed and told me anyway.

"Your mother was always fascinated with humans. She studied humans all the time, wanting to know everything about your kind. We were waiting for her to come of age so she could officially be sworn into the kingdom's circle of royal council. She was going to take on more advanced training to prepare her for when she becomes queen. When she ran away,

I didn't do anything to stop her. Like you, Marie had to take on the role freely. No one can force it on her."

Lolo paused, staring at a painting on the wall Mama made a long time ago. I waited for him to continue.

"I had no intention of looking for your mother after she ran away. It was a decision she made for herself. I was prepared to appoint another clan to the throne before the war broke out. But after the first war, I realized only a descendant would have enough power to impose order in Engkantasia. I could not choose any of my closest kins, knowing the forces fighting for the throne would overpower them. I needed Marie to come back," he whispered. I kept quiet, afraid to interrupt his story.

"I never realized until recently that Marie procreated while in the human world. Now I suddenly have a granddaughter, a half-human one at that. I not only have to protect my daughter, but also you. This crossover has become more complicated than I thought. But at the same time, it is also surprisingly fulfilling."

His lips moved, a small sign of a smile. Or perhaps not. It was hard to tell.

"What about Lola? Did she do anything to convince Mama?"

"Your Lola died when your mother was still very young. I guess in a way, your mother's training began earlier than it should have because of that loss. The distress of having no queen intensified the pressure to be the perfect heir. After she left, I asked some of my closest subjects to keep track of her. For some time, I'd watch her myself, making sure she was safe. But it became too painful and so I stopped."

Lolo rubbed his hands together gently, a slow rhythm familiar to me. Mama used to do that when she was feeling sad.

"What's Engkantasia like? Where is it?"

"Engkantasia has been around for as long as the Earth has been around. It mimics the reality of the human world but with more . . . intensity. Engkantasia and the human world are separated by a fortified veil, which can only be lifted by the royal family. This veil has protected Engkantasia from the harsh treatment the humans impose on its environment and on each other. Our waterfalls shimmer like diamonds, our sun isn't harmful, and our forests are filled with nymphs and various creatures no one has ever seen before."

"Have I seen any of your creatures before?"

"Probably not. We've kept our world as hidden as possible from humans. It wasn't always this way. Hundreds of years ago, the *engkanto* signed a peace pact with the human tribes after one of us fell in love with a human. It was a promising unity that ended in a horrible tragedy. My ancestor died of a broken heart and a very gruesome war ensued. Many of my people suffered at the hands of humans. Many of the humans shed their blood. It was then that my grandfather declared the infinite separation of our worlds—never to be connected again. We were forbidden from crossing over, and the veil was enforced to stop the humans from entering Engkantasia."

I knew almost nothing about this new world I was supposed to be a part of. From the books I had read, it was hard to know which ones were fiction and which ones were real. Although Lolo hadn't spelled it out, I was beginning to feel like I was the last resort, the only one who could save their kingdom.

"How soon do I need to go through the training?"

"You have to learn to control your abilities, and strengthen it."

"Strengthen? Why would I want to make my powers more dangerous than they already are?"

Lolo paused, hesitating to tell me more, probably because it was more bad news.

"At this point, your powers have already been made known to my world. That means, whoever wants to take over the throne will be trying to . . . "

"Oh God!" I gasped, not wanting to hear the rest of the sentence. "Am I in danger? Lolo, are there creatures coming to kill me right now?"

"That's why I'm here until you finish your training. I can teach you everything I taught your mother, and protect you at the same time. I want to start tomorrow. The sooner we do this, the better chance for your survival."

Survival. The word sounded so definite, like I had no other choice. I guess it was looking like that. Survive or die. And here I thought our biggest problem was looking for Mama. It looked like her disappearance was supernatural as well. I got up to leave the room and gave Lolo a hug. He patted me awkwardly on the back.

"Good night, Lolo. Thank you for being honest. I'll see you in the morning." And with that, I left the room. I went to bed without eating dinner. My stomach was tied up in knots, and I was too anxious to eat. I lied down, hoping for some reprieve, wondering what bad news tomorrow was going to bring.

Chapter Six

San Francisco Tribune, December 2012
Reward Offered for Information on Missing Migrant

The family of missing Filipino migrant Marie Harris has offered $100,000 reward for anyone who can give information on Harris's whereabouts.

Harris disappeared from her house in May this year shortly after arriving in the country with her family.

A spokesperson from the police department has admitted they still have no progress on the case. They are working with Harris's family to continue the search.

June 2015

You would think that given everything that had happened—turning sixteen, the yellow flower, Lolo—I wouldn't have to go to school. But "being normal" was something I needed.

My "training" was set to start Monday. I didn't remember saying yes to it but if there were creatures coming to kill me, I thought a bit of training wouldn't hurt.

There was some sort of relief in the knowledge that there was a reason why I felt so different from everyone else. I also found a bit of comfort knowing that there was a big chance Mama was still alive. Even when everyone else had lost hope, even when the authorities had switched the search for Mama to the retrieval of her remains, we never believed she was dead. You know how people who had lost someone said they could feel that their loved ones were still alive? Well, I knew in my heart she was, and every time I touched the smoothness of my necklace, I felt something more than hope, like an undeniable fact that Mama was still alive.

After school, I was supposed to go home immediately so my grandfather could share his knowledge of Engkantasia.

I went through my school day ritual barely speaking to Dad and Lolo. I knew it was supposed to be Mama's fault that I was oblivious to my other life, but I couldn't help but blame my father as well. Why did he marry her without knowing her full background? But then again, how would you do a background check on someone who didn't live in our world? It was all too convoluted.

I rushed through my breakfast and grabbed my bag to catch the car pool with Mark and Alyssa. The drive to school was quiet, too. None of us wanted to talk about things with Alyssa's mom there, so we kept our mouths shut until we reached school.

We practically jumped out of the car before it even fully stopped. Mark and Alyssa had so many questions for me, and I desperately needed people to talk to—people who were not related to me. But before we could discuss everything, I felt a tight knot in my stomach, like a giant arm was gripping my innards. You know that feeling of anxiety when you were about to do something you were afraid to do, like maybe do a presentation in front of the class when you were totally not prepared, or climb the rope during gym class? My insides felt like that but ten times worse. I wasn't sure why I felt it but it was so intense I had to grasp the rails to hold myself up.

That was when he suddenly appeared. There was a new kid in school and he was hard to ignore. We paused to gawk like the rest of the school as he strode to the entrance. Even Mark couldn't help it. His stature was a harmonious mix between royal and military, oozing confidence out of his pores. His skin was a perfect tan, his hair golden brown, but it was his eyes that shocked me the most. They were a piercing green with a hint of blue when he stood under the sun. I squeezed the rail harder as my innards continued to tighten.

He walked past everyone with ease, oblivious to the stares. But just before he entered the halls, he stopped and turned to where we were standing—looking straight at me ever so briefly. It was so quick I thought it never happened. The first period bell rang, giving us no choice but rush to get ready. English literature would not wait, even if I had a great excuse to skip it.

We spoke quickly as we hurried to our lockers. "Who was that?" Mark asked me.

"I don't know, why are you asking me?" I said a little too defensively.

"It's kind of hard to miss that he was looking straight at you, Karina," Alyssa said.

"He was looking at us. For all I know he was probably enchanted by your long blonde hair," I told Alyssa, hoping it wasn't true. She moved to her locker quietly but not before I glimpsed her little smile at my comment.

As much as I wanted to keep thinking about the new boy in school, the class bell didn't give me enough time to linger.

"I'll see you guys later."

I sat at my desk before the teacher came in for English class. Mr. Parish placed his things on the table, his red bow tie a great contrast to his blue suit jacket. He was one of the few teachers I liked. When I became a social pariah a couple of years back, Mr. Parish encouraged me to use my emotions in my writing.

The new student was a couple of feet behind Mr. Parish. He didn't scan the crowd or looked at the teacher, who was introducing him to the class. His gaze went straight to my desk, staring at me with what I could only translate as contempt. I felt my stomach squeeze itself into knots again and I could not help but feel angry at the new guy.

"Class, please welcome our new student, Jason Lund. He just moved from another school, but he is originally from

Norway and will be joining our class starting today. Jason, please have a seat," Mr. Parish said.

As the universe would have it, the only vacant seat was in front of my own. I sighed in relief, knowing he wouldn't have a chance to stare at me again. I tried hard not to glance at him as he settled in his seat. I fidgeted with the reading material for the class. We've been discussing Harper Lee's *To Kill a Mockingbird*. I was trying hard to concentrate on Mr. Parish's lecture but it wasn't easy. Aside from the nerves I felt about my first training session, I couldn't help but steal glimpses of Jason's back. You could see the contours of his back muscles through his school uniform. I suddenly felt a bit hot around the neck, like I was burning up inside. Maybe I was just putting too much meaning into his stare. It was probably not contempt. Maybe he was just nervous? Constipated? It wasn't like he had any reason to be mad at me since we had never even spoken to each other. I only saw him that day, plus I had never been to Norway.

Class was dragging by at an unusually slow pace, which was sad because I usually looked forward to English. It was one of my favorite subjects because, before this Engkantasia thing happened, I wanted to become a journalist or maybe a writer. I guess I wasn't really sure what I should be aiming for. If I ended up in Engkantasia, I wouldn't be doing reports from Darfur. I doubt they had CNN there or BBC.

When English finally ended, I breathed a huge sigh of relief. I didn't even notice I barely moved during the entire class so my leg fell asleep. It took me a while to get out of my seat and by then, I only had minutes to spare before my next class. I resolved to just go through the day and focus on the tasks in front of me. There was no point worrying about the training when I didn't even know what I was supposed to do.

At lunch, Alyssa and Mark waited for me at the cafeteria. We decided to take our food outside, away from the crowd where our conversations would not be overheard by anyone. As we settled on the grass, I spied Jason heading to one of the trees.

"I heard he's from Norway and his mom is from the Philippines," Mark said, taking a bite out of his sandwich.

"Really?" I said, trying to act nonchalant.

"Hey, maybe you guys have something in common. Might be a good conversation opener," Alyssa said, not too convincingly.

"Like I'd want to start a conversation with him. I don't think I'll be talking to him anytime soon."

"Why? What happened?" Mark asked in between bites.

"Nothing. Forget it," I said, dismissing the topic. "Besides, I have more pressing issues today."

Mark tried to suppress a laugh without much success. "I'm sorry, I just can't imagine you doing karate given your history with anything sporty. You can barely balance on a bike."

It was true. I think I was born with the worse sense of balance. I must have overslept on the day the heavens handed out balancing skills. I could swim and I did some karate classes while I was in the Philippines, but that was about it. I always ended up flat on the ground every time I tried anything complicated. That also translated to other types of sports. I tried basketball once and ended up with a bloody nose after the ball bounced on my face. I tried skating and biking, but again, the lack of balance and stupid gravity took hold of me. I couldn't even ride an electric scooter without falling.

"I doubt there would be anything physical required of me. I think it's just about practicing my abilities. Maybe learn to regrow avocados, that way we can always have guacamole when I want it," I joked unconvincingly. I sneaked a glimpse toward Jason's direction and I swore he was snickering, too.

"Can we watch your training?" Alyssa said.

"I don't think so. My grandfather wants everything to be as hush, hush as possible. Dad had to clear the garage so we can have somewhere private to train. But I'll definitely let you know tomorrow."

"Isn't it bizarre to find out that you're actually not half-Filipino after all?" Mark said.

"What do you mean?"

"Well if you think about it, technically Karina's mother is not a Filipino, is she? She's not from this realm," Mark said looking at me. I didn't say anything, letting the realization sink in. Mark was right—one of the identities I had known all my life had just been ripped off of me. If only I knew what being half an *engkanto* meant.

The bell rang and we rushed back to our classes. I caught Jason staring at us before he quickly ducked into the toilet. Maybe I would have the courage to talk to him, and maybe ask why he didn't like me. It wasn't important. I needed to focus on what was in front of me and that was it.

Although Lolo never asked me outright, I knew he wanted me to take the throne. I couldn't be forced so in reality there shouldn't really be any pressure. But why was I feeling the pressure? I really didn't have time to think of Jason's weirdness. Unnecessary distractions had to be placed on the sideline because I was going to make the biggest decision of my life.

Chapter Seven

House for Sale, January 2013
Rose Garden, San Jose

Perfect Family Home in a Quiet Cul-de-sac

This sophisticated modern style family home is ideal for comfortable suburb living. This stylishly renovated property boasts of an open-space layout with a great view of the city. A huge terrace entertaining area extends the lounge room space outdoors. The home is tucked in a peaceful elevated private location, featuring panoramic views.

- *Three bedrooms, main with WIR and ensuite*
- *Two bedrooms with built-in wardrobes*
- *Modern spa bathroom, separate internal laundry*
- *Spacious granite kitchen with dishwasher space*
- *Modern dining room with high ceilings*
- *Large living room, extending to terrace entertaining area*
- *Automatic garage, carport*
- *Huge basement area*
- *Sun-drenched lawn*

It is situated close to bus stops, schools, shopping centers, and train station. Auction is scheduled this Saturday, 3:30 p.m. Viewing and registration from 3 p.m.
For further inquiries, contact the real estate agent anytime.

The house was empty when I got home. For a moment, I almost thought it was just another normal day when Dad had to work late and I had to make my own dinner. But then I saw Lolo waiting for me in the backyard, and the anxiety crawled back. I took a deep breath and walked to the garage.

"Lolo, I'm ready, let's do this."

"I'm glad you're eager to start, my child. I've been waiting all day for you to arrive. Let's go to the training room."

The garage was dark, I fiddled around to find the light switch and walked to the center of the room. Lolo was staring at the pile of old things Dad had pushed to one side of the garage to make room for our training.

"It is still hard for me to grasp that my only daughter left our world to replace it with this one—a world where the main source of entertainment is a frame on the wall with moving pictures. Your Dad taught me how to change the picture by pressing buttons on the 'remote control'. But no matter where I changed it to, I still cannot understand why this would entertain anyone."

"It is a form of escape into another world, Lolo."

"Engkantasia is another world."

"Never mind."

"You have three months to learn how to fully control your abilities. I wanted you to stay home today so we can begin earlier but apparently, your human school is more important."

"I don't really agree with that. I could've used with a day off from school," I said. "What's with the three-month deadline, Lolo? What's going to happen in three months?"

"I have to leave in three months. But don't concern yourself with that for now. We need to focus on the task at hand," he said, brushing the topic aside. I could sense there was more to it but I decided not to press on.

"Have you heard from anyone in Engkantasia? I mean, do you guys use phones or something?"

"We communicate differently from humans. Already I can sense something is amiss in Engkantasia. The news has probably already spread that I'm in the human world and that the heir to the throne has used her power. By now, my enemies would be looking for ways to find you. It's only a matter of time before they figure out what is going on. We are losing precious time."

"So let's begin," I said, honestly eager to get things going. If I would be targeted by monstrous creatures, I needed to be able to defend myself.

"We will start with the manipulation of nature, something you've already done yesterday with great skill. It isn't as hard as you think. You've already figured out what you needed to do to make things happen. See it in your head, focus and believe. You don't even have to touch anything, just the mana, a form of energy coming from your hands, your feet, your eyes, will be enough to make things happen. Other beings from our world can't do some of these things, but because you are my granddaughter and your mother has bestowed her own powers upon you through the necklace she gave you, you have more inside you than most of the creatures in Engkantasia."

Lolo placed a seed on the ground and stepped back.

"I know this is only a seed but I want you to make it grow."

I blinked and looked at him to see if he was joking. Lolo's face was set, dead serious about what I was supposed to do.

"But it's only a seed. And there's no water, or sunlight, or soil. How can I make it grow? It's on concrete. You need photosynthesis to do this. I don't even know what plant that is. How can I picture it in my head when I don't even know what it should look like?"

"Do what you did yesterday. Picture the seed growing, taking root, growing a stem. But instead of thinking of how it should look like, ask the seed to take its own destiny. Ask the seed, like you would another person, to grow and embrace its life. Have you ever wanted to do something but your parents wanted you to do something else instead? Imagine that feeling of being able to do whatever you want and focus that on the seed—guide it like a parent would but without restrictions. Do you understand what I'm saying. Karina?"

I nodded. "I think I understand. I'll give it a try." I sat on the floor and focused on the seed, pushing my face close to the ground. Nothing happened.

"This seed is stubborn," I sighed.

"You have doubt in your mind, I can sense it. That's what's blocking your abilities. Why not try this: Do whatever it is that calms you. Your mother used to sing while using her abilities. Why don't you try that?"

"Singing? It might die on me if I sing to it," I chuckled. I had been known to make children cry just by the sound of my singing voice. But Lolo wasn't smiling, so I tried again.

I closed my eyes and started to hum to quiet myself, a lullaby Mama used to sing to me before bedtime. I clutched my necklace, letting its smoothness soothe me. After several seconds of humming, the seed started to exert tiny roots on the ground. The transformation started slow at first, but as I got more excited, the stem and leaves moved faster, revealing more and more as it grew higher. I continued to hum, this time smiling and slowly standing. Sensing something strong inside of me, like an adrenaline rush, I hummed a bit louder and saw the plant push several flowers from its stem, blooming in the dark training room, creating a stark contrast with the dreary walls.

"It's a Belladonna," I gasped at the beautiful plant now firmly rooted in the concrete ground of the garage. "How do I make it stop growing?"

"Just tell it to stop, in your mind or out loud, it doesn't matter. You can communicate with nature any way you want. Although in the human world, it might be best if you keep your thoughts to yourself. Your abilities need to stay hidden, as you can understand."

I knelt down to move my hand near the plant and its roots clung on to my arm, settling the plant on my palm. I carried it to a space in the backyard where it could grow. The moment it touched soil, its roots started digging, immediately knowing what to do.

"Wait, can your people sense me every time I use my power?"

Lolo nodded.

"But that means your enemies can sense it too, right? This garage will be like a lighthouse for those who want to kill me."

"I can assure you I've taken measures to hide you while you're inside your home. After what happened yesterday with your abilities, I needed to make sure everyone is cloaked from anything that's looking for you. And your necklace protects you as well."

"What kinds of creatures are after me, Lolo? How bad are they?"

Lolo sighed. I could see he was hesitating to tell me about the creatures that wanted me dead. His brows furrowed as he raised his head to look at me.

"It's not a problem at the moment. In due time, I will tell you about them. But for now, we need to focus on this."

"Making plants? Am I supposed to be raising a rainforest or something?"

"Patience, mija, patience. Nature is all around you and if you can manipulate it, then you are fit to rule the land," he said.

I cringed at his words. I wasn't sure I wanted to rule their land. But I couldn't tell him that because even though I hadn't decided yet, a part of me was also curious, even excited, at the notion of being queen one day.

"Karina, you are still so young. It wasn't fair to disrupt your life. But there is no other choice. It's not only your life that's on the line. Your world and mine will collide in a disastrous battle if nothing is done in the next couple of months."

I looked at my hands, so foreign to me now. I never imagined my hands could be responsible for such magnificent things. "Shall we continue, Lolo?"

"Yes. Let us proceed," he said, before taking two seeds out of the bag. "This time, do the same thing to two seeds, but don't stop until they've grown as big as they can grow." He nodded. "Let us begin."

Chapter Eight

June 2015

Dear Diary,

    Who would have thought I could grow plants by just using my mind? Definitely not me. It's only been a week, but already I can command several plants and trees to do what I wish them to do. It is the coolest thing in the world. One moment I'm just an ordinary girl and the next moment I'm Mother Nature incarnate. Well, maybe not mother, maybe sister nature. Little Sister Nature?

    Lolo has been patient with me and I've been enjoying our training sessions together. I've long accepted the fact that I don't have grandparents. My dad's parents never traveled while we were in the Philippines and by the time we migrated here, Dad's mom already passed away. Knoppy lives in Tasmania, Australia so we barely see him. Mama always said she's been an orphan for a very long time. But now so suddenly, I have a royal grandfather, and a whole world of relatives I haven't met yet. I am very much aware of the underlying responsibilities that come with the abilities. I am also aware that something is expected of me at the end of three months' training. But I need to just focus on the present, otherwise I wouldn't want to get out of bed.

    Mark and Alyssa have been quite supportive of my trainings, even if it means less time hanging out together. We managed to schedule it so that Friday nights are our nights. Given the circumstances, Dad has been very easy on me. I can stay at either Mark's or Alyssa's every Friday night. But we can't go out at night without adult supervision so we're pretty much confined to indoor movie nights and talking sessions.

    School has been quite bizarre as well. I would have thought it would be boring given my extracurricular activities but that Jason kid has made things more interesting. He never said a word to me during his first week at school. He never glanced at my direction nor sat anywhere close to us during lunch breaks. He seems to be quite contented interacting with other students, especially Melissa— all legs Saint Melissa. She's always hated that I am Alyssa's best friend but I never pay much attention to her, especially after she argued that "irregardless" was a word even after she's been corrected by the teacher!

Melissa has made it her personal project to help Jason out with everything. Within a week, she's moved him from his spot under the tree to "her" table. It doesn't seem to bother him but sometimes I catch a glimpse of him staring into space, like he was thinking about something deeper than the gossip. There were moments that I pitied the guy for being sucked into that group, but that changed rapidly after he continued ignoring me during our classes—even during the ones where we are sitting next to each other. Oh well, it doesn't matter. He's just wasted energy.

June 2015

It always amazed me how resilient some people could be. We would always adjust even if our 'normal' was actually quite strange to others. Me having powers felt regular. It was just another day, another lunch hour at school. I knew that I wasn't the same person I used to be last month, but the rest of my world was still the same. For years, no one tried to say anything to me that was unnecessary. Sometimes I got the occasional invites to parties, but I knew this was only because I was hanging out with Alyssa. There were times when I got a "good job" from some random student on a piece I wrote in the school paper, but nothing really earth shattering.

They still kept their distance, unsure of what to make of my "situation."

I decided to stay in the library for my lunch hour. I wanted some peace and quiet, away from the chatter of other people I didn't want to listen to. There was an old armchair tucked away at the back, between shelves of old books no one would really borrow. I sat there with a book on my lap that I intended to escape to. I opened the pages and inhaled the wonderful scent, a smile spreading across my face. But it quickly disappeared as I felt the painful jab in my gut, like a dull throbbing pain that had become familiar to me. I knew I wasn't hungry because I ate quickly before rushing to the library. It definitely wasn't constipation.

Like a scene from a romantic movie on perfect cue, I saw him behind the shelves. His eyes flickered quickly to meet mine and he walked toward me with deliberate steps. My skin prickled as he approached. I took a deep breath to contain the pain and when I looked up, he was already in front of me. The pain in my gut throbbed even more. I had heard of butterflies in the stomach but this wasn't it. That was supposed to be a bundle of nervous excitement. This one felt like dangerous pain.

"Hi, I'm Jason. You're Karina, right?" he said, extending his hand. I kept staring at my book.

"Um, yes, I'm Karina, and I know who you are. We've been sitting beside each other for over a week now," I said in my most detached tone, not bothering to shake his hand. I was not normally rude but I couldn't help it.

He didn't seem to mind this or my tone. He sat on the floor next to me—so close I could smell his shampoo, or maybe it was his cologne. He smelled of the forest and a hint of citrus, and his skin was so much smoother up close. How can a Norwegian be so tanned?

"I heard you're from the Philippines?" he asked.

I just nodded. I didn't want to get too friendly. After all, I was the last person in the school he actually spoke to and that stung a bit. He even talked to the school janitor at the gym, even if I was less than five feet away from him.

"My mom is from the Philippines as well. We moved to Norway when I was small but I still remember what it was like and I miss it sometimes. Don't you?" he asked with a shy grin that looked much too calculated.

I just shrugged my shoulders, "Sometimes." It was hard not to admire how he looked given how close he was. He was probably the only person in campus who could make the school uniform look hot.

"Can you actually talk or are you one of those one-liner type of girls? I mean, I've heard you talking to your friends so I know you can talk well," he grinned.

My heart jumped a bit, knowing that he actually noticed me before and he had been listening in to my conversations. I knew I should be worried in case he overheard some of my private talks with Mark and Alyssa, but knowing he noticed me excited me a bit. It was getting too hard to keep up the one-line responses, plus I wasn't really good at small talk so I decided to just be upfront.

"I do talk, really well, in fact. But I wasn't sure if I wanted to talk to you given how you basically avoided and ignored me since you arrived in school. I'm not really sure what I did to deserve it but if you're like that then I really don't want to get to know you," I said, more forcefully than I intended to. I was expecting him to get mad or walk away, but instead he let out a loud laugh.

"Wow, you don't mask your feelings do you? I understand why you're mad and I do apologize for being so rude. I just wasn't sure how to approach you. I saw you on my first day and you looked, um, aloof. Then you started talking in class and you are really smart. Normally, I don't talk to smart girls because they always see how dumb I am after a sentence or two. Probably like what you're seeing right now," he smiled.

I tried to suppress my smile, but it was impossible not to after his nervous blab. Another jab in my gut again, not as bad as before but still painful. It felt strange talking to another teenager. Yet it did not really feel like he was a teenager. The way he arranged his words and apologized for being rude, high school boys just would not say things like that unless in front of the principal.

I did my best to ignore him, hoping he would go away. But he didn't. He stayed beside my seat even when I pretended to read the book. I snuck glimpses at him as he took out an old copy of something from his bag and started to read it. He caught me watching him and he smiled.

"Tolkien. A very old copy. It was a present," he said, handing me the book. I couldn't help but take it. It felt heavy in my arms, wrinkled with age. I placed it close to my nose and inhaled its scent. When I opened my eyes, Jason was staring at me. I returned the book to him, embarrassed by what I did.

"I do that, too," he said quietly as he placed the book in his bag. He stood up and started walking away but then he paused, hesitating a bit.

"I'm sorry about your mom," he said, so low it was hard to hear him. He walked away without turning back. I felt my stomach settle and a heaviness lifted from my chest. I let out a huge sigh but I wasn't even certain what I was sighing about. I packed my bag to look for Mark and Alyssa. Suddenly, I didn't feel like being alone anymore.

I found them in our usual spot outside. I cruised through Mark and Alyssa's conversation, only half listening. I kept turning my head to where Jason was sitting with Melissa, and I smiled every time I caught him looking back at me. I felt like I had just added another complication to my life, but one that I wanted to have.

Since that day at the library, Jason found several excuses to come up to me at school to talk during the week. Sometimes, I found myself lingering a bit longer after class to see if he was around.

I opened my locker and caught something drop. It was a package covered in brown paper tied with a brown string. How strange. I looked around but no one was paying attention to me, as usual. I untied the bow and gasped as I took out the Tolkien book Jason was carrying with him in the library. There were no notes or markings to indicate who it was from but I knew it was from him.

I smiled and shook my head. It must cost a fortune. I couldn't possibly keep it, but a huge part of me was dancing inside. I had never owned a book as old and as expensive. I tucked it carefully in my bag and closed my locker door. I turned around and found Melissa and her pretty posse behind me. I stepped back, startled by their sudden appearance.

"Hi Karina, in a rush, are we?" Melissa said in her high perky, venomous voice. How could a person sound so friendly and scary at the same time?

"Hi Mel, what's up?"

"It's Melissa. Not Mel," she said, eyebrow arching. "I hear you're becoming quite close with Jason. Isn't that nice?"

"Yep, it's great. Can I help you with something? I really need to head out," I said, moving away from the circle. Melissa glided like a ballet dancer to block my path. I almost tripped trying to avoid bumping into her.

"I'm just curious, what do you guys talk about? He seems to be quite . . . expressive when he's around you."

"Books," I said quickly. I wasn't about to engage in a catfight with Melissa. The less I said, the better.

"Oh, you don't talk about your mother's case? I took the liberty of filling him in because, you know, someone has to warn these new students about the school's unusual situations," Melissa said, baiting me. I could see she desperately wanted me to snap.

I grinded my teeth and clenched my hands, calming myself down. I gave her my biggest and fakest smile.

"Thanks for filling him in, *Mel*. You're such a swell girl," I said, before roughly pushing past her. I walked away without looking back. In the hierarchy of things to worry about, Melissa was like an ant at the bottom of my list. I had to learn to let these things go. I walked faster, thinking instead of our Friday night ahead.

It was *the* Friday night. The night of the monster with bat wings and half a body. The night started out innocently enough.

We decided to crash at Alyssa's place for movie night. We wanted to call it a slumber party but Mark pleaded we spare him the humiliation of being part of a girls' slumber party. Mark provided the movies and I picked up the pizza and popcorn. Just as we were settling for our first movie, Alyssa suddenly remembered to ask about Jason.

"Are you guys, like, going out or something? You seem to be hanging out a lot at school. And every time you see him, you get that look on your face," Alyssa said, nudging me with her elbow. I saw Mark roll his eyes.

"Oh God, girl talk. I'm gonna get us drinks downstairs. Please be quick with this segment of the program so I can come back with my dignity intact. Quick gossip and that's it," Mark said, leaving me with Alyssa.

"We're not going out. I don't think so anyway. We just sort of, like each other's company. Maybe it's the half Filipino thing, I don't know. We barely talk about our cultural heritage. I just kind of, really, really like being around him."

"Well, Melissa is absolutely furious at you, even more now. If I were you, be certain what all this is about so you claim he's your man. Otherwise, the vultures will snatch him away."

"The thing is . . ."

"What?"

"Every time he's near me, I feel something strange," I said, hesitating to explain the jabs in my gut. Alyssa raised an eyebrow.

"Strange? Like what kind of strange?"

"It's hard to explain. It's like a pain in my gut. Like spider sense or something."

"Spider sense? Do you think Jason is dangerous?"

I shook my head but couldn't say anything. A part of me believed he was not dangerous, but another part was sending me mixed signals.

I sat there quietly for a moment, not really sure what to say. The more we talked, the more I was interested in him. But my life was much too complicated to add anything else to it. The problem was, how do I explain to a teenage boy that I couldn't hang out anymore because my destiny was set in another world? He'd probably think I was a freak if he ever found out — not that he would anyway. I turned to Alyssa and faked a smile, but she could read my face like a map.

"Honestly, I think it's about time you got interested in a boy. I was starting to think you were a lesbian. Not that I minded but people were starting to talk that we were girlfriends instead of girl friends, you know? Unlike you, I do actually want to date guys but they get confused because they're not sure if I'm straight."

"No way! No one thinks we're gay!" I chuckled.

"Why do you think they snicker and say LG when we pass by sometimes?"

"LG?"

"Lover Girls," Alyssa laughed. I couldn't help but laugh, too. It wasn't my fault none of the boys at school interested me.

I needed better conversations than Xbox games and basketball results. Plus, I wasn't interested at anyone who believed all the stuff that had been whispered about my family anyway.

After the laughter tapered off, Alyssa turned serious.

"How's your dad taking this whole thing?"

I let out a long sigh.

"To be honest, I'm not really sure. He keeps things to himself. But I could see how much it has affected him. He never expected how bad things would turn out after we moved here."

Our move to America was fuelled by an opportunity with Dad's profession. He was creating an app while waiting for his contract to finish in Manila. The app got bought out and with it came a job offer in Silicon Valley. It was good that we saved up the money he got from the buyout instead of travel the world. It supported us when Dad took time off work after Mama disappeared.

While Dad was buried in his grief, I took over the house budget and the chores. While other thirteen-year-olds were perusing celebrity sites, I was going through how-to articles on managing the household budget. I followed Mama's budget book and figured out her system. I didn't think Dad ever realized the transition. Or if he did, he never said anything. I guessed he knew he could trust me.

"Maybe you should reach out to him. You've taken on so much after your mother disappeared. You need some support. You are the only teenager I know who does the house budget, the groceries, the bills. It's insane," Alyssa said.

"We gotta do what we gotta do," I smiled weakly.

"Enough about that, let's talk about something else." Just then Mark walked in, carrying softdrinks and a tea towel.

"What's in the towel?" I asked.

"It's a little bird, I think it's still alive. It hit the window while I was getting us drinks and I didn't want to leave it to die," he said, placing the towel on Alyssa's bed. He gently unwrapped it, revealing a tiny gray bird with black stripes and a yellow beak.

"Oh, poor thing! It looks dead. What are we supposed to do with it?" Alyssa asked, looking at me.

"I don't know, don't ask me," I said, although I already knew what was going to come next.

"K, maybe you should try your powers on it. You know, bring it back to life or heal it or something," Mark pleaded. He had always been an animal lover and hoped to be a vet one day. He had been working part-time in one of the vet clinics nearby.

"You know I can't do that. I'm under strict orders not to try anything in case something bad happens," I told Mark. Lolo Magatu had warned me about the enemies sensing my abilities every time I used it outside our house.

"Just try it really quickly, only a couple of seconds, and if nothing happens then that's it. I won't force you to do anything else. We'll bury the bird and watch a movie," Mark begged. "Come on, you always asked what your powers are for. This is it—to help poor animals. At least, try anyway."

It was hard to say no to Mark after everything that he had done for me. He was right—a couple of seconds wouldn't make any difference. What was the use of my powers if I couldn't help anyone, right?

"Move aside. Here goes nothing," I said, rubbing my hands together and kneeling in front of the bed, close to the tiny body. I placed my hands above the bird and closed my eyes, trying to picture the tiny creature coming back to life. Maybe because it was tiny, or maybe because I had had training, it took only moments before its wings started moving again. I moved my hand away and stared as the little bird struggled back on its feet.

"Open the window, Mark, hurry," Alyssa called out. Mark rushed to the window and pushed it open just as the bird started flying. The bird did circles around the room, chirping gleefully like it was thanking me, before it flew out into the sunset.

"Oh, my God, Karina, that was awesome!" Mark said, hugging me and pulling me up on my feet. "You're like Mother Nature or something, so cool!"

"I hope they don't turn homicidal like the pets in *Pet Cemetary*. They won't, right?" I joked, but also a tad serious. I didn't really know what my abilities would end up doing and I had never brought anything back from the dead before. After the horror movies I had seen, it was normal to think that maybe they didn't always come back right. Or maybe this was the power of the *engkanto*, bringing creatures back to life, healing helpless animals. I made a mental note to ask Lolo Magatu about it when I got home.

"Okay, enough excitement. Let's just watch the movie and enjoy ourselves. Close the window and hit the lights. Let's relax a bit and watch something gory," I grabbed the popcorn and sat on the bed with Alyssa, while Mark made himself comfortable on the floor.

We decided to do a zombie marathon and watched the two versions of *Night of the Living Dead* and *Dawn of the Dead*. By the time we finished the third movie, we were all zombied out. It was a unanimous decision to leave the nightlight on all night.

Minutes after settling ourselves in, I woke up startled to hear a scratching sound on the roof—or was it on the window? I brushed it aside as bats or some wild animal when it suddenly got louder. I sat up and looked out the window just in time to see a wing move quickly past it. I gasped. My heart started to pound in my chest. I wanted to believe it wasn't real, but I knew something was out there. Something with wings, something huge.

I sat there, I didn't know for how long, just staring out the window, trying to convince myself that it was just my imagination—a product of the zombie movie marathon. But then I heard it again, on the roof this time. I shook Alyssa and threw a pillow at Mark.

"Wake up! Wake up, you two," I whispered in the dark. Alyssa rolled and grumbled while Mark continued to snore. I shook Alyssa again, harder this time.

"What? I'm trying to sleep here," Alyssa said, raising her voice.

"Shhh, there's something out there. I saw something outside your window."

"It's just bats. The fruit trees in our backyard are infested with them, now go back to sleep," she said, covering her head with a pillow.

"It's not bats. It's something else. Something huge. Sit up and look out the window," I pulled Alyssa to a sitting position. She managed to finally sit up and rub her eyes while looking out the window.

"There's nothing out there," she started to lie back down. Just then, the creature appeared again, this time slowing down enough for us to see its gigantic wings. Alyssa let out a scream, but I covered her mouth quickly.

Hearing Alyssa's scream, Mark sat up fully awake. "What? What's going on?!"

"Shhh. There's something outside the window. Alyssa, give me your phone, hurry."

I grabbed the phone from her hand and started dialing my grandfather's mobile phone. It rang several times but there was no answer. Frustrated, I dialed our home number, hoping my dad didn't turn the bedroom phone on mute. He answered after two rings.

"What's the matter, Karina?" he said.

"Dad, where's Lolo? There's something outside and it's huge. I think it's not from his world," I whispered.

"Hold on, I'll check on your Lolo."

I could hear him walking and opening a door. "He's not here, I don't know where he is. Stay there, I'm coming to get you."

"Dad, no, I'm okay. I'm not going to go outside. I'm safe inside. We don't know what it is and I don't want you in danger. Just try to contact Lolo for me. I'll call you back soon."

I got out of bed and sat on the floor beside Mark. I needed to know if this thing was trying to get inside the house. I couldn't let it harm us or Alyssa's parents.

That was when things became much worse and the creature tried to slice us with its tongue.

It went away, thanks to Lolo—leaving behind the images of jagged sharp teeth in our heads. The entrails hanging out. The missing lower half. The stench of rotting meat.

I didn't die that night but I finally saw the reality of the fight in front of me.

Chapter Nine

MAMA'S DIY
ENGKANTASIA BOOK

Manananggal

The *manananggal (sometimes confused with the wakwak) is not a mythical creature of the Philippines. It is an evil, man-eating and blood-sucking monster.*

It is hideous, scary, mostly female, and capable of severing its upper torso and sprouting huge batlike wings to fly into the night in search of its victims. The manananggal preys mostly on sleeping, pregnant women, using an elongated proboscis-like tongue to suck the hearts of fetuses, or the blood of someone who is sleeping.

The word "manananggal" originated from the Tagalog word "tanggal" which means "to remove" or "to separate." It literally translates as 'remover' or 'separator' or "one who separates itself."

The lower body of the manananggal is left standing, and it is more vulnerable of the two halves. Burning the lower half is fatal to the creature. The upper torso will not be able to rejoin itself and will die by sunrise.

I woke up to the sound of birds chirping outside my window, the sun streaming onto my bed, the sky cloudless and perfect for a day of picnic. I marveled at the beautiful scenery straight out of a travel show. Rose Garden was a gifted place and even with all the chaos we were going through, I paused to appreciate that we ended up here.

The weeks following the incident at Alyssa's place hadn't been good to my family. The strain caused by my heritage had doubled, maybe even tripled after we figured out what the creature was that night.

I was right. My little magic trick created a ripple through the human world and landed on the radars of the worst enemy of the *engkanto*—the *manananggal* clan. I guessed they were my worst enemy as well. Apparently, they had been trying to topple down Mama's family for hundreds of years—using everything in their resources to take over Engkantasia.

The *manananggal* clan did not share Lolo's view of separation of the *engkanto*'s world and the human world. They did not understand why my family was against taking over both worlds. Humans, to them, were toys and food—the bottom of the food chain. They had dark allies willing to give their lives for the cause, but it was the *manananggal* that was the most dangerous group.

Although Lolo didn't want to reveal the whole story to us, I insisted. If I was expected to fight these creatures, I had to know what my enemies were so I could protect myself better. He finally agreed, but on his terms. If I finished the next phase of my training, he would answer all my questions. I took a deep breath and started preparing for school, mindlessly putting my uniform together, not really thinking about the day ahead.

I knew I could do this double life, but for how long, I wasn't sure. Mama always used to tell me I was a clever little cookie with heaps of confidence to boot. I didn't really know what made her say that while I was growing up but those words were giving me some confidence.

I remembered when I was five, I chased around a bully to kiss him. He was scaring the other girls with spiders and various bugs and I knew it was only a matter of time before he did the same to me. I was scared of bugs—even today with my abilities and all, I'd still cringe at the sight of them. So I decided to take action instead of waiting around like a useless little duck. I told him not to chase me with bugs and in return, I wouldn't chase him around for kisses. He thought I was joking. Even though I didn't get him on the first attempt, I managed to catch him off guard during class recess. He screamed in disgust, wiping my kiss off his cheek with his arm. He never tried to scare me with bugs after that.

I wished it were that easy to solve things. I wish I could just kiss my enemies away and that was it. Unfortunately, violence was the only thing they responded to. After Lolo saved our behinds from the *manananggal*, he had been very civil to me. He didn't tell me off for being irresponsible. It was as if it never happened. I wanted so much to ask what he did to scare the creature away but I had to follow his terms.

It was hard not to think about it though. At school, it was all Alyssa, Mark, and I could talk about. We saw the red bulging eyes and the huge fangs salivating outside Alyssa's window. We didn't know what would have happened had Lolo not gotten there in time. Not knowing how to defeat the *manananggal* just made things worse.

The six weeks of training had been good, but I still had a hard time trusting that my new abilities could save me. I had learned how grow to plants, manipulate nature and elements like water, fire, wind, and earth. It had been a challenge trying to juggle several abilities at once, but Lolo was a great teacher. Still, it was hard to have faith in myself when I had never tested my abilities in a fight. Could I kill a *manananggal* by drowning it with water? Could I choke its sharp fangs with flowers and leaves? Was I strong and quick enough to think of a defensive move when I was being attacked? Based on what I saw, the *manananggal* was as nasty as nasty monsters would get, and I was certain they'd be more than happy to chew on my insides after they had ripped me to shreds.

I shuddered at the thoughts running through my head. Concentrating on my classes had been a huge chore given the things I had to focus on. Had it not been for Mark's help, my grades would have tremendously slipped. Dad thought having a regular life and focusing on school was more important than my training—like everything was going away after two months. I was torn. My world was splitting into huge chunks and I didn't know which way was the right way to go.

We started training on communicating with live creatures, animals and bugs. I found myself actually enjoying the process. I had always been close to animals. I had always found myself caring more for animals than humans. After knowing my history, I finally knew why. This skill was something I was looking forward to mastering. But first, I had to survive another day at school.

I walked to school on my own again, refusing a ride from Dad. I could see he was hurt that I was walking instead of our usual ride together. But I used that time to think and reformat my brain to being just a normal girl. It was my transition walk. Every step I took away from home was like a step to being normal. Not that they treated me any differently at school. In the three years of studying there, I had never had a boy ask me out, or heard of anyone having a crush on me. I had been plugged into a pigeon-hole and they were not letting me forget it. Being a pariah had its advantages though. For one, I never got picked on. I barely got invited to parties but at the same time, I also missed out on trouble caused by these binge drinking parties. It balanced itself out, or so I told myself.

I found Mark and Alyssa waiting for me near the gate. Alyssa had a bandage wrapped around her lower arm.

"What happened to that?"

"Training, the usual," she said, like it was the most normal thing for her.

I suppose it was. Since the *manananggal*'s visit, Alyssa had upped her Wing Chung training at the local sports center. She had always been athletic and loved being a cheerleader, but last year Alyssa decided to casually try out Wing Chung. She dropped her other activities and had been focusing solely on self-defense training.

"Try not to kill yourself, okay?" Mark said, worried about Alyssa's weekly injuries.

"I have to do something, right? And since I don't have your giant brain and your inventions, this is something that I can do to protect myself."

"Inventions?" I raised my eyebrow.

"Yeah, well, I've been reading up on your folklore and there are some weapons I've been trying to design to help us, in case, you know, they attack again," Mark said, almost shyly.

"You know those are only stories. We don't even know what hurts them and what doesn't. I'm going to get more from Lolo and I promise you will find out the truth. I want you to arm yourself the best that you can, but we have to get all the facts first," I said to them.

Alyssa placed her good arm around me, leading me in the building. Mark followed behind us, muttering something about finding resources for his work.

"Let it go, Mark. Let's just wait for the real information. Focus on the day ahead."

I let Alyssa lead the way, enjoying the few minutes when I didn't have to make a decision for myself. I had deliberately been avoiding Jason, too, knowing that I would probably get him in trouble if he got too close to me.

It hadn't been easy. I saw the pang of hurt in his eyes every time I changed direction when I saw him waiting for me. I made sure I was constantly with Mark and Alyssa during my breaks so he didn't get a chance to talk to me.

Once afternoon, I got a note in my locker, a white piece of paper with nothing but a question mark on it. I saw him watching me, as I crumpled the paper and tossed it in a bin. Better I hurt him now than the *mananaggal* later on.

When I finally finished for the day, I rushed home to start the animal training session with Lolo. I took a shortcut through the back streets to cut travel time. As I turned into an alley, the familiar jab in my gut knocked me over. I grabbed on to something when someone behind me caught my fall. I pushed myself off the person and knew immediately where that scent of citrus came from.

"Are you okay?" Jason asked.

"Yes, I'm fine. Thanks for your help," I said before turning around and resuming my walk much quicker than before.

"Did I do something wrong?" Jason asked as he followed me. "Was there an imaginary boundary that I crossed to piss you off?"

I said nothing and continued to walk. It was hard not to answer him. But I couldn't say anything without sounding like a liar.

"Karina," he said, grabbing my arm. A zap traveled through my body, burning the spot where his hand met my skin. I immediately pulled my arm away.

"Whatever it was that I did, I'm sorry. I didn't mean to offend you in any way. I'm not going to bother you anymore if that's what you want," his eyes pleaded.

All I could do was look at him because I was afraid if I opened my mouth I might actually tell him the truth. I started walking away.

"The book was my grandfather's gift to me before he died. I hope you appreciate how important it was to me," he said before disappearing around the corner.

I was tempted to run after him, to explain about my heritage and the creatures trying to kill me. To run to his arms with the perfect lighting of the golden hour, like in the movies. But I didn't. Instead, I kept walking home.

I found Lolo in the garage, standing tall, waiting for me. He didn't say a word, and I felt a pang of sadness by his cold demeanor. I could usually charm my way out of trouble with Dad, but with Lolo, I didn't know how. I nodded to him, walking to the center of the room and looking at the mouse in a box. I guessed communicating with animals would be much simpler if we started with a small one, instead of, let's say, a tiger.

I placed the mouse on my hand and focused on telling him what I wanted him to do. Its pink tail curled around my thumb as I stroked its white fur. I smiled and whispered to Wilbur—it seemed like an appropriate name for a mouse. Wilbur looked at me, standing still, waiting for my instructions. I focused even more and whispered for Wilbur to stand on two legs. Gingerly, the mouse uncurled its tail from my thumb and pulled itself up to a standing position. I gasped as quietly as I could, afraid I'd drop him on the ground.

"That's a good start, Karina," Lolo whispered, trying not to disturb the connection between Wilbur and me. "He is able to understand your thoughts, but now you have to try and comprehend what he's trying to tell you. Concentrate and feel the mouse's energy. Make your hand sensitive to its aura and let it travel through you. Each creature is made of mana, a form of energy that's abundant in Engkantasia. In order to communicate with each other, you only need to tap into their energy and let them tap into yours."

I reached for the necklace with my other hand and felt its power. A vision passed through me, of Mama and her training, her joy of mastering this skill. I saw Wilbur's essence in the colors of the sunset, covering my arm. I knew that my own emotions triggered Wilbur's emotions at once. We had become connected now.

I snuck a glimpse at Lolo and saw a deep sadness in his eyes. The necklace was showing me Mama's training. Lolo was standing beside her, beaming with pride. This had reminded him of Mama and the pain of losing her. He saw me watching him and he smiled the same smile he gave Mama.

I started humming the song I hummed when I had to concentrate and relax at the same time. I closed my eyes and took a deep breath. When I opened them, I was suddenly very aware that I had an extra sense that had come to life after being dormant for sixteen years. It started as a whisper in my head, a quiet nudge in the background. After focusing on the sound, I realized they were Wilbur's thoughts conversing with my own.

He wasn't speaking a human language. I wasn't really certain what language he was using but I could understand it like it was a language I had been using all my life. The excitement I felt after such a discovery rushed through my body, sending a jolt to Wilbur, who reacted by jumping up and down my hand. I started to giggle uncontrollably as Wilbur scampered up my arm to rest on my shoulder.

I wasn't entirely sure how the connection happened. All I knew was that I could understand Wilbur now, and it was very clear he wanted some food. I walked to my backpack and looked for leftovers in my lunchbox. I handed Wilbur a tiny piece of bread crust and he happily nibbled on it.

We continued the training, honing my skill to communicate with Wilbur even from afar. By the end of the session, Wilbur had become my new best friend. I decided he would be sleeping in my room from now on. The training had lifted my spirits more. Every session could only make me stronger and better.

"Nature is everywhere and it's everything. Imagine if you can communicate with animals. They can warn you of incoming dangers from miles away. If one of your friends is in trouble, a bird might spot them somewhere and contact you for help, a house pet can easily communicate with you or another creature who can relay the message to you. It's not just about growing plants and manipulating seeds. It's about harnessing the things around you for a good purpose. It's all connected together and you're at the center of it," Lolo said.

"But how do you kill a *manananggal*? Can I use fire or water? Can I use plants to kill it?"

"The stronger your powers become, the better you can control them. Think of it this way. If you punch someone and you've never trained before, your punch will be very weak and won't injure anyone. But if you've been training for a while and have mastered powerful punches, you can inflict really severe injuries on your opponent. Right now, all you can do is make vines grow, but imagine if you can make them whip someone or even stab a *manananggal*'s heart. That would be a useful skill to have."

I had to admit, it did sound very cool to be able to command nature. But I knew Lolo was just skirting around the real reason why we were having this conversation. I wiped my hands on my jeans, trying to get the courage to finally ask him.

"Lolo, you need to tell me more about our enemies. What are the *manananggal*?"

He sighed and sat down beside me. He hesitated, but I looked at him, waiting for answers.

"The *manananggal*, like the one you saw, are women who merged in the human world hundreds of years ago. At first, it was just an experiment to venture into the human world. But soon it became more of a quest for domination. It all started with the first *manananggal* who crossed over. Her name was Marila, a *manananggal* whose beauty was so alluring it stunned every human who saw her."

Lolo waved his hand, summoning light from thin air, creating a screen of some sort to show me his world. I saw a beautiful woman walking in the forest, her black hair reached to her thighs, perfectly framing her face and wonderfully contrasting her smooth, fair skin. She had the reddest lips and blue-gray eyes that would change color when the sun's rays hit them. She looked surreal, like she was designed by the gods themselves.

"Marila lived on her own in the thick jungles of Mindanao. She wanted to experience the daily grinds of being human and decided to try living with the folks of a nearby village. What she didn't realize was that no matter how common her clothes were, she could never hide the beauty that she radiated. Soon, the village men were smitten, even the married ones pursued her. She easily became the center of ire of every woman in the village."

The image on the scene changed. I could see Marila, walking on her own at night. Lolo waved his hand and the whole thing dissipated.

"Why did you stop?"

"It's not . . . suitable for you."

"Okay, tell me then. I can take it. I know how cruel the world is. I watch the news."

He sighed before continuing the tale.

"One night, several drunken men forced their way into her hut and abused her after she rejected them. She tried to fight them off, but Marila did not anticipate the violence she experienced from the men. Transforming in the human world was a slow process and by the time she had the energy to change, the men have already left, leaving her bloodied and bruised."

My chest hurt hearing Marila's past. No matter how many times you hear about it in the news, in the media, in movies, it still shocked me every time I heard about rape.

"What did she do after that?"

"She tended to her wounds, but she was surprised at the hatred she received from the women who accused her of seducing their husbands. Marila was not a kind-hearted being to begin with, and the incident brought out the worst in her. She realized how vile humans could be and justified that imposing her own sense of justice onto the human world was fair. Marila left her cottage and moved to a more secluded area in the jungle—preparing to unleash her wrath to the men who abused her."

Lolo waved his arm and put the images back on the air, showing me Marila's transformation for the first time.

"Are you sure you want to see this?"

"I have to, Lolo," I said, holding my hands together. He waved his hand and the image moved.

The sun was orange outside her hut as Marila wiped her body with something that looked like oil. Slowly, Marila's back curved, almost splitting her shoulder blades. The skin on her back cracked like dehydrated land and batlike wings pushed themselves out, stretching wide and long. Her hands shook and increased to twice their size. Sharp claws ripped out of her fingernails, designed to rip off flesh like hot knife on butter.

Once the transformation was complete, Marila flew to the village and waited for the men to stagger to their homes after a drunken night out. Seeing her chance, Marila attacked all five men with such speed and anger that there was barely time for any of them to scream for help. She sliced their throats and ripped their chests, pulling their hearts out of their ribs. It only took minutes for her to mangle them, leaving a bloody mess of flesh and entrails.

Without thinking about it, I grabbed Lolo's hand and he froze the image of Marila's face, bloodied and grinning with evil glee.

"Were you watching all this from Engkantasia?"

He nodded.

"But how can you just watch it and not do anything?"

Lolo sighed, placing his other hand on top of mine. "We don't intervene with your world. Only very few of my people cross over and we keep track of them but we don't do anything unless it threatens our whole existence."

I understood what he was saying, but I didn't agree with it. Whoever was king then was definitely powerful enough to stop what Marila was doing. Instead, he just watched because it wasn't important enough for his intervention.

"What happened next? I don't want to see the rest of this anymore," I said, turning my back against the image. Lolo wiped them off the air.

"Satisfied with her revenge, Marila took the men's hearts and flew back to her hut. She transformed back into her beautiful human form, cleaning herself off the men's blood and innards. Smiling and contented, Marila went to the kitchen and started cooking the men's hearts for dinner as the final act of justice, humming a lullaby to herself. She never had human flesh before and she was surprised to find that it was the tastiest treat she had ever tried. Her revenge changed something in her that night, but Marila never noticed it. She was much too enthralled by her newfound food. Although part of her knew her revenge had been fulfilled, Marila's anger wouldn't disappear."

"So she just kept on going then? Killing, eating hearts, and you just watched?"

Lolo was quiet for a while.

"Marila was the first of their kind. We had no basis on what to do with her. We had to deliberate the most efficient way of dealing with the situation."

I stayed silent, not knowing what to say. The images burned behind my eyelids. I shouldn't have watched it.

"What happened next?"

"The villagers thought they were attacked by beasts and stayed in their huts after the sun had set. Marila wanted to make the women suffer—those who accused her of seducing their husbands and shunning her from the village. The more she thought about it, the more her anger boiled. By the time she had transformed herself, Marila was convinced she was justified for seeking out revenge. One by one, Marila hunted the women. With every kill, she got hungrier and angrier. She became addicted to human flesh."

I grimaced at the thought of it all. It was a good thing my stomach was empty. I was feeling a bit queasy thinking about it.

"Marila's terror spread out further. Night after night, she moved from village to village, not caring about justifying her actions anymore. All she knew was that her discovery had woken something inside her and it was addictive. Each night when she prepared to transform, mild changes occurred in Marila. During the day, she was still the beautiful woman in human form, even more glowing than before she started eating human flesh."

Lolo showed me an image of Marila. Her skin was even more supple and creamy, her hair so silky it practically rode the air, her eyes were bright and her lips red as blood. But her transformation had gotten worse. She now looked more like a bat than human. Her sharp claws had grown longer, her teeth had turned jagged and pointed, her eyes had turned red, bulging out of their sockets. Her face had broken into a snout, her tongue had grown longer, and her arms had started to grow fur.

"Marila was too addicted to human flesh she didn't take notice of the changes happening to her. As the stories of a flesh-eating monster spread around nearby villages, the people started to lock themselves in their houses after nightfall. No one would dare walk close to the jungle once the sun had set. It became harder and harder for Marila to hunt at night, which angered her and increased her craving for humans even more. Her addiction intensified, driving her close to madness. She decided to take more drastic measures."

I saw Marila on top of a hut, brushing aside the nipa roofing wide enough for her to stick her mouth in.

"What is she doing?"

"Marila would extend her tongue until it stretched close to her target. It was enough to kill them and she got what she wanted. Sometimes, she victimized pregnant women, aiming for their unborn children."

"Oh, my God," I whispered, getting more scared of the monster I would have to face one day.

"She had her tongue cut out several times because of this, but still, it didn't stop her from going back for more. The villagers created a patrol to protect their families, armed with primitive weapons, spears made from bamboos, knives, and bolos. Knowing she would be in danger in the nearby villages, Marila moved on to farther areas, risking the extra miles she had to fly at night."

"Marila's transformation evolved over the weeks, designing itself around the single most important purpose in her life—hunting. During the day when she was in human form, Marila rested, not even bothering to cover up a pretense of being human anymore. She craved for the darkness to hide the form she truly wanted to be in. Since the farther villages had not been attacked before, they were very vulnerable. Her only fear was that the sun would be up before she was able to get back to her hut. She wanted to find a way to fly faster before dawn."

An image of Marila flashed above my head. She was preparing for her hunt, wiping extra oil around her midriff, coating the skin with the potent potion. As the transformation began, Marila scraped her stomach with her talons and pulled her upper body from her lower body, stretching the skin until it ripped.

She poured more oil onto her exposed midriff, screaming as the pain rippled through her body. Slowly, her tissues divided, separating her upper half from her lower half. It was like her body knew what she wanted and pushed itself to make it happen. She kept on pulling until only the upper half was flying around the room. Marila let out a loud triumphant shriek, feeling the lightness of her weight, giving her extra speed for her flight. She flew out the window, leaving her lower body on the floor inside her hut.

"Marila soon discovered how fast she could go without the weight of her lower half. She flew further and further away to a village she had never been before, salivating at the thought of a fresh fetus's blood. She was so engrossed in the hunt that she forgot to notice dawn creeping in the horizon."

I saw Marila flying back to the jungle, a blur in the coming dawn, the light chasing her until it caught a wing. It burst into flames, slamming her down into her hut. She attached herself back into her lower half as the morning sun hit her. Her entire body was engulfed in flames. She struggled to splash a jug of water onto herself. She sat on the floor, burns all over her body, her clothes singed, her arms bleeding. But Marila seemed to be oblivious to her pain. It was like something had clicked in her head, the power she had over the humans, the fear she put on them, and the taste of their flesh. She started to laugh, maniacal and sinister. If evil had a smile, that would be it.

I jumped, startled as Lolo continued with the story. "What Marila did to herself cost her everything but she didn't care. Because of it, she could not fly in the sun anymore. But it didn't hinder her plans to procreate with humans. She wanted to have her own army in the human world."

"Still, your kingdom did nothing but sit and watch as she ate one human after another?" I didn't even try to hide the contempt in my voice. Why would I want to join a realm that just sat idly by as humans were being murdered?

Lolo continued as if he didn't hear what I just said.

"Although she violated the rule of the land, she wasn't a threat to the kingdom. She was a threat to the human world, but Engkantasia saw that that was not our business. If the humans wanted to rid their world of Marila's cruelty, then they would have to find their own solutions. Engkantasia only intervenes when the kingdom is in peril."

"However, when Marila fell pregnant, Engkantasia feared for its safety. A half-creature could mean a future threat to the kingdom. Marila's evolution to a vile creature had been passed on to her offspring and no one knew what this would mean for Engkantasia once the creature came of age. So we sent a team of our top warriors to collect Marila and her daughter, Maita. Even with Marila's powers, she was helpless against the warriors. She had no choice but go back to Engkantasia where she was imprisoned indefinitely. As for Maita, no one really knew what happened to her. Rumors had it that some of Maita's clan members snuck her out of Engkantasia into the human world and hid her. She was taken as a baby and therefore she had no knowledge of what her heritage was. She would have come of age a long time ago, which meant her abilities and her transformation would have already happened. My father had no knowledge of Maita as this was before his time as ruler. There were stories that she found a way to get back into the human world to find her father and live a normal life. Every now and then, a team would be sent out into the human world to find Maita, but they would always come back empty handed."

Maita definitely lived her life in the human world. The fact that we saw a *manananggal* meant she survived all those years ago. Or maybe it wasn't her but her offspring. Whoever it was, she had been hiding all these years, trying to avoid the royals from capturing her. But now she had risked everything to get to me. That meant it was open season. And I was the prized deer.

I felt like there was an anvil on my chest, suffocating me. I was suddenly so aware of how tired I was. I excused myself from Lolo and headed off to my bedroom without any dinner.

Chapter Ten

MAMA'S DIY
ENGKANTASIA BOOK

Tiyanak

The tiyanak is a vampiric creature that imitates the form of a child. It usually takes the form of a newborn baby and cries like one to attract kindhearted people. Once it is picked up by the victim, it reverts to its true form and attacks. The tiyanak is the most scheming of monsters.

The tiyanak takes sinister delight in leading travelers astray or in abducting children. Sometimes, it may take the form of a specific child. Its face is part gargoyle and part demon with piercing red eyes. It has a strength that's unexpected from a small creature. Many underestimate it because of its size, which always leads to the victim's demise.

The size and speed of the tiyanak make it a difficult enemy to target. But once captured, the tiyanak can be overpowered by severing its head. During the day, the tiyanak can only take human form if it is out of its shelter.

Staring at my bedroom ceiling had become a sleeping ritual for me. I had memorized the almost invisible cracks, the flowery pattern, and the shape of my bedroom light. I stared at it like it held the answers to all my questions. I wasn't so interested about school anymore. If not for Alyssa and Mark, I would have feigned sickness every single day.

Jason was a promising and intriguing new friend, but it was better to keep my distance. What was the point of having a new friend when you couldn't really share anything with him anyway? He was probably back in the warm snuggly folds of a very happy Melissa. I hated him for giving up so easily, but I knew I shouldn't expect him to be waiting for me to warm up. It wasn't like he didn't have options especially with the way he looked.

I moved to my side to watch Wilbur sleep. He had taken so well into utter domestication. I made a bed for him using an old woven basket, fluffed with a soft pillow. His food and water bowl sat next to his bed. Being able to communicate with a pet had its advantages. I didn't have to worry about cleaning up his poop. He knew where to go after I explained it to him. I wanted to reach out to Wilbur but decided against it. I didn't want his little body to be riddled with the anxiety I was feeling about everything.

It made sense to me then, the little things I thought were pure fluke when I was a little girl. When I was four, I went to school a couple of blocks from where we lived in the Philippines. It was a short distance from our house inside a gated community so I used to walk on my own. We had an old dog named Juanito and every day he would walk me to school before walking back home on his own. When the bell rang at three o'clock, I'd find Juanito waiting outside the school, ready to pick me up after class. I was amazed that the dog knew my schedule and kept me company on the short walk home. Even then, I already must have some extra sense to connect with animals.

As much as I wanted to have a normal life, I knew there wouldn't be such a thing for me. Even after Lolo had left for Engkantasia, I still wouldn't be a normal girl. My abilities were here to stay. That I knew for sure. I would be hiding a secret for the rest of my life if I stayed here, and I would be leaving everything behind if I decided to take on the throne in Engkantasia.

I closed my eyes and forced myself to relax so I could finally fall asleep. Moments later, I sank into slumber, riddled with darkness and creatures I had never seen before. I was trying to fight something I couldn't see but none of my abilities worked. I was very aware of my mortality and the helplessness. I tripped on a tentacle sprouting out from a huge tree and fell into the gaping mouth of the earth.

I woke up drenched in sweat, my heart racing, and my head throbbing. Wilbur jumped out of his bed, too, startled by my fear. Although I knew it was only a dream, I felt motivated to train even harder. I knew I was up against unspeakable monsters whose ability I wasn't aware of. I needed to be prepared for anything. I slumped back down on the bed, hoping to catch a few more hours of sleep before going to school, but after much tossing and turning I decided to get up instead. There was no point forcing myself to sleep when I knew it wasn't going to happen.

It was only five-thirty in the morning. I couldn't even remember the last time I woke up this early, or if I ever did. I heard something downstairs, a cry. A baby's cry? How could that be? None of our close neighbors had children that young. I walked downstairs as carefully as I could, trying not to trip in the dark. The sound was coming from the front door. Had someone left a baby outside the house? The cry was getting louder, more frantic.

I stopped in front of the door, uncertain whether I should open it or not. We had enemies and I had to be careful. But a baby was just a baby. I opened the door for just a fraction, enough so I could see outside. There was a baby on the front step. He was naked and lying on the cold hard concrete. My heart broke for the little baby, alone out in the dark on a chilly night. Who could do such a thing?

83

I picked him up, looking around to see if the person who left him was still around but the streets were empty. I opened the door wider to take the baby in the house, humming a quiet song to calm him down. The baby stopped crying and looked at me.

"Karina, don't move," Lolo said. I didn't even hear him walk down the stairs.

"It's just a baby, Lolo. Someone left him near the front door," I told him, still cuddling the baby.

"Karina, listen to me carefully. Open the door and put the baby back where you found it. I need you to trust me on this," Lolo said, walking cautiously toward me. I looked up, confused by his instructions. The fear in his eyes caught me by surprise and I felt my pulse quicken. Why was he so scared of a little baby?

"Lolo, it's just a baby. This isn't a . . . "

"Tiyanak," Lolo said, finishing my sentence. My entire body turned cold. The baby had stopped crying but I couldn't push myself to look at it, afraid of what I might find.

I remembered the *tiyanak* mentioned in my old books. Being such a religious country, Filipinos believed that the *tiyanak* was an aborted fetus coming back from the grave to avenge its death. Old folks used this tale to scare pregnant women out of wedlock from aborting their babies. I always thought it was just a story, another one from the horror books. I wish it stayed between the pages.

I looked down to find my nightmare come to life, still clutched in my arms. The *tiyanak* flashed its fangs and jumped off me, scratching my neck with its claws. The pain caught me by surprise and I fell on my back. The monster let out a screech, running toward me with surprising speed. A flash of bright light threw the *tiyanak* back. It hit the wall with a thud, screaming in agony. Lolo aimed for the *tiyanak* again as the little monster struggled to get back up. I scrambled to open the front door, kicking the *tiyanak* out of the house like a soccer ball. Lolo chased it outside but it disappeared behind the bushes, running for its life.

The door was covered in bloody handprints and so were my pajamas. Blood dripped from the deep scratches on my neck. How was I going to explain this to Dad? Lolo saw the wounds and reached out to touch it. A warm feeling spread over me and when he took his hand away, my injuries had disappeared, like they never happened.

"We better clean this up before your father wakes up," Lolo said, spreading his arms wide. Vines, leaves, and flowers emerged from his outstretched arms, spreading over the areas where the fight broke out. In seconds, all traces of blood had disappeared. No one would ever suspect I got attacked.

"I don't understand, Lolo. Why would they risk sending only just one *tiyanak* here if they wanted to take me out?"

"I don't think that was what they were after. It's another way to test your abilities, to see if you are a threat to them or not."

Obviously, I wasn't a threat. It dawned on me so painfully just how unequipped I was to defend myself from my enemies. How was I going to defend an entire kingdom if a tiny little monster could take me down? Had Lolo not been there, I wasn't sure how I would have been able to defend myself.

"I better clean myself up," I said to him, grateful for the excuse to hide and cry in the shower. I placed my pajamas in a plastic bag and stuffed it in my school bag. I wanted to find a place to get rid of it on the way to school.

After putting on my school uniform, I grabbed a couple of accessories from my jewelry box. I rarely decorate myself at school but since my eyes obviously had dark circles around them I might as well wear something colorful to draw the attention away from my face.

Breakfast was a choice of various leftovers from the last two nights. Since I started training, I found myself always hungry in the mornings. Lolo said it was the energy drain from all the work we had been doing. Usually, he said, the *engkanto* could just tap into any source of energy they wanted when training in Engkantasia. But since we were in a garage in the suburbs, we were limited in our options.

I piled my plate with spaghetti bolognese, roast chicken, rice, and a side of chopsuey. I placed the plate on a breakfast tray and decided to eat in front of the TV. I took my time eating breakfast, zoning out while stuffing my mouth. I started to finally feel at ease again. Relaxed. Even normal. As I watched the sun slowly rise outside the house, I decided early mornings would be my time. Minus the *tiyanak*.

By the time I arrived in school, I had already managed to shake off some of the morning's fear. While walking, I realized something. They would keep sending someone to kill me. I couldn't stop that from happening. But I could do something about it. I could focus on my training and find a way to make sure that the next time they sent something, I wouldn't be caught off guard. Do what you could to solve the problem. Mama always used to say that to me.

I didn't notice I was smiling when I reached school. Mark gave me a quizzical look.

"I had a good morning."

Given that a little critter just attacked me, I was surprised I felt okay. Newfound confidence. I hoped it would last long.

Jason was with Melissa, heading for class. He turned to look at me and I gave him a shy smile. It took him by surprise and he lingered before heading inside the classroom.

I didn't really expect to hear from Jason again, especially after our last encounter. So it was quite a surprise when he sat beside me on the grass outside during lunch break. I felt the tug in my gut and inhaled his familiar scent even before I saw him—another perk from the training was gaining a hound dog's sense of smell.

"And here I was thinking you never want to speak to me again," I said before he could open his mouth. He looked at me, confused, like he was about to give me a nasty remark, but decided against it.

We stayed quiet for a while. I sighed, trying to avoid his gaze. "I'm so sorry, Jason. I was going through something really difficult and I didn't want any distractions."

"Am I a distraction to you?"

"I didn't mean it like that. It's just that, I really like you and well, I didn't know how to juggle the stress at home plus the stress of Melissa wanting to kill me for stealing you."

He grinned that lovely grin.

"Melissa doesn't own me, and you never stole me from her. I tolerate her company because she's very accommodating, and very pushy. She's nice enough, but there's only so much celebrity news I can take."

I smiled back. "I'm sorry, I never meant to hurt you. I just really needed the space. There's still some drama going on but I didn't want to put my life on hold just because it's there. If you let me, I can make it up to you."

He smiled and gently tugged my hair. "There, that was my revenge. Now, how are you going to make it up to me?"

My smile widened. "You're so juvenile. How about a movie? My treat. This weekend."

"I should really make you suffer a bit more, but I really am a sucker for freebies. Pick you up at your place?"

I hesitated, not really wanting him anywhere near the drama at home. "How about we meet at the cinema? I'll check the schedule and text you the time, is that okay?"

"Okay, it's a date," he stood up as Mark and Alyssa approached our spot. He waved goodbye and smiled at my friends.

"What was that all about?" Alyssa said.

"Nothing, we're just watching a movie this weekend, that's all."

"You're going on a date?!" Alyssa squealed with delight.

"Shhh, it's just friends going out. I wanted to make it up to him for snubbing him the last couple of weeks. It's not a big deal."

"Melissa will kill you, you know," she warned.

"If the the *manananggal* doesn't get to me first."

"I think the *manananggal* would be more merciful with you. Once word gets out that you guys are going on a date, hell will break loose, like literally," Alyssa said.

"Figuratively. Literally means the devil will be coming out of the ground to kill us all," Mark corrected her.

"Look at you, Oscar the grouch, what's with the 'tude?" she said, a bit hurt.

"I can't believe you're going out on a date at a moment like this. You have more important things to think about than a date. There are things out there that want you dead. Don't you think that requires more attention than your social life?"

Mark was the one most disturbed by the appearance of the *manananggal*. He blamed himself for the attack since he felt he pressured me to bring the bird back to life. No matter how much I told him it wasn't his fault, he still wouldn't let it go. I decided not to tell them about the *tiyanak*.

"My enemies will always be there. My future will always be undecided for the next couple of weeks. If I lock myself up in the room and think about all this all the time I'm going to go mad. I need my life back, or at least some part of it. When will I ever have a chance to go out with someone if I don't do it now?"

"I doubt your dad would let you go though," he grumbled.

"He will. He already feels guilty enough for everything I've gone through. Plus, if I promise not to use my abilities, he'll feel much safer. My Lolo is literally only a call away, and I mean that literally. He can hear my cry for help even if I were ten feet underground. So stop worrying about Dad, I have it all figured out."

Mark dropped the subject and quietly chewed on his tuna sandwich. I obviously hurt him but I couldn't help it. This was my only chance to have some semblance of a normal life and I expected him to be supportive. Alyssa couldn't stop gushing, asking me all sorts of questions about what I was going to wear, how I was going to do my hair, if I was going to use makeup or just a light touch of mascara, and so on. I half listened to her drone on about my "date", thankful that at least I had some support about my decision to go out with Jason. I didn't really know where my sudden optimism came from but I didn't want to let it go just yet.

As expected, it wasn't too hard to ask my dad for permission to go out with Jason. I sprung it on him as casually as possible on Saturday, hours before I was going out. Dad almost looked relieved. Unusual, yes. From what I heard, dads were supposed to be strict with their kid's dating life. But then again, I was not your usual teenager—not anymore, anyway.

Dad cleared his throat and attempted to put on a tough face. "Is he old enough to drive? Who's going to take you home?"

"We're taking the bus, Dad, no one is driving. He's meeting me there and then I'll take the bus home."

"What? He's not even going to take you home? What kind of a man is that? During my time, we take our dates home safe and sound."

"It's not really a date, and it was my decision to take the bus. It's convenient and practical. He's new to the country, there's more chances he's going to get lost if he takes me home."

"So I'm not even going to meet him?"

"Really? You want him here? In our house, with all of Lolo's . . . talents floating around?"

"Just . . . be careful. I think that's what normal dads are supposed to say," he said, giving me a kiss on the forehead.

I smiled and headed to my room, nervous about my date. It was an entirely new experience for me and I wasn't sure how to act. I sat on the bed, silently contemplating things, thinking how it was such a huge milestone for mothers and daughters.

How would our conversation go if she were here? What would she tell me? How would she react to her daughter's first date? Would she know I have butterflies in my stomach the size of a dinosaur? What advice would she give me? Will she tell me to be myself? I once had a crush on this boy when I was younger and Mama said that if I pretended to be someone else, then I'd never know if the boy really liked me for me. But being myself means talking to animals and growing plants from nothing. Maybe I should just be a bit like myself but not too much.

I felt the necklace's smooth surface and took a deep breath. There was an ache in my chest, the familiar pain of not having my mother around.

The funny thing was that after everything that had happened to us in the last couple of weeks, the very normal date was what felt surreal. It was true what they say, you get used to whatever was handed to you and adapted to changes. My closet was a jumble of school uniforms and very basic casual clothes. I had never gone out on a date before and so I had nothing that seemed appropriate to wear. I threw out several tops and jeans, piling them on my bed until I could barely see the mattress. I understood then why teenagers on TV kept saying they had nothing to wear. My nerves were not helping, too. I felt like I had to pee every couple of minutes.

After almost an hour of trying on clothes, I decided on wearing my dark denim skirt, red halter top, and a nice pair of sandals. I let my hair down and wore a pair of stud crystal earrings, applying a bit of red lip gloss before heading out of the door. I looked like myself, although a tad girlier than usual. Too late to change my mind.

I rushed to the door before anyone saw me. But as I got out of the house I saw Dad waiting for me beside the car.

"I'm driving you to the cinema, and that's that."

I should have been mad but all I could do was smile. I guess my dad really didn't want to miss his only daughter's normal date out. It probably crossed his mind that this would be the first and only time he could drive me to one.

"Only a ride, okay? You take me there then drop me off. You're not going to stalk us in the cinema or anything, right?"

"Yes, Ma'am."

We drove in comfortable silence, listening to a local '70s FM station. When he finally said something, his voice was so low I barely heard what he said.

"Have fun tonight, cupcake. Make sure you have a great time. You deserve a good normal break."

"Thanks, Dad," I smiled at him. I had been so wrapped up in my own issues that it didn't really occur to me just how hard my dad was taking all these changes. He was probably preparing to fend off my suitors when I turned sixteen, but instead he was facing the real possibility of fighting monsters to save me, or losing me altogether. The realization hit me hard, and I felt the weight of my responsibilities. Dad seemed to sense the sudden turn in the atmosphere and tried to lighten the mood.

"If he ever does anything dodgy, or you know, make a pass at you or something, don't be afraid to spray him."

"Spray him? With what?"

"This," he handed me a small bottle of what looked like breath spray.

"A breath spray?"

"It's only the bottle. I wanted to make sure it's disguised so you don't look too conspicuous. The liquid is my own concoction. I got it online."

"When did you have time to do this?"

"I did this before your sixteenth birthday. You know, just in case."

I placed the bottle in my bag and laughed. I wondered if the spray would work on a *manananggal*. I bet no one's even tried it.

We got to the cinema with ten minutes to spare. I quickly got out of the car and waved goodbye before rushing off to the theater. Dad honked and left. I inhaled deeply and walked to the cinema, hoping I was the first one there. But even before I turned the corner, I could already smell his scent.

He smiled when he saw me, grinning from ear to ear. I couldn't help but smile back. He was contagious. And totally breathtaking out of his school uniform. He was carrying a brown paper bag in one hand and two large soft drinks in the other.

"I thought you might want something to snack on," he said, handing me the bag. Inside was a big bucket of cheese and bacon popcorn, one big bucket of caramel popcorn, and an assortment of chocolate bars. I laughed at the ridiculous amount of food he brought for a two-hour movie.

"You don't expect us to eat all these, do you?"

"I've seen you eat at school. This is nothing compared to the lunch you bring," he grinned.

I felt my face burn, thinking about the times I had packed my entire fridge to school after being so hungry from my training sessions. I jabbed him on the shoulder. "I don't eat that much! Well, some days I don't. Let's get in the queue before it fills up."

"I already got that sorted. I went online and bought us the tickets. You can pay me back later for the food, too."

"Well, don't you just think of everything," I smiled.

"It's our first date, I wanted it to go smoothly," he said. There was no denying it anymore. It was officially a date and my palms started to sweat.

It didn't take us long to find our seats. We watched the movie in silence, occasionally stealing glimpses at each other. Our hands sometimes touched as we grabbed for the food in the bag, which turned into a mix of confectionery by the end of the movie. Each time his hand brushed mine, it lingered a bit, sending goosebumps all over my body. It was only a second or two but I held my breath forever, exhaling slowly so he wouldn't notice how tense I was. I wondered if all our dates were going to be this way. I feared I wouldn't be able to last five dates before I had a heart attack or an ulcer. What was I thinking? Several dates? I wouldn't even have time for another one!

The movie was a blurry memory, a jumble of dialogues and actions in between moments when our hands touched. I felt disappointed when the credits finally appeared. We had no excuse for contact and I wanted so much to hold his hand. I looked at him as we stood and wondered if he was just as disappointed as I was. We strolled lazily out of the cinema, lingering at shops and trying to stretch our time together. As we neared the bus stop, I was disappointed to see that my bus was almost there. I had no excuse to stay and chat with him longer. I was about to say goodbye when he started walking with me to the bus stop. I looked at him, confused.

"I'll take you home."

"But you'll be late getting home," I said tentatively, wanting him to come with me.

"That's okay. I'll send mother a text message to let her know."

My heart skipped a beat as he sat next to me. I didn't know where to put my hands, or what to do with them. The sun was already glowing orange red, signaling the end of the day. It would be dark by the time we got to the house. I was not naïve, I knew what was expected after the first date. There was supposed to be a kiss of some sort before he'd leave. Should I close my mouth? Leave it open? French? Why was it called French kissing anyway? Did they invent it?

"Are you okay? You've been very quiet since we finished the movie," he asked.

"I'm okay. I just didn't really get the movie, it was a bit confusing."

"Yeah. I know what you mean. I wasn't sure what to say about it, and I didn't want to sound stupid making shallow remarks."

"I think there's no other remark but shallow for that movie," I laughed. He showed me his crooked smile.

"So are you okay now? I mean have your problems been resolved? I really don't want you to give me the cold shoulder again. It was a bit miserable for me."

"But you had Melissa to keep you company," I teased.

"Yes, that's why I said it was miserable for me."

"My life drama hasn't gone away yet but it's manageable. Besides, I've decided not to let it get in the way of my social life."

"Can't you tell me about your problems? Maybe I can help, you never know."

"Thanks for the offer, but it's kinda personal, you know, family stuff. I really don't want to drag anyone else to my family drama. It's complicated."

"Okay, but if you ever need anyone else to talk to, I'm here."

I looked into his eyes and knew he meant every word. It warmed my heart knowing he really cared about my secret issues, even if I could never tell him about it. I smiled and put my hand over his. "Thanks."

I changed the subject before things got too intense.

"So, tell me about your family, your parents. What are they like?"

He shifted in his seat and rubbed his hands on his pants, hesitating.

"I didn't mean to pry, we don't have to talk about your family if you don't want to," I said quickly.

"No, that's fine, I'm just not used to talking about my family, that's all. Mother is an extremely private person," he paused a bit, unsure what to say next. "She makes most of the decisions in the house. My stepdad loves that about her because he's the 'going with the flow' type of person, you know, a bit of a hippie. She can be a little demanding at times but I know her intentions are good."

"Why did you guys move to California?"

"My stepdad's work. He travels a lot though so we don't see him much."

"Wouldn't she be mad that you're out so late tonight?"

"No. She was the one who encouraged me to go out, you know, be a normal teenager. Make friends."

I wanted to ask him another question when he started again. "What about your family? What are they like?"

"Well," I hesitated, not really wanting to lie to him. "We're pretty tight, very close. Mama was a hairdresser and Dad's in IT. I don't really know what he does but his job took him to the Philippines where he met my mom. We moved here when I was thirteen after he got a better deal. There's nothing much to say really, we're pretty normal." As normal as a supernatural family could get.

He didn't say anything and for a moment, I almost thought he didn't hear me.

"I don't believe any of it, you know. The things they say about her, about your family, about you." He took my hand in both of his.

"Why don't you believe them?"

"I'm more clever than you think," he winked then turned serious. "Sometimes, people are just like that and there's nothing you can do about it except ignore them. Their simple life revolves around local gossip. It says more about them than about you."

I couldn't help but smile, knowing he saw past the rumors circulating around school. I realized I had subconsciously written off dating after my family's life became a source of constant gossip. I welcomed the little good surprises in my life no matter how brief.

The bus was almost at my stop and I pressed the button to get off. I stood up to move to the exit but stumbled back as the bus abruptly stopped. Jason wrapped his arm around my waist to catch my fall. My heart stopped.

He led me out of the bus, his hand still around my waist. I never wanted the moment to end. I felt my body's disappointment when he finally let go. My house was two blocks from the bus stop and we walked in silence, trying to slow our steps to stretch time.

I could see the sun's last rays in the horizon as the stars took over the skies. I felt his hand brush mine and when I looked down, he was already holding my hand. I squeezed his hand back and smiled. My heart was pounding in my chest and I felt a bit faint being so close to him. His grip was warm and strong. I never wanted to let go.

We walked in silence, not knowing exactly what to say but also enjoying the comfortable quiet between us. I used to complain that our house was too far from the bus stop, but tonight I silently regretted it wasn't two blocks further. We stopped near my front door and he took my other hand. I looked at him and felt my senses heightened. I noticed the specks of gold in his eyes, the musk of his body, the smoothness of his face. I wanted to run my fingers through his hair, feel his skin close to mine.

"I had a great time tonight. Really great. I'm hoping we can do this again sometime," he said, moving closer.

"I had a great time too, and yes, I'd like to do this again."

"What about this week?"

"I can't go out during school nights, but maybe Friday or Saturday?" I said, very much aware that his hand was stroking my hair.

"That would be great, I'll give you a call. I know you usually hang out with your friends at school, but can I hang out with you at lunch? I promise not to cramp your style."

"I'm sure that can be arranged. I'd like that. Wouldn't Melissa get mad at you though?"

"Yes, oh the tragedy of that. How will I ever survive?" he said.

I wanted to tease him some more but he lowered his head and kissed me. My heart jumped to my throat. I closed my eyes and felt his soft warm lips on mine. I didn't know how but I suddenly just knew how to kiss him, tenderly then with more urgency. His arms wrapped around me tightly. Time stopped. We were in a bubble under a starry sky. I wanted it to never end. I opened my eyes to watch him kissing me. Out of the corner of my eye, I saw the flowers in our front yard blooming, sprouting seeds and coming alive. My emotions had caused our plants to bloom everywhere. The gardenias we left unattended, dying in the front yard, were sprouting flowers. I pulled back fast, stopping the plants mid-bloom. Jason's brows furrowed, confused at my sudden reaction.

"Sorry, I thought I heard my dad."

He brushed my lips with his hand and leaned to kiss me again. The porch light suddenly turned on. I pulled away and smiled at him, disappointed that we had to end the kiss but also glad I had an excuse to go inside.

"I guess I should go," he said, squeezing my hand. "I'll see you at school."

He walked away, looking back to wave. I waved back before moving to the door, glancing at the wonderful work the kiss had done to our front garden. I had to be very careful about my emotions. I needed to keep myself constantly in check in case I created something similar somewhere public.

Dad was sitting in the living room, pretending to watch TV when I got in the house.

"Hi Dad, I didn't know you were into *Girls*."

"I wasn't watching it. I was just channel surfing," he said, changing the channel quickly. "How was your night?"

"Good. We skipped the movie and got matching tattoos instead. Night, Dad."

I ran to the bedroom smiling to myself. Apart from the garden show, my day was as normal as normal could be. I felt elated being just another teenager on a date. I still couldn't believe I just got back from my first date. My first kiss. It was everything I imagined it would be and more. Lolo was right about my powers. It was closely knitted with how I was feeling, so much so that when Jason's lips were touching mine I felt the warmth of my surroundings. I felt my own emotions were amplified. It was like I was singing and the flowers were my backup singers.

I touched my lips and smelled my hand, inhaling his scent. Nothing could ruin this moment. Nothing. I was glad to have this night because no matter what happened after, I would always have this one perfect night to look back to.

Chapter Eleven

The Filipino American Gazette, March 2013
Migrant Still Missing

The Filipino-American community is calling for police support on the continued search for Marie Harris, the Filipino migrant who went missing in San Jose May of last year.

Members of the community are disgruntled from the lack of interest from authorities after months without lead. There has been no new information from the public despite the sizable $100,000 prize money offered by the family.

The community continues to offer their support to the Harris family.

June 2015

It had been two weeks since my first date with Jason. We had gone out on a second date and that went just as splendidly. I was grateful for the training with Lolo because the kiss on the second date didn't result into a flora carnival in my front yard. I was able to focus on one particular plant that was dying near our home. By the end of the kiss, it had started to sprout lemons. I hoped it was a lemon plant.

It was official now, we were going out. We got together during our breaks at school, or sat somewhere for a while to chat before heading home. It felt so natural to be with him, like I had always known him all my life. It was getting more difficult to not talk about what I was going through, but I had to protect him from it all. I tried not to think about what would happen in a month when I had to decide to leave the human world or not. If I left, at least I had made memories I could bring with me.

Melissa didn't stop trying to get Jason back until after the second date. I commended her efforts, really. But she didn't bow out gracefully. There was a bit of a scene at the cafeteria one lunch period, where Jason heroically intervened by addressing Melissa loudly so everyone could hear it.

"Is there anything my girlfriend can do for you, Melissa?" he said, addressing the hushed cafeteria audience more than Melissa.

"Nothing, I was just admiring her necklace," Melissa said coldly before stomping out of the room.

I felt embarrassed but also special at being confirmed as his girlfriend so publicly. After that, Melissa kept giving me her coldest and sharpest stares. I just smiled back. For once, something in my life was going right.

As for the training, well, things had become even more interesting. Controlling and manipulating plants, animals, and the elements had been fun. But our sessions required more advanced skill. I was a bit nervous as I didn't know what was expected of me, but it was made even worse by the presence of Mark and Alyssa. We managed to convince Lolo to let them see what I could do if they promised to stay out of the way.

"You want me to what?!" I asked, surprised at the task.

Lolo was standing in the middle of the room, ready for our multitasking session. Mark and Alyssa were sitting quietly in the corner, staring at the menagerie in the room.

"You've mastered your abilities one skill at a time. Now I want you to apply all of it at the same time."

Our garage had been turned into a mini zoo, with lines of seeds and plants on one side and various animals in cages and nets. There were ten mice in a cage, a hamster running in his roller in another, a goldfish in a bowl, and our neighbors's cat, Tricky, hanging from a net on the roof. Lolo walked toward me, slowly listing the things I was expected to do simultaneously.

"I need you to grow these seeds from the ground, make the vines cross the room and open the cages, while making sure the cat doesn't eat the fish. When the mice and the hamster are out of their cages, I want you to line them up and make them wait patiently for your instructions."

I stared at Lolo, dumbfounded at what he just said. I could see the confusion on Mark's and Alyssa's faces. They had never seen me in action before except for the thing with the flower and the bird. I felt a bit of performance anxiety coming on.

"How can I do all that at the same time? I'm not ready, Lolo. It's too much. What if the cat eats the mice? Have you seen how quick Tricky is in action? That cat's feral."

"Then you have to make sure the cat doesn't kill any of the other animals," he says. "Start communicating with the animals. In the count of five, you will begin."

"One."

I sensed the confusion in the room. The mice panicking, the hamster oblivious in its endless marathon, the goldfish calmly swimming around, and Tricky, hungry for the feast in the garage.

"Two."

I held the smooth rock around my neck and told the animals to calm down, to relax, to listen to me and only me.

"Three."

I saw Tricky licking her lips and I gave her a look that briefly made her pause, but I guess primal hunger took over more because she still kept eyeing the mice.

"Four."

"Hold on, Lolo, I'm not ready yet."

"Five."

I sent the seeds flying to the ground, burying themselves through the concrete, while the vines climbed around the walls, reaching the cages on the other side of the room. Lolo let Tricky out of the net and she landed on her feet, immediately going after the mice. I heard a loud crash as the goldfish bowl shattered on the floor, tipped by one of the vines. My head was fighting to focus on all of the tasks at the same time. My heart was racing and I feared I wouldn't be able to save any of them from Tricky's hunger. The vines opened the mice and hamster cages, and they all panicked, scrambling around the room, trying to get away from Tricky who was now in full hunting mode. I felt the gasp of the goldfish, drowning on the floor, and I quickly lifted it in the air just as Tricky had reached the spot. My focus started to waver and my confusion kicked in. I looked around the utter chaos and felt the helplessness of the situation. I was not ready. I was not from their world. It all felt impossible.

The plants on the ground were starting to wilt and I felt the immense fear of the mice and hamster as they raced for cover from Tricky. Before I could say anything, I heard Alyssa's voice echo in the room.

"You can do this, Karina! Keep going!" Mark was cheering, too, whistling and clapping. My personal cheer team.

Their energy gave me a boost and I closed my eyes to focus. I could see in my head what I wanted everyone and everything to do. I saw how I wanted them to act and what I needed them to show me when I opened my eyes. The image in my head was so clear. I was calm, confident of what I would find when I opened my eyes. I saw that everything I pictured in my head had been copied in real life. From the cat sitting quietly away from the mice and hamster, who were staring at me, standing on hind legs, to the vines on the wall, the plants flowering on the floor, the gold fish swimming in a filthy plastic cup, and Lolo smiling in the corner.

"Well done, Karina. Very well done."

I gave Lolo a look, unsure about what I did exactly. I knew I made everything happen, but did I just move him from his spot, too? Or did he move all by himself? Seeing my confusion, Lolo offered an explanation.

"Your mind is stronger than you think, mija. When you saw me in your head, I presumed you wanted me out of the way so you can arrange everything else. Although I could have moved, your abilities placed me in the spot you wanted to put me."

"He literally floated to that spot, it was awesome," Mark said, jumping out of his chair.

"Can I really do that? Move people?"

"Yes, you can. It would have been harder for you to do it had I resisted your abilities. You will know this when you face your enemies. But the stronger your powers become, the easier it will be for you to fight them."

Tricky was still looking hungry so I led the mice and hamster back in their cages and opened the back door to let the cat out. I pulled the plants out of the concrete and off the walls, and added them to the increasing number of flowers in our backyard.

"Okay, show's over. Back to normal life," I nudged Mark and Alyssa to follow me in the house. Lolo stopped me near the doorway.

"Tomorrow, we need to do more, Karina. There are still a lot of things you need to learn."

I nodded and walked away. I understood why he was doing what he was doing. Still, I couldn't help but question whether it was to help me with my enemies or if it was to help him and his kingdom. I was still unsure whether I cared about Engkantasia or not.

I found Mark and Alyssa in my room, playing with Wilbur. I sat on my bed and realized how hungry I was. We all walked to the kitchen to fix ourselves something to eat. We had been doing this on our own for a while now.

When Mama disappeared shortly before my fourteenth birthday, I had no choice but to learn how to take care of myself and Dad. Mama used to do everything for us. She once told me she found peace in the day-to-day chores. When she disappeared, I had to learn quickly how to cook, do the groceries, do the laundry and ironing, manage my own life, and more. I couldn't rely on Dad. He was unreachable for some time, locked in his own head, obsessed with various ways to find Mama. I didn't hold that against him. We were a team. So while he looked for Mama, I took over doing the things she used to do.

Mark was making a huge batch of two-minute noodles while Alyssa and I made the sandwiches. I couldn't count the number of times when we had done this in my kitchen, working like a well-oiled machine, handing condiments to each other without a word. We carried the food to the dining table and sat down in silence. Finally, I couldn't stand it anymore.

"I know you are bursting to say something, so spill."

Mark and Alyssa looked at each other, hesitating for a bit. Alyssa gingerly started, unusual since she had never been afraid to tell me anything.

"Watching you do all those things, well . . . " She looked at Mark for confirmation. He nodded.

"What?"

"It just made things more real, you know? More final. Our lives are never going to be the same again."

I looked at their sullen faces and knew they were right. The changes in my life would not only affect me, or endanger me, but them as well.

"What do you want to do?" I asked quietly, not wanting to know the answer. What if they wanted to sever ties, stay away from me because of my new life? I didn't think I could do everything I needed to without them.

"If you want to stay away, not be friends anymore, I will understand."

"What are you talking about?" Mark said, surprised. "Is that what you want?"

"Of course not, but I won't be surprised if you guys want to stay out of my chaotic life. I'm putting you guys in danger just by being near you."

They looked at each other again, a little coded message streaming between them.

"What?" I asked.

"That's not what we want at all," Alyssa started. "We feel a bit useless around you, like there is nothing we can do to help. So, while you've been training, Mark and I have been talking."

"We know you've been distressed after finding out about the *manananggal* so Alyssa's been helping me with a little project . . . to help you out."

"What project?" I asked, now really confused.

"We're a team, that's never going to change. So we wanted to be useful to you, so you don't worry about us too much. Mark and I came up with some gadgets." Alyssa's excitement was showing in her face.

"What kind of stuff?"

"I think it's better if we show you after dinner. I packed them in my bag before coming here today. They're in your room."

"It's utter genius, absolutely," Alyssa gushed, and I could see Mark blushing a bit. We finished our food quickly and placed everything in the dishwasher.

Mark rushed to my room and we followed him. He unpacked a huge gym bag and set the gadgets on my bed. The contraptions looked primitive, like a science project from your garage, which was, I guessed, what they were. Mark held up one of them, a wristband of some sort.

"After you told me about the origins of the *manananggal*, I thought about creating something that would deter them from attacking us. So I came up with this," he said, attaching the wristband to my arm. He turned the bedroom light off and turned the wristband on. It spread a purple bluish light around the room in different angles, like a disco ball.

"It's a compact UV light emitter that I've rigged so that it's portable and pushes the light in different angles. You mentioned that the *mananangal* couldn't survive in the sun when they're in monster mode. So a pocket UV light will come in handy," he said, looking mighty pleased with his invention.

"Look, he even made one for me as a necklace so it's not too conspicuous," Alyssa said, showing off a round flat metal necklace that would look at home in a rock concert.

"This is amazing, Mark, you've outdone yourself!"

"I know, right? Finally, something that actually has a good purpose," Alyssa teased, referring to the dozens of times Mark had come up with a new gadget in his little workshop.

"There's more," Mark said, ignoring Alyssa's joke. "I've also designed a vest and a couple of mega torches. I thought it might be something you can wear, or carry around or something. Just in case, you never know."

I looked at the weapons Mark designed and felt a surge of happiness knowing that these people would always have my back no matter what. The way they had always been there for me in the past.

"I can't ask you both to give up your normal life to be part of mine. But know that I am eternally grateful for your support."

Alyssa hugged me while Mark awkwardly patted my back. He was never big with emotions. But his geeky face said it all.

Now if I could only keep them alive.

Chapter Twelve

Mama's DIY Engkantasia Book

Engkanto

The engkanto has many similarities to humans. An engkanto ages, although not as quickly. It can suffer from illness, and can die. Male and female engkanto are very beautiful, have intense eyes, fair complexion, and luxurious hair. They look very human that it is hard to distinguish them.

The engkanto gets its source of mana (energy) from its surroundings. This, however, is not as abundant when it is in the human world.

The dwellings of the engkanto appear as natural features, like large rocks or trees. Although to humans befriended by the engkanto, the houses can appear as grand palaces. These creatures prefer large trees such as the balete, which can also be an entrance to Engkantasia.

Since everything started, I had been updating my journal more. I took out the binder from under the bed, filled with memories. Good ones and bad. I started it when I was nine, scrapbooking photos and writing my deepest thoughts about my life. Well, as deep as a nine-year-old could be.

After Mama disappeared, I compiled all the news articles I could find about her case, hoping that one of them would hold the answer. At the peak of it all, Mama's disappearance became the face of various political agendas. They made special features about it on TV and interviewed some people who claimed to know her in the Philippines. Half of them were total unknowns. People we had never even met. That was when I realized you couldn't rely on what you'd see in the media at all. If we ever had a chance of finding out what happened to Mama, we had to do it ourselves.

As I prepared for my session with Lolo, I tried to gain the courage to ask him more about what he knew about Mama's case. I felt like he had deliberately avoided having that conversation with me. I walked to the garage to find him sitting with Wilbur. It was a Saturday, and I decided to spend the whole day training. I wasn't going to, but the last couple of nights had been distressing for me. I had been having constant nightmares, riddled with *manananggal*. In the center of the chaos was Mama, helpless and bloodied, lying on the ground. Every time I tried to reach her, a *manananggal* dragged me away. I always woke up unable to save her. I was tempted to shake it off as my subconscious' way of sorting things out, but something clicked in my head. The place where my dream occurred was always the same. The same spot, the same surroundings, the same walls and floor. It was a place I had never been to before but I couldn't help but think it was a real place. What if it was a vision and not a dream? For the first time, I felt hopeful about finding Mama.

I stood there watching Lolo play with Wilbur, a smile spread across his face. His veil was down and I saw a boyish twinkle in his eyes as he let the little mouse skitter around him. I wondered if he used to smile like that as a child, or when he was training Mama. I touched my necklace, a habit I noticed I had been doing more frequently. As my hand felt the smoothness of the rock, I was transported to an unfamiliar environment. A beautiful place with trees of vivid colors—purple, red, yellow. Green clouds floated in the sky like fairy floss. Birds flew in a flock of multiple colors that changed as they moved.

It was Engkantasia.

There was laughter. A little girl playing with droplets of fire. They danced on her hands and she giggled as she made them explode above her head in a glittering display of fireworks. A man was standing beside her, applauding her efforts. The man turned. He was a younger version of Lolo. It must be when he was training Mama as a child. She was jumping around, whirling waterpools in the air above Lolo's head, getting him wet. He ran as she chased him with it, splashing him with water.

A tear ran down my cheek. I didn't even realize I was crying. There was so much joy and love between them. They were close, like Dad and me. It broke my heart to know that this bond was broken.

109

"Are you okay?" Lolo asked, putting Wilbur down. The vision dissipated, taking me back to the garage. I wiped away the tears and sat next to Lolo.

"I'm fine, Lolo. It's nothing."

"Do you want to talk about it?"

"No, I just want to train. Get my mind off it."

He squeezed my hand, letting the silence sit between us for a while.

"Let's begin then."

He moved toward the table. It had a bowl of water and a candle on it. Lolo lit the candle with his finger.

"Today, I will teach you how to manipulate the elements. Fire, water, wind, lightning. Whatever is available to you. The concept is similar to what you did with the plants, but with these you have to be more confident. Natural elements are temperamental. A slight doubt can be devastating."

"Devastating?"

"Trying to control fire, for instance, means you have to make sure you don't get burned yourself. If you doubt that you can do it, the fire can engulf you instead of your enemy. The same with wind, lightning, water—they can all turn on you, injure you if you're uncertain."

"Great," I muttered. Already I was starting to doubt myself and we had not even started.

"Let's begin with water, something relatively harmless. The water in the bowl is clean. I want you to drink it."

"That's simple enough," I said, reaching for the bowl.

"Drink it without lifting the bowl," he said, stopping my hand. "Take the water out of the bowl and direct it to your mouth. See in your mind's eye where you want it to go."

I remembered the vision from the necklace. Mama creating whirlpools in the air, chasing Lolo with it. I smiled and moved toward the bowl.

"Focus," Lolo said.

I stared at the water for a couple of minutes but nothing happened. I moved closer, dipping my finger and whirling the water around until it created a small whirlpool. The water was cool on my finger. The swirling was relaxing me and I started to loosen up. I lifted my finger out of the bowl, letting droplets fall into the little whirl I created. But instead of falling, the droplets floated in the air, suspended by whatever force was there. I lifted my finger higher and more droplets followed the direction of my finger. I walked away, slowly, opening my hand, drawing the rest of the water out of the bowl. It moved, like waves in the air, following my hand. I drew the water high above my head, letting the drops fall into my mouth. I heard a loud sound near the door and I lost my concentration. The water fell on me, drenching my head. I saw Dad with his mouth hanging open.

"Hi Dad," I smiled at him. I felt guilty, like he had seen me doing something I shouldn't have. I realized Dad had never seen me in training before. Lolo had told me several times that he was welcome to watch, but he never wanted to. When he knew we were having a late session, Dad would always stay at work. He was still in denial. As long as he didn't see what I was doing, then maybe he could think it didn't exist. He picked up the phone he dropped on the ground and walked out the door.

"Dad!" I ran after him but Lolo stopped me.

"We have work to do, mija. Let him think things through. You can talk to him later."

I stood there, staring at the door, feeling sad and guilty. I didn't know why I was feeling guilty about what I was doing. It was not like I had a choice. I was training to protect us from whatever it was that was out there trying to kill us. I half-heartedly tried the water trick again, and as expected, it didn't work. It took me a while to get back into things, focusing on what Lolo wanted me to do. Finally, Lolo decided to raise the stakes.

"I know you're disappointed by your father's reaction. But you have to realize that you don't have the luxury of being distracted anymore. You need to learn this now, master it. Your family's life depends on it."

His words made sense but I couldn't help but be angry at him. I didn't choose to be like this. I wanted my old life back, the one that had my parents eating pancakes together on a Sunday morning. The one that didn't have monsters flying outside my bedroom. The one without nightmares haunting me each night.

"My family is my dad. Mama is gone. I don't know where she is and it looks like you don't either. So yes, I am distracted because the only family I have left is feeling worse than he felt after Mama disappeared. What do you know about family? Your own daughter ran away and you just sat there and watched her go. That's all you do. Your kind just sits and watches as the world gets eaten by your creatures. I don't want to be like you. I care for the people I love and I will do everything in my power to help them."

Lolo looked at me, sadness flickered across his face. "You're right, Karina," he said, leaving me in the garage on my own. In a span of mere minutes, I managed to alienate my dad and offend my grandfather. Brilliant. There was still plenty of daylight. I cut our training short, very short.

I decided to continue with the training on my own, starting with the water on me. I needed to do something productive. If I could drain it from the bowl, could I drain it from my body and clothes? Wasn't it just the same principle but in smaller amounts?

I began with the water on the floor, separating the drops from the concrete, molecule by molecule. I looked at my body, my clothes, my hair, careful not to lose my concentration. As a ball of water formed in front of me, I moved toward the candle, still burning low. I used my other hand to take the flame off the candle and float it beside the water, like bubbles in the air. I didn't know what it was inside of me that was making me do these two new things at the same time. Maybe it was the anger or the confusion, or the pity I felt for my dad. Maybe it was my sudden resolve to find Mama no matter what. It didn't matter really. It was time for me to stop sitting idly by while Mama was somewhere, probably suffering, being tortured by whoever took her.

Unsatisfied with just water and fire, I created a small whirlwind on the ground, spinning like the red top I used to play with as a child. I sat on the floor, lining up the water, fire and whirlwind, now rotating in small circles. It was hypnotizing watching the spinning elements. It was relaxing me, clarifying my thoughts, taking me back to my dream. Then it hit me, so clear I wondered why I never thought of it before. The walls, the floor, Mama's prison, it was enough of an image to send the animals to find.

I threw the ball of fire hurling across the room, hitting the bin and setting it on fire. On instinct, I threw the ball of water in the bin. The fire fizzled out. I focused on the whirlwind, now the size of a plate, sucking bits and pieces from the garage into its center. It occurred to me, without a single doubt, that if

I wanted to I could create a tornado. One that could decimate the whole neighborhood, even maybe the whole city.

This utter clarity and confidence were liberating. For the first time since all of it happened, I knew I was strong. Stronger than my enemies probably gave me credit for. I split the whirlwind into two, then three, then four, until they all disappeared into the breeze.

I sat on the floor and tucked my legs in, closed my eyes and hummed the song that calmed me the most. I reached out to any creature I could find around me—Tricky, the mice, the birds, my neighbors's golden retriever, Zeus. I reached as far as I could and called out for help. I explained what I wanted them to see, the room, the floor, the walls, my mother lying there, still in the nightgown she was wearing the day she disappeared. I forced myself to remember more details, like the color of the bricks, the cracks on the wall, the lack of windows, a solitary lightbulb, a bucket in the corner, the grime on the walls, maybe some mold or a slimy green substance. I didn't know how many animals I had reached. I kept my eyes closed and sent the image again, just for good measure.

When I opened my eyes, I gasped at the sight in the garage. There were animals everywhere, filling every inch of space. They sat there silently, staring at me, letting me know they heard what I just sent them. Birds, cats, dogs, butterflies, squirrels, the ones I called creepy crawlies—spiders, worms, caterpillars, snails, and more. I stared back, smiled, and said thank you. They scampered out as quickly and as quietly as they came in.

I walked to the house to talk to Dad. I found him in his office, hunched over paperwork but not really reading. I sat on the chair behind him, tucking my legs under me. Before I could decide what to say, I heard him say something, so gently I almost missed it.

"She's not dead, you know. I know it in my heart. Like I know the sun is going to come out tomorrow."

"I know what you mean," I said.

"I'm sorry. For not being there. For checking out, leaving you on your own."

"I understand. You don't have to apologize." He turned his chair to look at me, eyes full of pain, of things he'd left unsaid for so long.

"I'm supposed to be the parent."

"I know, and you provided for me. We're a team, right? That's what Mama always used to say. I wanted to help out in any way I can. You didn't abandon me, Dad. You were coping the way you knew how."

We fell silent, not knowing what else to say. There was something I had been meaning to ask him for a while but didn't know how to start.

"Dad, did you ever have any suspicions about Mama and her past?"

He looked at his hands, hesitating. Maybe I shouldn't have asked him. What good would it do? It would only hurt him more. Just when I thought he wasn't going to answer, he started to talk.

"I knew she wasn't telling me the whole truth about her past. She was always vague about it when I asked her. But it didn't matter to me. We all have our secrets. I just never realized her secret was this big."

"How did you guys meet?" I had never asked my parents about their love story. It wasn't that I had never been curious, especially given how obviously in love they were. I always thought there would be a perfect time when I could ask them. Then Mama disappeared and that changed it all. I guess it was as better time as any to know about their past.

I could see a sad smile forming on Dad's lips. Despite everything, the memory of their first meeting still brought him happiness.

"We met while I was finishing my contract in Manila—a very populated and polluted city if I ever saw one. I said yes to that job mainly because of the money and the adventure. I've never been to Asia and was curious about the place and its people. I never had any intention to meet anyone and get into anything serious."

He raised his head and looked at me. "Your mother changed all that."

"I was invited to the wedding of one of my workmates. I chatted a lot with the bridesmaids and basically hung around with the ladies more than the men. Somehow I ended up in one of the hotel rooms where the bride's entourage was getting ready. Your mom was the hairdresser for the event and although there were heaps of gorgeous women there, I couldn't take my eyes off of her."

He ran his hand through his hair, clearing his throat and wiping his eyes.

"She was quiet most of the time but there was just something about her that caught my attention. She was effortlessly beautiful even with her messy ponytail and makeup-free face. She wore a shirt and paired it with jeans and slippers. It was very simple but she carried it with an aura of grace. Now I know why. She was royalty."

Dad continued, "I didn't know how to start a conversation with her because she never looked at my direction. So after the last of the bridesmaids' hair was done, I took the seat in front of the mirror and asked her to fix my hair."

Dad let out a surprising laugh. "I was sporting longish hair back then, I thought it was cool. I sat there looking at her while she combed and cut my hair. I wasn't paying much attention to what she was doing because I was trying to get some words out of her, which was quite difficult. It was like squeezing water from a stone."

I moved closer to Dad and held his hand, loving the happiness that briefly crossed his face as he recalled that day. As our hands enclosed each other, a jolt of static electricity traveled through me. When I opened my eyes, I was there, in the room with my parents—a younger version of them from the day they first met. I was standing in the room but also very much aware I wasn't part of the scene.

"Karina? What's wrong, honey?" Dad said, bringing me back to the present.

"I can see you and Mama. I can see you guys on that day, that memory you have in your head."

"How?"

"I don't know. When I held your hand, it's like the memory went through me. I want to try again, Dad, I want to see."

He took my hands and held it between his. "What do I need to do?"

"I think you just think of that day, remember your first meeting."

Dad closed his eyes and I felt the jolt again, taking me to that day. I could see the great resemblance between me and Mama. She was so beautiful.

"How long have you worked as a hairdresser?" Dad asked.

"Long enough."

"Are you from Manila?"

"No."

"Where are you from?"

"Central Philippines."

"Which island? Visayas?"

"Around there."

"Are you living with your family?"

"No."

"Husband and kids?"

"No"

"Boyfriend?"

"No."

"Girlfriend?"

Mama stopped what she was doing and looked at him, raising one eyebrow and shaking her head, exasperated by his barrage of questions. It didn't discourage him though. He was determined to get more information out of her.

"Did you always want to be a hairdresser?"

"No."

"What did you want to do for a living then?"

"A serial killer," she deadpanned.

"Cool, you'd be great at it since you're very well equipped already. Those scissors are sharp."

Even more silence. Not even a smirk. I applauded Dad's patience.

"So how do you know the bride and groom?" Dad tried again.

"She comes to the salon regularly."

"Are you friends with both of them?"

"No."

"Just the bride then?"

"No."

"You look like you have mixed heritage. Are you half-Spanish or half-Chinese or something?"

"No."

"Have you traveled a lot?"

"No."

"I'm from Australia. It's a great country, you should visit it some time."

"I'm done," she said, turning the chair so Dad could see the haircut. He looked in the mirror and froze. Mama had turned his longish hair into a mullet. She must have used her powers because I was sure Dad's hair wasn't long enough for a mullet.

"It suits you," she said.

Dad laughed so hard there were tears in his eyes. "I guess I deserved that," he said. "I apologize if I made you uncomfortable. I promise to shut up if you fix my hair before the wedding."

Mama paused and thought about it. "If one more word comes out of you, I will stop what I'm doing and I won't fix your hair until after the reception."

"I promise," Dad said, putting his hand on his chest.

She started working on Dad's hair again, cutting up the mullet.

But Dad just couldn't resist it. "I'm not trying to crack on to you or anything. I just really want to get to know you."

Mama stopped what she was doing and started putting away her tools. Dad quickly realized she was dead serious about the "no talking" rule.

"I'm sorry, I promise I'll shut up, please," he pleaded but it was too late. She had already packed her things and was ready to head out the door. She turned around and gave him a card.

"This is where I work, you can drop by anytime and I'll fix your hair for free. But for today, you'll have to go to the wedding with half a mullet," she said before slamming the door behind her.

Go, Mama.

Dad just sat there, stunned and staring at the door. He turned around to look at himself in the mirror and was horrified to see he only had half a mullet. It looked even worse than a full mullet.

I let go of Dad's hands and returned to the present, laughing so hard, tears started coming out of my eyes. I looked at Dad and he was laughing too, a real belly laugh that I hadn't heard in a long time.

After the laughter tapered off, I watched Dad as he wiped his face.

"What did you do after that?"

"I couldn't find any scissors and so I was forced to go through the entire wedding ceremony and reception with that haircut. I had to tell everyone I had an accident with my head shaver in the hotel room. As it was a wedding, there were heaps of photos of the event. Later on after we got married, your mom contacted my old friend and asked for a copy of one of the wedding photos with me in it—half a mullet and everything. We still have the photo somewhere."

"Mama was a tough nut. She was amazing."

"I realized very quickly that she was very different from any of the women I've ever met, which meant I had absolutely no idea how to ask her out. I presumed none of my old tactics would work on her. I went to her workplace the very next day and begged for her to fix my hair. She made me wait for an hour before giving me a proper haircut and I didn't say a word the entire time she was doing it. After she finished, I went to the cashier and paid for the service, even though she said it was free. I turned around and gave her my card and said thank you before I left."

"That's it? You didn't ask her out?"

"It took me a while to have the courage to talk to her again. I had to go back to the salon several times for my haircut. I dyed my hair so many times in so many shades before I finally asked her out. By then, I think I've worn her out with my almost weekly 'haircut' trips, my incessant questions, and my blabbering. It took some time before she finally warmed up to me, and even longer to finally become my girlfriend. It was extremely hard work. She was always very private about her personal life even after we started going out."

"Even her workmates at the salon knew very little about her. She kept to herself and only joined gatherings every now and then. Her workmates told me she's had so many men pursue her but they all eventually gave up—some much quicker than others. I didn't know why she went out with me. I only found out about it later on when I finally asked her why she picked me out of all the men who wanted her. She said she could see my heart and that my intentions were pure. I thought it was a euphemism for women's intuition. Now I realize she really did have the ability to read people."

Seeing my parents together so vividly warmed my heart and strengthened my resolve to help them be together again. No matter what the cost. I had been reading about earth-shattering love stories in books but I never thought about looking at my own parents' story.

"I know everything is going to be fine, Dad. I know it."

I saw him smile, briefly, but I was glad it wasn't one of his half smiles. "What I did in the garage . . . "

"Don't worry about it," he said. "It was just a surprise. I've known you're amazing since the day you were born, but to see what you've been doing, it's just beyond words."

"Are you scared?"

"Yes, but seeing what you've been doing has helped, I must admit. I know the training will help you with whatever it is that's out there. I want to know that you can defend yourself even when I'm not there. I would have been okay with karate lessons but this is good, too," he smiled, a twinkle in his eyes. There were moments when I caught the old dad, the joker who wouldn't let up, who always found the fun things in life and always perked me up. I cherished the rare moments when I would see that Dad again.

"So you're okay with it?"

"Do what you need to do. Don't worry about me. Listen to your Lolo. Although he makes me uncomfortable sometimes, I know he only has your best interest at heart."

"Speaking of Lolo, I better go find him and apologize."

"Why?"

"I think I might have offended him a bit with a small rant." I got up to leave when I heard Dad standing up, hugging me from behind, kissing the top of my head like he used to.

"I love you," he whispered.

"I love you, too, Dad."

I headed to the kitchen to find Lolo when I heard voices coming from the living room. Visitors? That was odd. We never had visitors. I walked into the room to find the most bizarre vision I had ever seen. Lolo was conversing like old friends with several creatures. Ones that I read about for a long time in popular Filipino folklore.

The booming voice was coming from a *kapre*—a huge hairy man, over ten feet tall, sitting on the floor, trying to be comfortable next to the floor lamp. He was wearing clothes made from animal skin, I think, and trying hard not to hit the ceiling. He was holding a gigantic cigar in one hand, fidgeting like he wanted to light it. Sitting beside the giant was a *duwende*—a small man, probably less than two feet tall, wearing clothing made of leaves that glimmer under the living room light.

I moved closer to the group to see another creature sitting on the couch with Lolo. A *tikbalang*, unmistakable as there was nothing like it in books. He was tall, maybe seven feet, very hairy that you could hardly see any skin and only had a loincloth on. But although his body was that of a human, his head was that of a horse—like a reverse centaur. Then finally, there was a couple sitting across Lolo. A beautiful woman dressed in white with the longest hair I had ever seen. Her skin shimmered like it was encrusted with millions of tiny diamonds, with a tinge of blue and green hues. I could see patches of scales on her back. A *sirena*, or mermaid, as others knew them. Next to her was a *syokoy*. They always traveled together, according to tales. He protected her when she had a tail in the water and when she had feet on land. Instead of skin, the *syokoy* was covered in scales. His face resembled a fish, complete with gills. I was curious as to how he was breathing above water.

It looked like a meeting of leaders from a comic convention. The room fell silent the moment they sensed me. It was a surreal experience staring into the faces of creatures so familiar to me but also so foreign. They were from my books and they had come alive.

"Karina, come and sit with us. Let me introduce you to my old friends," Lolo said, beckoning me to sit close to him.

"'Why are they here?"

"I called them here after . . . " he paused, referring to my earlier rant.

"Lolo, about what I said, I'm so sorry," I started to say but he cut me off.

"Don't worry about that. You were right. That's why I called them here. We are finished watching. It's time to act," he squeezed my shoulder, and turned to the sitting giant smoking a cigar.

"This is Kamudo, the leader of the Kapre tribe. Here is Pili, the leader of the Duwende tribe," referring to the tiny man beside Kamudo.

"This is Gulat, the leader of the Tikbalang tribe," he said, pointing to the horse head. "And these are Serra and Yukoy, the leaders of the Serena and Syokoy tribe, the kingdom underwater. I invited them all here tonight for a crucial meeting and to meet you."

I moved closer to Lolo, not uttering a word. Things just became very real for me. My home was actually hosting a conference of leaders from creatures of a parallel land. Was I expected to step up to this? What did they want from me? Should I make a welcome speech or something? I was very much aware of how plain I looked beside them, sweaty in my training clothes. Before I could say anything, Serra, the beautiful underwater leader, spoke.

"We are here to meet you, Karina, that is it. We don't expect anything. We are just very eager to finally see the heir of Hari Magatu."

"Serra is a reader, she can sense emotions and read thoughts. I haven't taught you how to block that yet but I will soon," Lolo said.

"Welcome to my house. Do you guys want anything to eat? I mean, not that I know what you eat."

"No, we've eaten. Thank you so much for the offer," the *kapre* said.

"We can speak openly in front of Karina, so please continue," Lolo said.

"As I was saying," Pili said, "we are sensing a stirring in the kingdom. The clans are getting scared of the uncertainty of our future. There are talks of factions, tribes trying to get as much supporters as possible to try and take on the throne. The *manananggal* clan is even starting to consider looking for Maita's heir."

"The *manananggal*?" I asked.

"Those creatures are not like the one you saw outside the window, Karina. These are the original *manananggal*, untouched by the gruesome transformation of the one you saw," Serra said, reading my thoughts again. "They do not like how Marila turned out but they were also not happy about banishing Maita to the human world. Although they've been fairly loyal to the crown all these years, they still remember the pain and would not hesitate to follow a *manananggal* who wants to overthrow the king."

"So what can we do?" I asked.

They looked at each other, preparing to announce what I could only gather as bad news. I shifted in my seat, uncomfortable at the silence.

"We only have five weeks before your training ends," Serra paused, hesitating to say the next line. "But because of the uncertainty in Engkantasia, we will need to know your decision before this week ends. We need to send out a message to appease the kingdom before chaos ensues. Your great-great-grandparents placed those rules to protect both worlds. We're afraid that if word gets out that there is no heir, some might break the rules, perhaps even cross the boundary between the two worlds."

"So I have a week to decide," I said quietly. A giant rock sat heavily inside me. "But I am half-human. Wouldn't that fact cause even more chaos in Engkantasia? Will they respect me if I decide to take on the throne?"

"Just because you're half-human doesn't mean you're less powerful. You have the essence of pure *engkangto* royalty coursing through your veins. That is more than enough reason to earn the tribes' respect," Serra said.

"But what about Mama?"

Again, more silence and hesitation. Even with all their powers, it was hard for them to find the strength to say the words they wanted to say. Mama was collateral damage. Finding her wasn't as important as saving Engkantasia. I wondered if these creatures still considered her as one of them given how long she had been away from their world. I looked at Serra, hoping she was reading my thoughts. Finally, Lolo answered my question.

"Your mother was most likely taken by forces from Engkantasia."

"How can you be so sure?" I asked, not wanting to believe him.

"If she were just taken by humans and hidden in your world, I would have been able to sense her. I would know if she was dead or alive. But right now, none of us can sense your mother, which means she has been cloaked and only our people can do that."

"So she's still alive then!"

"There is a chance but . . . " Lolo paused.

"But what?"

Lolo looked around the room, but no one wanted to meet his eyes. They, too, were thinking the same thing. Mama might already be dead.

"She's been gone for a long time, Karina," Serra started. "None of us can assure you that Marie is still alive. If they've cloaked her, then . . . "

"Then even her body will be untraceable to us."

It hit me then, so clearly and so vividly. Mama was not a priority for these leaders. None of them believed she was still alive. None of them had my connection to her. Even if I tried to convince them she was not dead, their main focus would still be saving the two worlds. The need of the many outweighed the need of one.

I was on my own. I knew I should be more focused on the bigger picture, on the catastrophe that was upon us. But my family was my world. They had always been my world. What kind of a daughter would I be if I let go that easily? And what about Dad? I couldn't just give up. Not for his sake.

Without a word, I stood and went to my room, locking the door behind me—not that it would stop anyone. Lolo could easily open it, and Dad had spare key. But somehow, that one act of defiance gave me some control over my life just when it seemed to be spiraling out of control. I sat in the dark for some time, not moving, just staring into space, trying to stop myself from thinking. No one came after me, not that I was expecting them to. Everyone in that room knew the weight of the decision I had to make.

Five weeks. Something was going to end in five weeks. It was either my life in this world or an entire civilization. I felt my cheeks getting wet but I didn't remember crying.

Something clicked in my mind and before I knew it, I was off the bed and packing clothes in my overnight bag. I changed to my jeans and shirt, and stuffed everything I could think of in the bag. I opened the window as quietly as I could. I had to get out. I needed to be somewhere else. I ran to the bus stop with my bag and took out my mobile phone. There was only one person I could think of who was detached from all this madness.

Chapter Thirteen

Mama's DIY
Engkantasia Book

Tikbalang

The tikbalang is a creature that lurks in the mountains and forests. It is very tall, bony, with longer limbs than normal that when it squats, its knees reach above its head. It has the head and feet of a horse.

The tikbalang is mild by nature but is also a great trickster. It confuses its victims so that they keep returning to the same spot no matter how far they go or where they turn.

The tikbalangs are the brave guardians of Engkantasia. These creatures are found standing at the foot of large trees, guarding the entrance to the engkanto's territory.

"Come in, Karina, I'll take care of the cab fare, don't worry," he said, looking fabulous even in his pajamas.

I held my bag close to my chest, very aware of my vulnerability. Jason's house was almost palatial. The metal gates were so tall and meters away from the front door, protecting the family's privacy. The front lawn stretched with lush green grass, tall trees lined up against the gate, adding extra protection from prying eyes outside. I felt Jason's arm around my shoulder. He took my bag and guided me toward the house.

"I am so sorry for calling so late and for putting you on the spot. I just didn't know who to call. I hope your parents are not mad," I said to him, embarrassed at my situation. What am I going to tell him about why I ran away?

"It's okay, don't worry about it. My stepfather is traveling so it's just us and mother. My parents are very hospitable people and they know I care about you a lot. They understand."

I felt his whole body contract as we neared his house, like he was anxious about something. I didn't want to push him about it but it seemed like he was just as scared as I was. Knots were forming in my stomach again, getting worse with each step.

He opened one of the enormous double doors, leading into the living room. There was a very expensive-looking leather couch suite across a giant TV, complemented by other artsy furniture and high-end hi-fi system. The room was littered with souvenirs from all over the world. The windows were covered with heavy curtains. I knew they were rich but I didn't know they were mafia rich.

I didn't get enough time to admire the rest of the house as Jason pulled me toward the staircase where a stunning woman was descending. I could see the resemblance and somehow I knew that she was Jason's mother, even though she seemed far too young to be his mom. To say she was a sight to behold was an understatement. Her long black hair was made even darker by the contrast of her flawless skin. Her lips were full and red and her eyes glittered with different shades of blue and brown. The resemblance was uncanny. I knew then that Jason would still look marvelous even as a woman. Not that I wanted him to turn into one.

"Hello Karina, welcome to our home. I am so delighted to finally meet you," she said, extending a well-manicured hand.

127

I accepted her hand and held down a shudder as I felt her firm ice-cold handshake.

"I'm so sorry to be disturbing you like this. I really appreciate your help, Ma'am," I said. Another chill traveled up my spine.

"Nonsense, you are not disturbing us at all. And please call me Mirasol. Any friend of Jason's is a friend of the family. I hope you find your stay comfortable. And please, feel at home. Don't hesitate to ask us for anything," she said, touching my hair before going back up the stairs.

"Jason will show you to your room. Good night," she said without looking back.

"This way." Jason took my arm and led me to the other side of the house. We went through the kitchen and out the back door. I began to think they were putting me in the garage when I saw the cabin on the other side of the garden. Jason opened the door, revealing what looked like a room from a five-star hotel. The king-sized bed with a very plush duvet was the center of the room. Across it was a huge LCD TV on the wall, a Blu-ray player, and a small refrigerator under it. There was a round breakfast table with two chairs close to the bed, while on the other side was a huge closet with a floor-to-ceiling sliding door mirror. He showed me the bathroom and I had to suppress a gasp after seeing the spa bath and huge vanity mirror. Towels, bathrobes, and various toiletries were already laid out for me. Jason said the refrigerator was also fully stocked with food I might like.

"This place is amazing. I don't know what to say," I said, in awe of everything.

"It's nothing. Mother always makes sure we have a good guest room wherever we are. The phone connects to the house, and I've left my extension on your bedside table in case you want to, um, call me or something."

"Thank you. Thank you for everything," I said, taking his hand.

"When you're ready to talk, I'll be really close. Just let me know and I'll be here in a flash," he said, before kissing me. "Good night Karina, rest well."

I locked the door after he left and sat on the bed. I didn't really know why I ran away. It was impulsive and irresponsible. All I knew was that I needed to get out. I sent Dad a text message telling him I was okay and that I would be home soon. I crashed on the soft expensive bed in my clothes, tired from the day's drama, and fell into a dreamless sleep.

Sunlight filled my room and dragged me out of a very restful sleep. I must've forgotten to close the curtains after collapsing from exhaustion. I was still in the same clothes I wore last night so I started stripping to get in the shower. I heard a knock on the door. I opened it to find Jason standing outside.

"Is everything okay?" I said, wiping my eyes, all too aware of my state.

"I'm so sorry to disturb you. Yes, everything is fine. I just wanted to make sure you were okay. Did you sleep well?"

"Yes, I did. Very well, thank you."

"Breakfast is in the kitchen if you want to join me. Mother is still sleeping so it's just us."

"Sure, that would be great. I'll just change and meet you in the kitchen."

I closed the door and showered quickly before leaving the guesthouse. I walked to the kitchen to find Jason and his mother waiting for me. She looked amazing in her white flowing nightgown—perfection incarnate. She would have made millions as a model had she taken that path.

"Good morning, Karina. I gather you slept well?"

"Good morning, Mirasol. I slept very well. Thank you so much for your hospitality."

"My pleasure. Enjoy your breakfast. If you'll excuse me, I need to go rest. I had a long . . . work night last night."

She nodded and turned to walk back to her room. I turned to Jason and smiled, looking fresh and beautiful in the early morning sun. We sat together in silence, smiling as our fingers touched. The table was filled with food. The croissant was warm next to the fruit platter. The scrambled eggs, mushrooms, and bacon were still hot. The bread was perfectly toasted and came in several flavors—raisins, date, caramel, and plain. There was a variety of cereal, fruit juice, and beverage—tea, coffee, hot chocolate.

"This is unbelievable," I gasped at the sight.

"Mother always does this when we have guests. If you stay with us longer, this will be waiting for you every single morning."

"I better not stay long then or I'll never leave."

"You're welcome to stay here for as long as you like, you know that, right?"

I nodded.

"I know it's probably none of my business, but would you like to tell me why you ran away?"

I fell quiet for a while, unsure of what to say. I knew he was going to ask me but I hadn't decided what to tell him.

"It's quite complicated. I can't really explain it to you. Some . . . relatives arrived at our place last night, and they all just sort of started planning my future. Or pressuring me about a decision I need to make about my future and it just became too much for me."

I paused again, taking a small bite of the croissant. "It's been building up the last couple of weeks, but last night . . . it all became too real. I just needed to go somewhere safe, somewhere neutral, you know?"

I saw him wince, a fleeting moment, but it was there. Then just as quickly it disappeared.

He took my hand. "I'm here if you need anything. I'm always here."

"Thank you. I owe your family so much for this."

He let go of my hand and poured juice in my glass. "Now eat up. We have heaps of stuff to do today. Anything you want. Anything at all. We'll have a great day."

"If you don't mind, I'd rather just stay in. I don't want to bump into anyone I know. Besides, you still haven't given me the full tour. This place is absolutely huge."

"Okay, if that's what you wish. We do have a great home theater system here. We can just do as much movie marathons as you want. The pool is also at the back of the house. I'm sure my mother can get some spare swimsuit for you. My father set up a game room in the pool room so that's another option. I don't use much of it all. Not too fun when you're on your own."

"Your house is like a teenager's paradise," I said with a big smile. I felt my heart warming, almost forgetting the decision I had to make.

"Eat up then. We have a great day ahead of us."

After breakfast, he took me to see the entire house, pointing to happy family snapshots from all over the world. We spent most of the morning in the game room, playing foosball and air hockey, or just sitting around talking.

Mirasol left us alone all day, giving us the space to do whatever we wanted in their house. She must trust Jason that much if she was okay to leave us unsupervised.

I found it very easy to be with him, like I could tell him everything, except that I shouldn't. Unlike other guys at school, Jason was so much more mature. Maybe it was because he had traveled all over the world. He didn't worry much about anything, like the world is a worry-free zone. But then again, a life of riches and leisure would make anyone carefree. I saw glimpses of his serious side, when his brows would meet, like he was thinking deeply about something. But it was always fleeting.

The sound of guns blazing jolted me back to the present. I smiled at him, sitting beside me in the entertainment room with a huge bucket of bacon and cheese popcorn. We decided to watch a movie before lunch.

"Jumpy, aren't we?" he teased.

"It caught me off guard. I'm only human," I said, reaching for the popcorn.

He organized lunch so we could have a little picnic out the back, under the tree. It was quiet and peaceful, with only the sound of the birds chirping every now and then. The sun was perfectly warm high up in the sky, trickling in between the leaves.

The afternoon was spent swimming in the indoor pool. Jason gave me a pair of new bikinis, which puzzled me.

"Mother is a distributor of various clothing lines around the world," he explained.

"I could get used to this."

"Me, too. I want this day to last forever," He leaned over to kiss me. "You can stay here forever, you know. My parents would definitely not mind."

"I wish I could, I really do. You have no idea how much I just want to be doing this. To not have responsibilities."

"What's bothering you, Karina? You can tell me. Maybe I can help you. You sound so troubled, it pains me to see you like this," he said, gently touching my cheek.

"It's hard to explain. I just have to make a decision, and one of the decisions requires me losing the life I want to have."

"You'll figure it out. I know it. In one of your choices, will you be moving away from me?"

I nodded, fighting the tears in my eyes. I didn't even know why I wanted to cry. He should be the least of my worries. Leaving my world should be what pains me more, but I couldn't help it. Losing him was just another one of the setbacks of what I needed to do.

"I know it is selfish but I hope you won't choose that path. I'm starting to get addicted to your presence. I'm not really sure how I'll cope without you." He kissed me hard, caressing the back of my neck with his fingertips. I lost myself in the moment, enjoying the bubble we were in, hoping that it wouldn't burst too soon.

As the sun went down, we changed to dry clothes and headed for the entertainment room. Everything was custom-designed, right down to the details of the chairs. The room could fit fifteen people and was equipped with plush reclining seats. I picked out our line-up for the night, a hefty dose of horror and sci-fi movies. Dinner was laid out on a table near the door, our pick of movie food—from burgers, to fries, fish fingers, and chips. They really went all out for their visitors. Or maybe it was because Jason wanted to impress me. My cheeks warmed at the thought.

We watched two movies and consumed most of the food. Jason seemed to be having a great time, and I relaxed next to him. I turned off my phone since last night, turning it on only to send a text message to Mark and Alyssa so my family didn't send the police out to look for me. I started to wonder if Lolo was leading a search party himself. I knew he could sense my powers so if I used them, he would definitely be able to find me.

Jason excused himself to say good night to his mother, leaving me to my thoughts. If all runaways ended up in a place like this, they would never go back home. When I ran away, I was expecting to crash on his couch or spare room, not a plush guesthouse.

I never had to lift a finger since I arrived. Everything was prepared for me. In my entire life I had never felt this luxurious, like some sort of celebrity. Mirasol's hospitality was unbelievable, and quite a bit daunting, too. I wondered if she treated all of Jason's girlfriends like that. She was quite a woman, very elegant and sophisticated. Watching her move so fluidly was mesmerizing, like each step was carefully calculated. I would never have thought she was Filipino. Maybe she was one of the aristocrats from the rich Filipino-Spanish families in the Philippines.

But as warm as she seemed to be, I still couldn't shake off the uncomfortable tingling in my spine. I wasn't really sure why but I tried hard to ignore it. Maybe the paranoia was getting to me. I felt everyone was out to get me. They'd been nothing but generous and I had to make sure I didn't seem ungrateful. Jason came back carrying a bucket of warm popcorn and sat next to me.

"I thought you might need a refill. This is bacon and cheese flavored."

I smiled and reached for the bucket. "You spoil me so much. I might never leave this house."

"Fingers crossed," he said, kissing my hand.

We spent the rest of the night watching four movies and polishing several more buckets of popcorn. I wasn't sure if they paid overtime for their house help since the food and drinks seemed to be pouring in endlessly even in the wee hours of the night. I felt very content watching the movie while leaning my head against his shoulder, his arm wrapped around me. Every once in a while he'd lift my head with his hand and kiss my lips, the tip of my nose, my forehead and go back to watching the movie without saying a word.

It was already two in the morning when we finished the last of the movies. I knew it was a Sunday night but I didn't even care that I'd be missing school the next day. I was exhausted with the day's activities and although I didn't want to go to sleep, my body was ready to hit the sack. I tidied up the mess but Jason stopped me.

"Leave it. They'll take care of it tomorrow. I'll walk you to your room."

We took our time walking the short distance from his house to the guesthouse. I was happy to know I wasn't the only one who wanted to prolong the experience. He took my hand when we reached the door.

"No matter what happens in the next couple of days, no matter what you decide to do, I just wanted you to know I would never trade this day for anything in the world. I am so happy you are here with me and I hope you feel the same way, too."

"I do. I feel the same way," I said, tilting my head to kiss him. I opened the door and waved goodbye, wishing it could be like this every night. I sat on the bed wondering what to do. I knew I had to go home sometime and I knew I couldn't skip school for long. This running away business could only last over the weekend. I had to go home tomorrow and make a decision. I took out my phone and turned it on, sighing from the seemingly endless beeps of unread text messages and voicemails.

"Whr r u? Everyone is going crazy," from Mark.

"Please come home. I'm about to call the police. We are very worried about you. We can talk about this, just come home," said a really worried voicemail from Dad.

"Karina, I can't believe you won't tell me where you are! I'm your best friend! Call me!" a frantic message from Alyssa.

All the messages were in the same line except for the last one from Mark. "Karina, your grandfather told me to tell you this. He doesn't want to alarm anyone but he says you are very close to danger. He can't seem to sense where you are exactly but he knows there is danger nearby. Please be careful. And come home."

The hair on the back of my neck stood up and goosebumps spread all over. The fear I tried to suppress after coming to Jason's house resurfaced with a vengeance, setting my heartbeat to panic mode. There was something off about the place and Lolo could sense it, too. I touched the necklace around my neck. What would I do? It was two in the morning. I couldn't just leave. But what if Lolo was right? What if I was in danger? No one could come to help me. They didn't know where I was.

I took my bag out from the closet and started to pack my stuff. It wasn't wise to be traveling at dawn but I had to be prepared just in case I had to leave fast.

I didn't really know what I was running away from or if I was even being rational. But instinct took over and I knew I had to get out of the place as fast as possible. I would find an excuse for Jason once I was out. I closed the closet and looked in the mirror. I gasped when I saw Mama behind me, wearing a torn and bloody nightgown. She was saying something I couldn't hear. I tried to read her lips and realized what she was trying to say.

Run.

I turned around but she was gone. Oh God, what have I done?

I grabbed my bag. I stepped outside the door. Then I heard it—the unmistakable flap of huge wings swirling close by. The same sound I heard outside Alyssa's house that night. I dropped my bag in shock. Lolo was right, I was very close to danger. I took a step back, trying to find the doorknob to go back in the room, listening to where the sound was coming from. I felt a gust of wind coming from above and a trickle of hot liquid on my skin. The *manananggal* had found me even if I didn't use any of my powers. It knew where I was and it was going to eat me. I shouldn't have run away. I should've stuck with the leaders where it was safe. I struggled to remember my training but my mind went blank. I couldn't figure out what I could do to protect myself.

I ran back inside, locked the door and moved away from the windows. I tried to follow the sound of the wings. I heard it going past the guesthouse, moving toward the house. It was heading to Jason's place. I peeked outside to the direction of the house. Although it was dark, I could make out a form in the moonlight. A huge creature with wings moving fast toward the top floor. It slowed down and circled the house before landing in the balcony of one of the rooms. I knew from the house tour that it wasn't where Jason's room was located but I wasn't certain whose it was. He never showed me the rest of the second level of the house.

I moved away from the window. My whole body trembled. I looked down to see my arms bleeding. No, it wasn't my blood but it was starting to burn. I ran to the bathroom, rubbing the substance off my arms under the faucet. It stunk of rotting meat. It was slimy and dark, like the color of dead blood. My skin was burning from where the blood hit me. It must be the *manananggal*'s blood. Had it been wounded? It couldn't be human blood. No human blood smelled that horrible, nor does human blood burn skin. It was the *manananggal*'s and it landed on Jason's house. I wiped my arms and ran back to the window, peeking outside for any sign of the creature.

There was nothing outside. I decided to wait until dawn to see if the *manananggal* left the house. Surely it couldn't stay in there until daytime. It had to reunite with its lower body, wherever it was.

Unless, its lower body was already in the house. Unless, the *manananggal* lived in the house. What if it lived in there? What if it was someone Jason knew? What if it was . . . no. It couldn't be Jason. It wasn't him. It couldn't be him.

I felt very alone. I gathered my belongings and waited for light. I wanted to get out of the place as fast as possible. It was a mistake running away. No matter how much I wanted to escape, there was no turning back. I had a decision to make. Others relied on this decision. I couldn't turn my back on my responsibilities anymore. It was time to face it.

Huddled in the corner of the room, I drifted in and out of sleep, constantly waking up at the tiniest of sounds and checking outside for any signs of the *manananggal*. Being away from those I trusted most was not a good idea. I had to get back home fast.

Chapter Fourteen

MAMA'S DIY ENGKANTASIA BOOK

Sirena

The sirena is an aquatic creature with the head and torso of human female and the tail of a fish. The sirena clan is the guardian of the bodies of water.

The sirena has a very beautiful and enchanting voice that can attract and hypnotise males, especially fishermen. It is an empath. It can read minds and is sensitive to the pain of the creatures it reads. Although it is more vulnerable out of water, do not underestimate the sirena's ability to fight on land. In the water, however, it can be very deadly.

I didn't sleep all night. I saw the orange streak of dawn in the horizon and immediately knew that I was right. The *mananaggal* lived in Jason's house. I wanted to scream, or cry, or punch something but I couldn't move. I was frozen in my spot in the corner of the room, near the window. I took deep breaths, trying to find a way to get out before the whole house woke up.

I knew I could figure it out. I had to. I sent Dad a text message with Jason's address on it, giving instructions not to sound the horn when he arrived. I took my things and crawled out of the room, staying in the shadows. The drops of *manananggal* blood were still on the ground, trailing all the way to the house. I ignored the stench of rotting meat and kept going until I was close enough to the gate.

The gate.

It was electronically locked. I had no choice but to go over it. I ran toward the trees near the fence and looked up to see which tree could give me the best footing. I was so tempted to use my powers but it might trigger the *manananggal* inside the house. I strapped the backpack behind me and started climbing. It wasn't as easy as I thought it was going to be. The last time I climbed a tree was in the Philippines and I was seven years old. Still I kept going, pushing my skinny limbs to its limit until my arms started to shake. I turned to reach for the fence and pushed myself over. But instead of climbing down slowly, I lost my balance, flipping over the fence and dropping on my back on the other side. I let out a groan as I hit the ground, my back screaming in agony. I stayed there for a while to recover from the fall. I heard a car stopping and turned my head in time to see Dad rushing toward me.

"Karina, are you okay?"

I saw the wave of relief on his face and I felt a knot in my stomach—guilt. He picked me up, like he used to when I was a little girl, and put me in the car.

"Daddy, I'm so sorry I ran away."

"It's okay, hun, really. They're all waiting for you, let's get you home, okay? Are you okay? Are you hurt?"

"No, I'm okay Dad. Let's go, hurry."

We didn't speak in the car. But I finally let the tears out. Dad stopped a block from our house and faced me.

"Talk to me, Karina. What happened?"

I took deep breaths as the sobbing continued, wave after wave of misery came crashing on me. Finally, I managed to calm myself down enough to tell Dad what I discovered.

"Someone in that house is a *manananggal*, Dad. I don't know who but I saw it with my own eyes. It was wounded and its blood burned my arm. I'm so scared. I don't know who it is. I don't know if it's his mom or if it's . . ."

He hugged me tight, stroking my hair. I stayed like that for a while, crying in Dad's arms, letting go of everything I had been afraid to admit. That I didn't like how my life turned out, that I didn't want to grow up too fast anymore, that I just wanted to be normal, that I wanted him to be the parent again. I cried until there were no more tears, and then I fell into a deep, dreamless sleep.

The sound of loud arguing downstairs woke me up. I recognized the voices—Lolo, Dad, the other clan leaders. It was starting to get dark outside. I must have slept all day.

I got out of bed slowly, trying to ease the pain on my back. I missed school but I didn't really care.

I hesitated to put proper clothes on because it meant I would have to face the people downstairs. But I had no choice. I slowly peeled off my clothes and headed for the shower to clean myself up. I passed by the mirror and paused, waiting to see if I would see Mama again. There was nothing but my own reflection. She tried to warn me. I knew in my heart she was still alive. But in what condition, I didn't know. She looked tired, bloodied, like she had been tortured.

It dawned on me that I knew very little about my own mother, that the childhood tales she shared with us were probably all made up. Were they tales of the life she saw while she was growing up as a princess? Whose childhood did I admire? Some random Filipino living somewhere in the Philippines?

I remembered the best stories that she told me. Like the one where she had to wade through the flood walking back home from school because they didn't own a car or didn't have a phone, and the public transport was on strike. She said she walked miles and miles in her raincoat because the school didn't close for the day even if there was a storm coming. By the time she got home, part of their roof was leaking profusely that she ended up having a shower in the rain inside their house. Still it was all worth it after having a bowl of warm stew to eat afterward. I thought how brave she must have been as a child to go through that on her own.

They were all just lies. Maybe a figment of her imagination, or an experience she saw in the human world that she decided to use as her own. I put on some clothes and walked near the stairs, trying to catch bits and pieces of the argument.

"It was Maita's descendant, I am telling you it was her. She is in the area and she knows we are here. We have to take drastic action," said Pili.

"We know where she is now. We can go there and take her down," said Gulat.

I knew what they were talking about. They wanted to take down the *manananggal*, attack during the day when she was most vulnerable. But what if it was Jason? It was hard to tell whether the form was female or male. It could be anyone. And if it wasn't Jason, they could easily harm him in the crossfire. What about Mama? What if the *manananggal* had her hostage? I couldn't let them just raid the house without knowing the real identity of the enemy. I walked into the living room, cutting short their conversation.

"We're not going to attack. We don't know who it is or if it has my mother. We can't go in there blindly without knowing more. I know my mother is not your priority but if you disobey this, I swear I will never set foot in Engkantasia. You follow my request and I will leave the human world to save yours."

No one talked. They eyed each other, trying to decide what to do next.

"What do you propose we do?" Serra asked.

"I'll finish my training while you try to discover the *manananggal's* identity. I only have a couple of weeks left, so we need to act quickly. We need to investigate. We need more facts, not just sheer brutality."

For the first time since everything started, I felt in control. It felt good. I walked toward the kitchen for some food when I sensed someone following me. I turned to see Serra, hesitating for a second.

"What is it?" I asked. Among all the clan leaders I met, I liked Serra the best. She was calm and collected. You could relax just listening to her talk.

"Can I have a word with you?" I nodded and led her to the kitchen. We sat together.

"I felt your pain. When you stepped out of the window to run away, I felt it. I sensed your need to escape and so I didn't alert the rest of the group about what you were doing. I don't blame you. It was a mistake pushing you so hard like that. We've been old for so long that we have forgotten what it was like to be young and impulsive."

"How old are you?"

Serra let out a delicate laugh that sounded like tiny bells in the wind.

"Over two hundred, give or take." She laughed again, seeing my mouth wide open.

"You are a very brave girl, Karina, much braver than you give yourself credit for. You have handled yourself well given that you've been shoved in the middle of a conflict that's been happening for hundreds of years."

"That long?"

"One day I will tell you more about your heritage but for now you need to understand that the *manananggal* clan has always been cruel and deceptive, even when they were in power a long time ago. Blood was shed from both our worlds and it took an epic battle to end their tyranny. They are trying to get that power back now and we have to do everything we can to prevent that," Serra said, taking my hand in hers.

"If it's been going on for a long time, how come we never knew about it?"

"But you do. It's your mythology. In the human world, the truth about the great war has degenerated into a form of mockery, dishonoring the blood that was shed all those years. I guess this is the only way humans know how to cope with distress and fear."

I shook my head. The horror of the past had become nothing but plots in human storybooks. We kept the truth buried in the fantasy world and used the stories to scare children into behaving well.

"It has been so long since anyone has made contact with the humans that all we remember are the bad memories and very little of the good. I am quite certain that the main reason why we allied with your clan is because it is still a better alternative than having the *manananggal* in the throne—even if the Magatu family's lineage has been . . . compromised with human blood."

"Compromised?"

"All I can say is that not all of us welcome the thought of having a half-human in the throne. I mean no disrespect. It's just that, we remember the past and we know the weaknesses of humans."

"Then you also know well the strengths of my kind," I said, almost angry at Serra, even if she was only telling the truth.

"I apologize if my words offended you. What I wanted to say is that if we know the weaknesses of humans, then I'm sure our enemies know them, too. They will use that weakness against you, no matter what the cost," she said, before getting up to leave.

I made myself a sandwich to take to my room, hoping to have a bit of peace. I walked toward the stairs as quietly as possible, hearing snippets of the conversation still going on in the living room between the clan leaders.

"By now she's figured out we're all together in this. She's probably already formed a plan, maybe even called for an alliance herself," said a small voice, probably Pili.

"He is right, Hari Magatu. By now, she's already realized that our presence here has something to do with you. She is badly wounded. It might be advantageous for us to attack," Yukoy said.

So they were the ones who wounded her. How did they track her down? I had to find out more. Maybe they know the identity of the *manananggal*. I moved out of the shadows and joined the group. They all fell silent.

"Tell me what happened last night," I demanded. They looked at each other before Serra answered.

"It wasn't intentional. We were looking for a place to rest when we sensed her presence. Kamudo saw her from a distance as he was perched on top of a tree and lunged at her, knocking her on the ground. We caught her by surprise. Yukoy managed to throw a spear through her, but she got away."

"Do you know who it was?"

"It's hard to know their human features when they've transformed but if I smell her again, I will be able to tell," said Gulat.

The trail of blood from Jason's house flashed in my head, making me shudder. I knew it wasn't Jason. It had to be female. The male kinds of manananggal were unheard of. That was what I thought.

"But can you be sure it's female and not male?"

They looked at each other, puzzled by my question.

"There is no such thing as a male *manananggal* and even if there was, I saw the attacker that night. She was definitely female," Pili said, eyeing my reaction to the news.

A lump disappeared from inside my chest. I felt like I could breathe a bit better. It wasn't Jason. But that meant it was someone in Jason's house, and Jason knew everyone in that house. A feeling grew inside me, a certainty I didn't want to acknowledge. The *manananggal* was always gorgeous, with beauty that couldn't be human. I closed my eyes and an image of Jason's mother flashed in my head.

It was her. I was so sure of it. The ice cold feeling I got when I first shook her hand. It was a sign, one that I wanted to ignore.

I looked up to find the group staring at me.

"Karina, what is it?" Lolo asked.

"I know who it is. I know who the *manananggal* is."

Chapter Fifteen

MAMA'S DIY
ENGKANTASIA BOOK

Syokoy

The syokoy is a member of merfolks. It is a humanoid that has a scaly body, webbed hands and feet, and fins on parts of its body. It has the head of a fish.

Compared to the sirena who has human features, the syokoy looks more like an animal in physical form. It is loyal to its sirena, who is its partner for life. The syokoy will die to protect its sirena.

I was forced to go to school even if I didn't want to. Dad was convinced school was the safest place for me—away from the clan leaders. He didn't know that Jason's mother was the *manananggal*. I did not tell him that to spare him from even more distress.

I found Mark and Alyssa waiting for me outside the school, shifting uncomfortably.

"What's going on? Why do you guys look like you've stolen something?"

A look passed between them.

"You say it," Mark nudged Alyssa.

"Coward," Alyssa hissed at Mark.

"What?" I said, getting impatient.

"When you ran away the other day, we sort of asked around if anyone had seen you, and some kids at school found out," Alyssa said.

"So?"

"Well, Melissa's best friend, Natalie, lives near Jason and she's been telling everyone at school that she saw you stay at his house."

"I don't see that as anyone's business. And so what if she did see me? It's not against the law."

"Well, now they're spreading rumors about you and Jason," Mark whispered.

"Guys, this is not new to me. It's happened before when my mom disappeared. I'm quite used to it so don't worry. I have worse things to think about."

Everyone stared at me as I walked in the hallway, a definite sign that something was up. But I ignored them and headed straight to my locker.

The word "whore" was written across my locker door in red lipstick. My face started to burn. I clenched my fist to contain my anger. I looked around. Everyone was still staring, waiting for me to do something.

I started counting to ten in my head to calm myself down. But then I heard it, the sniggering a few feet away. I turned to see Melissa and Natalie whispering to each other, laughing while stealing glimpses in my direction. I didn't know if they wrote the words, nor did I care. All I knew was that the anger I had been keeping inside for the last three years had finally reached a tipping point. All those years I tried to ignore the taunting and stories behind my back came crashing down on me. I walked toward Natalie, dropping my things along the way. Before she could move out of my reach, I grabbed her throat and slammed her against the lockers. I heard gasps all around. Natalie dropped her things and stared at me, eyes wide with fear. She tried to say something but my hand was choking her neck.

"Next time you spread lies about me, make sure you are prepared to move to another city," I said, slowly, in a voice I barely recognized. I let go of her and walked away. I could hear her gasping for air, coughing to breathe. My arm hurt but I didn't rub it. Everyone gave me room to move while Mark handed me my things as we walked to class together. They didn't say anything to me but I could see they were afraid of me, too. What was I turning into?

Luckily for me, none of the teachers saw what happened. It was also a miracle that none of the students told on me. I wondered about this until Mark explained it to me during lunch.

"They think you're insane and therefore dangerous," he said, chewing on a sandwich halfheartedly.

"No one wants to cross your path now because they don't know what you are like. They've always seen you as quiet and meek even after all the rumors about your mom. Then suddenly you go all alpha female on the top girls so now they think you're just nuts," Alyssa added.

I didn't say anything but I could tell they wanted to say more.

"What is it?" I asked.

"We're worried about you," Alyssa hesitated. "We've never seen you like this, Karina, and to be honest, I'm a bit scared after seeing you choke Natalie. I mean, she totally deserves to be taught a lesson but it's just that . . . "

"What?"

"It looked like you wanted to kill her," Mark finished. "I've known you for a long time and I've never seen you look like that before. It's not a nice thing to see. It's downright scary."

I should be defending myself, tell them I was still me, that I was not homicidal. But I couldn't deny the fact that for a moment I felt powerful. That I could easily take on Natalie and Melissa and everyone who had been gossiping about me.

"I'm sorry for scaring you guys. I don't know what to say."

"Just try not to go all psycho on us again, okay? Save it for the real enemy," Mark smiled a bit. I nodded and went back to my lunch.

The choking event totally eclipsed the news about knowing who the *manananggal* was. Fortunately, Jason didn't go to school so I didn't have to worry about seeing him. I wondered what happened. I wondered if the clan leaders were right, that they were planning an alliance with the dark clans. Thinking about being enemies with Jason hurt my insides. I wanted to be sick.

"What happened last weekend? You haven't said anything about your little stunt," Mark asked.

I didn't know where to start. I knew I could trust them but I couldn't bring myself to admit that Jason might be the enemy.

Still, I needed all the help I could get. So I told them. I told them everything. After I finished, no one spoke. Alyssa's mouth hung open, and Mark looked bewildered.

"So they really have their own entertainment center?" Mark said. Alyssa and I looked at each other and laughed. For the first time in a really long time, I let out a full-on belly laugh, not caring that everyone was looking at us. When the laugh tapered off, we looked at each other. I could almost see Mark's mind ticking.

"Okay. So we have to come up with a plan, right?" Alyssa asked.

"I'm not sure planning will do me any good at this point," I said quietly. Mark hadn't said anything for a while but I could see he was deep in thought. He had this look, like the world didn't exist and his mind was in outer space.

"Mark?" I asked, waving my hand in front of his eyes. He looked at me but not really, like he was only half with us.

"I'll figure something out, I promise," he said.

I smiled at him, not knowing what to say. I doubt he would figure out anything that could save me but I couldn't tell him that. He needed to work on this. It was what comforted him. So I let him.

Chapter Sixteen

August 2013

Hi Patrick,

My sincerest apologies, but like what I said on the phone, there is no trace of your wife. I've coordinated with my contacts with the authorities as well, and I'm on a dead end. This is a very unusual case.

When I took on your case, I was certain that the police missed something from their investigations. To be honest, sometimes they don't really look close enough especially when it's a migrant—a new one at that.

From my experience, these cases never happen. There is always a trace of something, or someone seeing something. But nothing has turned up. I will keep digging but at this point, it's not looking good.

I don't want to waste your money, but if you want me to keep looking for your wife, I will.

Again, I am so sorry.

Sincerely,
David McPaul
Private Investigator

June 2015

Lolo promised to restart my training so I hurried home. I opened the door to the garage, surprised to see what Lolo had done with it. The garage had been turned into a training gym, complete with a punching bag and wooden dummy.

"Um . . . Lolo, what is all this?"

"Today, we focus on your physical side. I will teach you how to fight."

I picked up the sword hanging on the rack from the wall.

"This is a real sword, Lolo. Are you expecting me to actually use this?"

He took the sword from me and put it back on its rack.

"Yes, I am, but not today. I know you have doubts about your physical abilities. But this is essential to your training. You need to be able to defend yourself with whatever is available in your surroundings, and to be able to adapt to any given situation. You need to be able to defend yourself so you can defend the ones you love."

I thought about Jason and cringed. Would I have to fight him? Would I have to kill him and his mother? There was probably more chance of him hurting me than the other way around, given how uncoordinated I had always been.

"Lolo, I'm good at swimming and I took a couple of karate lessons as a kid but I am nowhere near skilled enough to hold any weapon."

"By the end of this week, you will be. Trust me," he said with a hint of a smile. I had never really seen Lolo smile so I took it as a good sign that he was confident about our training.

"After the physical training, we will then train to incorporate all your abilities together. You will become a kick-ass fighter."

My mouth fell open. I laughed uncontrollably, gasping for air.

"I may have been watching too much of your human entertainment machine," he said, smiling fully this time.

"That was an awesome first attempt, Lolo. I am proud of you," I said, giving him a big hug. His arms tightened around me and he patted my head awkwardly after letting me go. It had all been very business-like with Lolo for the last couple of weeks. Having that moment with him was the closest normal contact we had had as grandchild and grandfather. I wished in my heart there would be more. I wanted to get to know my grandfather, not just the ruler of Engkantasia.

"Okay, so where do we begin? Pick up the jacket, put the jacket back on?" Lolo stared at me, confused. "We better get you started on *The Karate Kid* DVDs tomorrow, Lolo. I need to educate you about Bruce Lee, too." I smiled and took the spot beside him.

The two-hour session was brutal to my body. I didn't know I could physically hurt like that, or have muscles in places I didn't know about. Lolo was a great teacher but he was determined to create a fighting machine by the end of the week.

I wished I could say I was a quick study. In my head, I pictured me in a fancy movie montage, getting things right on the first go. Unfortunately for Lolo that wasn't the case. I dropped things. I nearly maimed myself. I destroyed furniture. I damaged my own body parts and almost broke Lolo's family jewels. It was a good thing we used mock weapons. I would've been dead before the real fight began.

I limped to my room for a hot shower. I just wanted to stay in bed all night but my stomach was growling. Although I was in agony, I couldn't help but smile at my reflection. Aside from my hug with Lolo, I was also feeling very good about myself. I always thought I was going to suck at anything physical so I never pursued any sort of sports or physical activity. I didn't dance. I didn't do baseball or basketball. I didn't even ride a bike. But after the training, I was starting to rethink things. Maybe it was just my fear that held me back. Sure, I almost maimed myself, but I was still able to do the punches and kicks properly. There was hope for me yet.

I walked to the kitchen to find dinner waiting for me with a note. Dad was working late again but he wanted me to have a good dinner. It had been a while since he had made dinner for us. I opened the lid and smelled the aroma of his homemade roast chicken and veggies, with rice on the side. My favorite.

153

I started to eat, fast and eager, surprised at just how famished I was after training. My phone beeped. It was a message from Jason, asking why I left without saying goodbye. I deleted the message and put the phone on mute. He never tried to contact me after I left. I wondered why.

Still, I couldn't have anything to do with him. He was the enemy. He was the son of a *manananggal*. That made him one, too.

I took the plate in the kitchen and searched for Lolo. I needed to ask him if there was a chance that Jason was a *manananggal*. I needed to know.

I found Lolo in the living room, sitting with his eyes closed. The lights were off except for a small lamp in the corner. It looked like he was meditating, his chest barely moving.

"Lolo?" I called out quietly. He opened his eyes and looked at me.

"What is it, mija?"

I sat on a nearby chair. I wanted to know the truth but I was afraid to ask, because I didn't want to know if I was right about Jason.

"Is it possible to have a male *manananggal*?"

Lolo looked at me, knowing fully well what I didn't want to hear. "There's never been a full-grown male *manananggal* before, apart from the old king who was killed by his wife. Every century or so, one would be born, but it would never survive to become a full-grown man. It was always hunted and killed not just by us but also by the dark clans."

"Why would it be such a threat if it were male?"

"A female *manananggal* can only give birth to one child at a time. But a male *manananggal* can impregnate as many women as he wanted, increasing the race of the clan at an alarming rate. This threat scared everyone, but every time we wanted to intervene, we were always too late. The dark clans always beat us to it. In a way, I am thankful for that. I don't know if we would have been able to terminate a child."

"Then how were they able to repopulate their clan?"

"The dark clans have an alliance of sort. Creatures like the *aswang* and the *wakwak* help the *manananggal* create their young. You must understand, the dark clans are eternally paranoid. They have their own system to balance each other so that each clan doesn't have too many offsprings. They don't want one to be more powerful than the other."

Lolo sighed, clasping his hands together, hesitating.

"What is it, Lolo?"

"You must understand that if Jason is indeed a *manananggal*, then we don't know what he is fully capable of. We've never had one created in the human world before. Let alone one who has survived this long."

"Jason can't be a *manananggal*. I would've sensed him, right? My new abilities would have warned me about it if it were true," I asked, but even I knew I was grasping at straws. The knots in my gut every time he was near me—those were signs. Signs I ignored.

"I don't know, mija. No one knows what abilities a male *manananggal* possesses. We've never fought or met one who survived."

Maybe it was not his mom. Maybe it was one of the help. Maybe someone close to the staff. Perhaps. Or perhaps I was just making excuses because I didn't want to face the reality that Jason was a monster.

As if he could read my mind, Lolo took my hand.

"No matter what happens, we will be here to help you. No matter who it is, we will be here to protect you."

But could they protect my heart?

"There is something else I need you to know, mija," Lolo said, almost a whisper. My heart beat faster. It was going to be bad news. I just knew it.

"In order to be the ruler of Engkantasia, you have to leave the human world and never look back. You will be bound to your duties and rule Engkantasia until you produce another heir. The life you now live will be left behind, and you will never experience the world of the humans again."

I stared at him, my head pounding, unable to process what he just said. He continued to talk but my mind was spinning. It was hard to listen to him.

"If you decide to stay in the human world, then I will go back to Engkantasia and surrender the throne to the next ruling clan. I will not have a choice. I, too, am bound by the rules of our world."

Leave my world. Leave my friends. Leave my dad. Or both worlds would collapse. My choices were clear.

"What's so bad about handing the throne to another clan? Why can't that work?" I asked, hoping this is a good alternative, even when I already suspected it wasn't.

"The two strongest clans are ours and the *manananggal*. If I hand it to another clan leader, they can be defeated if the *manananggal* decides to take the throne."

"So I have to leave this world forever. Can't I take Dad with me?"

Lolo shook his head.

"The veil between our worlds is getting weaker and weaker, which means more creatures can go through anytime they want. We need to seal that veil completely. No one can get in and no one can get out. Separate the two worlds forever. Humans in the human world and the *engkanto* in Engkantasia."

No room for humans in Engkantasia. That was what Lolo was saying. If Mama were here, she would take on the throne. Maybe that was what she was trying to tell me the night she disappeared. Maybe she always knew that she was going to go back. But she was not here and I had to make the decision. What else was there to decide though? Could I really live the normal life I wanted here, knowing that I had put both our worlds at risk by doing so? I would never be at peace.

My mind was suddenly so clear. I felt the pain in my chest as I made my decision.

"I know what I must do."

Lolo nodded and squeezed my hand.

I hugged him, clutching his robe as I stifled a sob. I had to keep it together. I needed to focus on what had to be done. I couldn't fall apart. Not now.

It occurred to me that Lolo had been training me not just to defend myself, but also to possibly rule an entire kingdom. He waited to tell me until I knew more about what was at stake. Maybe he was afraid I'd be scared and run away like Mama did.

I let go of Lolo and wiped my tears. If I was expected to survive this, I needed all the information I could get about Engkantasia.

"Lolo, I need to know our enemies. You mentioned other dark clans in Engkantasia. What are these creatures and how can we defeat them?"

"It's late, mija, you need to rest. You have school tomorrow."

School. It was ridiculous to be thinking I should be going to school when I probably wouldn't be living here anymore by next month. I was tempted not to go but it meant missing out on my time with Alyssa and Mark. These may be my last weeks to experience school. After that, who knows what my life would be like. I had to go. My last moments of normalcy before entering the unknown.

I started for my bedroom but not before making Lolo promise to tell me what I needed to know. He said he was going to ask Serra to come over after training to show me what I wanted. I climbed to my room and sat in the dark for a while, letting the tears fall. My life wasn't really mine after all.

I tossed and turned through the night. I dreamt of mother again, bloodied and in pain, screaming for me to save myself. I tried to reach for her hand but a glass wall fell between us, sealing her from me. I couldn't break the glass. I couldn't hear Mama. We were separated forever. I screamed and banged on the glass but it was too hard to break. I saw Mama being dragged by her legs into the darkness. I woke up sweaty. My heart was racing, and I knew that I had to find Mama before the veil shut forever. It was my only chance to see her again.

Chapter Seventeen

Mama's DIY Engkantasia Book

Duwende

The duwende is a goblin-like creature that lives in rocks and caves, old trees, and unvisited and dark parts of houses. Although good in nature, it can be irritable and grumpy. It often plays with children.

This little creature can provide good fortune or bad fate to humans. It sometimes comes out at 12 noon and during the night. Muttering words like "tabi apo" (excuse me) will appease a duwende that has been disturbed from its naps. It can be mischievous and take human things and laugh when you can't find it. It only gives the thing back when it feels like it or if asked nicely.

I had gone to school hundreds of times in the past, but it seemed different. I noticed the noise of the chattering students, the smell of food coming from the cafeteria, the colors on the walls covered by the occasional graffiti. I wanted to remember every single detail. I was lucky that we managed to keep me in the same school even after everything. We had to move to a smaller place so we could rent out our old house. Dad said we were 'downsizing' but I knew it was because he used up a lot of the money to hire private investigators to find Mama. The school was the only thing that he didn't want to change. I was grateful for that. I didn't think I would have survived moving away from Mark and Alyssa after Mama disappeared.

I was looking for my friends when I sensed him, so strong it felt like I had been punched in the chest. I knew it was him. I could smell him. I could feel him. His strength, his blood, his poison. I knew even before I turned around that he was there. I didn't know how he managed to hide it from me all this time. Or maybe how I felt for him clouded my judgment. He wouldn't do anything in the middle of a crowded school so I knew I was safe. Still, I couldn't stop my heart from beating fast.

I saw him walking toward me. His face was unreadable. Even after being certain of what he was I couldn't stop myself from wanting to touch him. I had dreamed of caressing his face again, pressing his lips against mine. That was never going to happen again.

He stopped inches away from me and I could smell a different side of him. A damp room mixed with sickly sweet fruits, almost rotting. He wasn't hiding who he was from me anymore. Did that mean he was ready to show me who he really was? To scare me? To show me who was stronger? Did he know who I was all this time?

He reached out to touch my face and I quickly moved away. He looked puzzled. I didn't want to play games anymore.

"I know what you are," I whispered to him.

"What are you talking about, Karina? What's going on? Why haven't you called me after leaving my house?"

"Stop it," I hissed. "Stop pretending. It's over. I know what you are. I know your mother is a *manananggal*."

There. It was out. I looked at him and saw a different Jason from the one I kissed just the other day. His face turned dark, dangerous. His eyes flashed red. He clenched his fist and I could see dark veins rippling through his arms. This Jason scared me. The one who could barely control his anger, who could turn into a monster. But just as quickly as his anger manifested, it passed and disappeared.

I touched his face as gently as I could. I was afraid his anger might poison me, too. I let him feel how I felt—the rollercoaster of emotions that had been going through me the last couple of weeks. The love, the happiness, the heartache, the betrayal, the fear. It flowed through me like an angry river, rushing to him, drowning him with my tide. He gasped. A tear fell down his cheek before he moved away from me. He rushed toward school without saying a word.

I sat down on a nearby bench, taking deep breaths. I wanted to cry but I held myself together. Not here, not where everyone could see me breaking down. I saw Mark and Alyssa walking toward me and I told them about my encounter with Jason.

"I'm so sorry, Karina," Alyssa said, hugging me.

"I knew it. I knew there was something off about that guy. I mean, he can't be all that great," Mark said, shutting up after Alyssa gave him the evil eye.

"Anyway," Alyssa changed the subject, "Mark and I have been talking and we think we should go to your training from now on."

"What? Why?"

"We are with you all the time, it makes sense to prepare us, too, just in case. Remember, the first time we saw a *manananggal*, we were all together. I need to at least arm myself with extra training. Plus, it will help someone's fighting skills," Alyssa said, pointing not so secretly at Mark.

"You don't have to rub it in, I already agree with you. The nerd always dies first," Mark muttered. "I am totally into preparing myself. Some of it will eventually stick with me enough to give me a chance to at least escape."

If I left this world, they would be safe. I would treasure any extra time I have with them from now on.

"Okay then. My place after school. Bring extra clothes and drinking bottles. It will be exhausting."

"Awesome, I can't wait!" Alyssa said. I could see her easing into it quite well, given what she had done in the past. But Mark would be tricky.

"So after your training, can we go back to our regular Friday nights together?" Mark asked.

"Sure," I nodded and smiled, unable to meet his eyes. I hated lying to them but I had to. I needed to delay the pain for as long as I could, even if it meant suffering in silence.

"And another thing . . . " Mark said, looking at Alyssa for approval. She nodded.

"What now?" I was a bit impatient for being out of the loop, not liking their secret signals at all.

"We installed a camera near Jason's house," Mark whispered.

"But that's illegal," I hissed at him. I should really be thankful for their ingenuity especially since I was curious about Jason's family, too. But a part of me didn't want to have evidence of their *manananggal* side.

"Only if you get caught," Alyssa said. I looked at her and raised an eyebrow. This surprised me especially since Alyssa had always liked following rules.

"What?" she asked. "Now is not the time to be moral about these things. These creatures eat people. They want to eat us. We need more information about them so we can be prepared."

I knew they had a point but I still felt uneasy about the whole thing.

"Just be careful okay?" I said to Mark. He smiled a bit. I think he was really enjoying this whole cloak-and-dagger business.

"I'll let you know if I find anything, I promise," he said.

Lolo didn't really welcome my friends with open arms when we arrived home. But I explained to him why I wanted them there and he acquiesced. I gave him a grateful hug before we started.

The second day was weapons day. I was armed with a long wooden stick. Not really what I would consider a weapon, but Lolo thought it would be better for me to start off with a "safer" one. Lolo showed the motions slowly, using the wooden dummy to exhibit the best blows we could use. He gave the stick to me and I tried to copy what he did, very unconvincingly. Mark took the stick and tried the same thing, hitting his shin in the process. Alyssa grabbed the stick from Mark and hit the points on the dummy in one continuous motion, like she had done it a million times before. I felt a tinge of jealousy watching her perfect the maneuver. I had never been jealous of Alyssa in my entire life until that day. I felt she'd make a better heiress than I would.

Lolo sensed my jealousy and approached me while Mark and Alyssa continued to hit the dummy. He took my hand and placed it on the necklace Mama gave me.

"If you can't find the strength in you, find the strength from your mother. When she gave you that necklace, she knew the things that you were capable of doing. Channel your mother's essence. Trust her."

It never occurred to me to use the necklace to help me with the physical side of training. I always thought it was more for the powers. But I guess it made sense given that all of Mama's memories were stored inside the little rock.

I wrapped my hand around the stone and closed my eyes, taking deep breaths, thinking of Mama. At first, I felt nothing but the coolness of the stone in my fist. Then a warmth came over me, traveling inside my body, like a hot cup of tea on a winter's night. I felt her strength, her love, her confidence. I saw a flash in my head of a younger version of Mama, holding two swords and swinging them around like a well-trained warrior. I forget sometimes that Mama had gone through the same training I was going through with Lolo.

I took the wooden stick from Alyssa and stood in front of the dummy. I gripped it tightly with both hands, determined to get this right. I hit the dummy on the face, the neck, the ribs, and legs before cracking between its legs, all in one swift move.

"Ouch," I heard Mark behind me.

"Well done, Karina," Lolo said. I couldn't help but smile. I didn't even break a sweat.

"Where did that come from? I've asked you so many times to come to training with me and you always say no because you have no coordination. You little liar!" Alyssa said, slapping me in the back. I felt guilty for being jealous when she had always been supportive of me.

"Let's do that again," I said. Lolo grabbed a stick of 163 his own.

We kept training all afternoon, taking turns with the dummy and trying the techniques on each other. Lolo paired up with me while Alyssa helped Mark with his moves. Two hours into it and I was already able to handle myself, blocking Lolo's attacks while creating my own series of offenses.

I was about to jump on Lolo with a strike from above when I felt an urgent pull from outside. I rushed to find where it was coming from but there was nothing in the yard. I still felt it though, a heart beating so fast, the fear and panic. I looked up to find a white bird flying toward us, carrying something in its mouth. It landed a foot away from me, dropping what looked like a mouse on the ground. I leaned down to pick up the familiar little creature in my hand and realized it was Wilbur. How did he get out? When did he get out? I didn't close Wilbur's cage but he never ran away so it was never necessary. I let go of my stick and picked up the bird with my other hand, bringing them inside the garage.

"What's going on?" Mark asked, fascinated by the two animals.

"I don't know, I have to see what they want me to see," I said, closing my eyes and opening myself up to the wild bird and Wilbur.

I saw images in my head from Wilbur, getting out of the room, running out of the house and traveling into backyards, through houses and streets. I saw him enter a familiar place. Jason's house. What was Wilbur doing there?

Wilbur showed me an image of the day I summoned the animals to help me find my mother. He was doing his part to help me. I felt a rush of love for this little creature. Tiny yet so brave, so willing to endanger itself to help me.

At first, Wilbur just sneaked around Jason's house, looking for cracks and holes to investigate. He moved toward the guesthouse where I stayed in when I ran away. It seemed like a million years ago now. Wilbur stopped near the old shed, sensing something nearby. He entered it through the gap in the door. There was nothing there but gardening tools and an old mower. Wilbur kept sniffing on the ground, looking for something until he found a tiny crack at the back of the shed, just big enough for him to squeeze through. He dropped inside and stumbled several steps down. A staircase! There was a hidden staircase underneath the shed.

My heart raced. I felt Wilbur's excitement as he scampered off again quickly. I could sense how tired he was but he kept going down, deeper into the secret room under the ground. It felt like an eternity but Wilbur finally reached the end of the steps. It was a metal door, sealed from corner to corner with a giant lock attached to it. He sniffed around, looking for a way in but couldn't find anything. Just when I thought there was no way to know what was in that room, Wilbur stopped to listen. He fixed himself on the biggest crack he could find. I heard what he heard. It was quiet but it was there. The distinct humming of my favorite lullaby.

It was Mama's voice.

K.M. LEVIS

Chapter Eighteen

MAMA'S DIY
ENGKANTASIA BOOK

Kapre

The kapre is a tree demon of sorts. It is enormous, almost seven to nine feet tall, brown, bulky and covered in fur. It has a distinct smell that would attract human attention.

It dwells in big trees and are mostly seen sitting under them. The kapre wears an indigenous loincloth known as bahag. It has the ability to be invisible to humans. It has a penchant for tobacco, which is why its smell is so potent.

The kapre is not necessarily evil. It sometimes interacts with humans to offer friendship. Sometimes, it falls in love with a human. If a kapre befriends a human, or loves one, the kapre will follow the person all through his or her life. But this has not happened in hundreds of years.

The clan leaders were in the living room, watching me pace around like a madman. I asked Lolo to contact them so we could meet and find a way to rescue Mama from her underground prison.

I knew Lolo disapproved of what I did with the animals but he didn't say anything. I didn't regret doing what I did.

Someone had to do something to find her. What were my new abilities for if not to help those I love?

I heard Dad's car parking in the driveway. I called him to come home quickly for the meeting. I wanted everyone there. Mark and Alyssa had made sandwiches for everyone but no one was touching the food. Everyone was as anxious as I was.

Dad burst into the house and dropped his work bag near the door.

"What's going on, Karina? Why is everyone here?"

"I know where Mama is," I said to him, afraid that if I didn't say it out loud she would disappear again. Dad froze, his mouth gaping open.

"Where is she? How did you find her? Why didn't you call the police?"

"Patrick," Lolo said, walking toward my dad. "It's not that simple. Marie is being held captive by our enemy. The *manananggal*."

"Where?"

"At Jason's," I finally said, revealing one of the secrets I had been hiding from him. "His mother is a *manananggal*, and Lolo thinks he is one, too. They've been keeping her hostage all this time."

Dad walked away, running his hands through his hair. I felt a knot tightening in my stomach. He had dedicated the last three years to finding Mama and it turned out she wasn't that far away. I felt bad for keeping things from him, for being secretive about everything. The last thing I wanted to do was hurt Dad.

"So what now? What do we do?"

"We haven't gone that far ahead," I said.

"We may have something. It might work," Mark said. Everyone looked at him. He stood with confidence, something I rarely saw Mark do. He had a look usually reserved for when he was revealing one of his brilliant inventions to us.

"It is risky but it might just work," he continued. I saw Lolo nod at him. "We need to go at night. I know it's when the *manananggal* is most dangerous but we can't walk around with the clan leaders during the day."

"We?" Dad asked. "No, you kids are staying here. It's too dangerous." I knew that he would protest to us joining the rescue mission. It was his job as a parent to keep us safe, but the decision had been made.

"Dad, we are coming with you. Mark and Alyssa are coming, too. They've been working with me. They can help. And I don't have to tell you the things that I can do. If there is a good time for me to use my abilities, it is now, to rescue Mama."

Dad grimaced but didn't say anything. He knew I was right.

"As I was saying, we go at sundown. Karina can draw us a map of the place as she's been inside before. I can be the lookout. We've set up a camera to watch Jason's place. Once you're in, you can set up two more. I only have three earpieces to communicate with you guys so I'll give one to Karina and one to Hari Magatu. That way we can talk to each other."

I didn't even ask where he was getting all this gear from. Mark knew people from his line of "work"—the one that wasn't entirely legal. He told us about it vaguely one time, but we didn't press because we knew his family needed the money.

"What are you going to do?" I asked Alyssa.

"I'm the getaway car," she winked.

"We stay together, we watch each other's backs," Lolo said.

"Okay, let's get to work," I said, taking a paper and drawing the map.

Dad drove Mark and Alyssa to their place to get the equipment and Alyssa's mini van. I felt much better knowing that both my friends would not be with us when we go in. I wanted to stop Dad as well but I knew I wouldn't be able to.

THE GIRL BETWEEN TWO WORLDS

Being so close to saving Mama had renewed his hope, giving him a new bout of strength.

I walked upstairs to change to more comfortable clothes. When I came down, I heard hushed conversations somewhere in the kitchen. I walked quietly toward it, feeling guilty for eavesdropping. But then again, they wouldn't be whispering if they wanted to share their thoughts with everyone.

"For as long as I can remember, the King has never been as vulnerable as he is now. Even when his daughter ran away from our world, he has remained stoic and firm. He runs the kingdom like the person who ran away was just another Engkanto—and not his own flesh. He continues his reign for many years, acting like the royalty everyone has expected him to be. But in this world, he is different. When Karina ran away, I saw the fear and worry in his eyes even before I sensed it. His love for his granddaughter is so strong that it makes him vulnerable. This is something his enemies can easily use against him if they ever find out."

It was Serra talking to someone I couldn't see. I knew Lolo loved me but he could be so distant that I sometimes wondered if he really cared. The fact that Serra sensed this made me happy but also scared me. She was right, they could easily use me to take him down, especially since I was the weakest link. My powers were not as strong as the clan leaders' and Lolo's. But I wouldn't let that happen. No one else was getting hurt, not because of me.

"She is tougher than you think she is. I can sense her strength. Karina can take care of herself, I can assure you that," I heard the *kapre*'s voice say.

"I know she is strong, much stronger than she thinks she is, but I'm more worried about her affinity toward the *manananggal*'s son," Serra stressed.

My chest hurt after hearing Serra's doubts about me. It was right of her to think my feelings for Jason would get in the way. But I was certain about myself. I knew my allegiance would always be with my family.

I heard a car outside and I looked out the window to check. It was Alyssa and Mark.

Alyssa was dressed all in black and wore one of the UV gadgets around her wrist. Mark got out of the van and grabbed a huge bag.

They went inside the house, and Mark opened the bag on the dining table. We watched as he took out one thing after another. I was sure the clan leaders didn't know what all the gadgets were, but they kept quiet and waited for his instructions. Mark took out the cameras. They were tinier than I expected. It must have cost him a fortune. That would be, if he bought them.

"Find a place where you can stick this in where it won't stand out too much. A bird cage, a tree branch, a statue, or in a corner somewhere. Stick it then turn it on. That's it," he said.

He handed me the cameras then took out the two earpieces and gave it to me and Lolo. I attached it to my ear and Lolo copied what I did. After testing that they worked, Mark took out his laptop and fiddled with it before packing his equipment.

We piled into Alyssa's van, not saying anything. I saw that Dad was wearing one of Mark's gadgets and I gave him a small smile, grateful that at least he had something to protect himself with. The *kapre* and *tikbalang* were on foot as they didn't really fit in the van. By on foot, I meant they were jumping from tree to tree, barely shaking the trees despite their size.

"Are there any dogs there? Like guard dogs or attack dogs?" Alyssa turned to me.

"No, they don't have any dogs, or any pets for that matter," I said. There were plenty of houses without animals but it did seem bizarre that a house that grand had no guard dogs. I didn't think the *manananggal* worried about home invasions, given how powerful they were. They would probably just eat any poor bastard who would attempt to rob them.

We drove toward Jason's house, parking a couple of meters away. Kamudo and Gulat were already there waiting for us. Mark set himself up in the back of the van, giving Alyssa instructions. I hugged them both before leaving with the group. We walked around the block, staying in the shadows. I heard Mark's voice in my ear telling me to go around the corner to the next street. The mansion's land took up two blocks, making it easier for us to find the spot closest to the shed.

"Stop," Mark said. "That's the place. Start climbing."

None of us were using our powers tonight, not until we need to. We couldn't afford being detected before getting close to Mama. I pointed to the fence and signaled for them to climb over. Kamudo grabbed my dad before he could react and leaped over the fence effortlessly. Gulat took me by the waist and pushed himself up. For a second, it felt like we were flying. Then I felt the thud of his hooves on the ground inside Jason's familiar backyard. Serra, Yukoy, and Lolo climbed over the fence, not breaking a sweat.

Mark's instructions were perfect. We were standing behind the shed. I looked around for a good spot to attach the camera. I remembered the little owl statue near the guesthouse. I crawled toward it and inserted the camera in its mouth. I moved quickly back to the shed where Kamudo had already pulled the lock free. I found a spot between the cracks of the roof and stuck the second camera in there, turning it on.

We walked down the steps, trying to find our way in the dark. I heard a crack, then a neon glow stick came to life. Dad remembered to bring one tonight. He threw it in front of us, landing near the door at the bottom of the steps. I hurried down, trying to get to Mama as fast as I could.

The door was made of steel, solid and tight. The plan was to break down the door. We were going to be quick, in and out, before they sensed us. But before Kamudo could smash his way through, Dad stopped him and moved closer.

"Let me. We'll get more time if we're quiet," he whispered.

He grabbed something from his fanny pack. I didn't even realize he had it. He put on his cap, the one with the LED lights in front of it that he used when he was fixing things. Then I saw a small black case I had never seen before. He opened it to reveal a set of tiny silver instruments, almost like the ones the dentist uses. Dad took two of them and inserted them in the keyhole. I stared at him dumbfounded as he twisted the tools around, picking the lock. In my entire life, I never knew my dad could do this. He sometimes alluded to his wild youth but never really gave any specifics. I wondered how wild it actually was.

After what felt like hours, we finally heard a distinct click and the door opened. Dad stashed his tools back in the fanny pack and stepped in the dark before we could stop him. We heard him drop on the ground with a thud, groaning from the fall. I took the glow stick and threw it in. Dad was lying on the floor a couple of feet down, clutching his leg. I saw the steel ladder attached to the concrete wall under the door, and rushed down to help Dad. Everyone else jumped down without difficulty.

"Are you okay? Dad?"

"I'm okay. Go find her. Hurry," he said, still clutching his leg. Serra helped him sit up and I walked into the darkness. It was freezing and foul. I almost gagged at the smell of old blood and human excrement. How could someone survive being locked in here? I couldn't tell how big the room was so I took the neon light and threw it across the room. It bounced on the wall and dropped on the floor, next to a shape lying on the ground.

I let out a small gasp. She looked dead. It couldn't be her. She couldn't be dead. She couldn't be Mama. She was wearing the same nightgown, her three-year old nightgown. It was ragged, covered in dirt and what looked like blood. I didn't know how long I stayed like that, staring at her, frozen on the spot.

The woman on the floor moved her head, turned around and locked her familiar eyes with mine.

"Karina?" she said, brushing her tangled hair away from her face, the hair I had envied for so long and brushed so many times.

I ran to Mama, hugging her with all my might. She was alive. I felt her wince and I let go, afraid to hurt her. I knew she was hurt but in the dark, it wasn't easy to see just how much damage they had done to her. I called Kamudo and he swept her into his arms easily. Yukoy and Gulat helped my dad while Lolo led the way. Slowly, we crept back up into the backyard. We were close to the door when I heard Mark's voice in my ear.

"Karina, they're coming. It's not the *manananggal*. It's . . . it's something else. I can see three creatures. I don't know what they are but they're heading your way. Get ready."

I told everyone what Mark just said and they looked at each other. I saw the panic in Serra's eyes.

"She must have summoned the leaders of the dark clans," Lolo whispered. "If that's the case, we need to split up. You and Kamudo have to take your parents over the gate fast. We will distract them. Kamudo, can you carry both of them?"

He nodded before Dad could protest. I didn't know what the dark clans were like but if they were anything like the *manananggal*, I didn't want my parents to be anywhere near them. Kamudo held my parents, one on each side. I stared at their faces. If we survived, I would never waste a single moment with them again.

Lolo pushed the door open and ran ahead, away from where we were heading. We moved out next, Kamudo following me toward the fence. I smelled the stench of rotting flesh before I felt the fear inside of me, gripping my insides. They were very close. I didn't know how many but there was definitely more than one. I heard huge wings, screeches of a wild animal, and something else I couldn't understand. I turned around, trying to see where the sound was coming from but it was too dark. I said a silent prayer for Lolo.

We moved quickly toward the fence, finding the same spot we climbed before. We were a meter away when I saw him emerge from one of the trees. But it didn't look like him. Not my Jason. Not the guy I kissed that night in the front yard of my house, causing the flowers to bloom.

The thing in front of me was a monster. He was wearing jeans but he was far from being human. Dark veins rippled through his arms, down the length of his giant hands that ended with long sharp claws. His body was covered with spikes in different sizes, protruding out his back and chest. But it was his face, his lovely face, that was utterly disfigured. He had a snout, snarling, baring its jagged teeth. His eyes flashed red with anger. I could feel him wanting to kill us. I couldn't see the Jason I knew, but I could still sense a part of him. He was there, inside this hideous creature.

"Jason," I said, hoping he was listening to me. The beast snarled, drool coming out of its jaw. "I know you're there, Jason. I can feel you in there. I know you can feel me, too. Please, help us. I need you."

He growled, taking a step toward us. I didn't flinch. Instead, I moved toward him, extending my hand slowly.

"Remember me, Jason. Please. I know you care for me," I said, lifting my arm higher. He reacted to my movement and slashed my arm with his claw, ripping through my clothes. Blood trickled from my arm. It felt like a hot knife just sliced through it. The pain surprised me and tears started to blur my vision. I had never felt pain like that before. Once when I was five, I accidentally sliced my hand with a knife but it was only a small cut. This one stretched across my entire arm. I looked at him and he saw my tears. His eyes were Jason's again. He was staring at me with guilt and sadness, so much of it.

"Go!" he screamed. "Hurry!"

Before I could say anything, he leaped away, leaving me with my family. I felt a giant arm wrap around my waist, squeezing me against Mama. Kamudo leaped over the fence in one jump. I heard the screech of wheels as Alyssa stopped in front of us. Kamudo pushed all three of us inside the van and disappeared into the trees.

Alyssa sped away, leaving tire marks on the road. We were the only ones in the van and I started to panic.

"Where are the others?" I asked Mark.

"They're okay. They got away. I've told your grandfather we're heading back home."

I breathed a sigh of relief. The pain shot up my body. I almost forgot about my arm. My shirt was soaked with blood but it was hard to see in the dark. I could almost laugh at how ridiculous our situation was. A family of three, all wounded, bleeding, and probably maimed. But at least we were together again. Mama was holding on to Dad's hand, squeezing it tight. I smiled as I watched them. It was the last thing I remembered before everything went dark.

Chapter Nineteen

MAMA'S DIY
ENGKANTASIA BOOK

Wakwak

The wakwak takes humans at night as its prey, just like the manananggal. The wakwak can fly but it has no ability to separate its torso from its body. It prefers to hunt in rural areas.

The wakwak makes a sound by flapping its wings while flying. The wakwak's sound, which sounds like its name (waaak-waaak), also indicates that it is searching for victims. It rips and maims its victims and then feeds on their hearts.

The creature has long sharp talons and a pair of batlike wings. Its claws are used to slash victims to retrieve their hearts. A wakwak can also transform into a wolflike beast to disguise itself.

A dream. I knew it was a dream because I was extremely happy. Everything in my world had sorted itself out. My parents were smiling, sharing a private joke. My friends were playing around as usual. Jason had his arms around me. No one was sad, tortured, or in pain. A part of me never wanted to wake up and just remain in the happy little place in my head. But there was also a big part that was screaming to get out, forget this silly little fantasy, and sort things out in the real world. In the end, the realistic side won over and I woke up wincing from the pain in my arm.

Someone had cleaned up the blood and placed a clean bandage on it. The sun was already high in the sky. Another day at school missed, but who cared really? It wasn't like I could use my diploma as ruler of Engkantasia.

Last night's rescue mission rushed through my head. Mama in the underground cage, bloodied. Jason baring his teeth, his claws ripping my flesh. I wanted to cry. There was joy in finding Mama, but there was also sorrow in losing someone I had come to love. The problem was that I still loved him, despite what I had seen him turn into. Was it possible to be in love with a monster?

I headed to my parents' bedroom to find Mama. I could hear hushed conversations downstairs. Mama was lying on the bed, her eyes closed. She looked serene and beautiful. They must have tended to us last night after I passed out. I wanted to talk to her but I also wanted her to rest. I stood staring at her when she sensed me and opened her eyes.

"Mija," she said, extending her arms toward me. I ran to her, embracing her, smelling the familiar scent of my childhood. Tears rolled down my cheeks and I sobbed like a little girl. Great big sobs of joy and sorrow all rolling into one. Mama didn't say anything. She touched my back, caressed my hair like she used to when I was little. When I finally stopped crying, I looked at her and smiled. I could see the mother I lost three years ago. Age had caught up with her a bit while she'd been imprisoned but she still looked absolutely beautiful.

I traced the lines on her face with my fingertips, scars that were not there before. Her arms were the same. I could see healed wounds, big scars that lined from the top of her arm all the way to her back. I wanted to see how far the scar went but I also didn't want to see it. I wondered what they did to her down there. I wondered how much pain they put her through the last three years. She saw the pain in my eyes and took my hand, kissing it gently.

"Don't worry about that. They don't hurt anymore."

"But they did at some point," I said, choking back the tears that threatened to spill again.

"Your Lolo healed us as much as he could. There are still scars and some wounds and bruises, but not as severe as last night. We will heal faster. You'll see," Mama said.

"What did they want from you, Mama? Why did they keep you?" If they wanted to rid Engkantasia of an heir, they could have just killed Mama, then killed me. I didn't understand why they took her and kept her alive all these years.

She sat up and took both my hands into hers. She tucked my hair behind my ear, a familiar act that made me want to be four years old again.

"I gave myself up to them."

My brows furrowed, shocked at what she just said.

"You went with them willingly? But why?"

"I started sensing a presence days before I disappeared. I knew it was only a matter of time before they figured out about you and your powers. I wanted them to believe I was the last heir. Once they got rid of me, they would leave you alone."

"But that's not what happened. They kept you alive. Why?"

"They wanted to get my father here, in this realm. They thought keeping me alive would push him to cross the portal. But then your powers started to emerge and they sensed just how dangerous you can be to them. They wanted information from me. They wanted to know what kind of powers you have, how to defeat you, how to defeat us all. But I refused to tell them anything. I refused to summon my father here."

They. Meaning it wasn't only Mirasol who hurt my mother. Jason did, too. I didn't know if I could keep loving him after this. I knew I shouldn't.

"Why did they want Lolo here?"

"I don't know. It felt like a personal vendetta, something that Mirasol have against my father."

I wondered if it was a family grudge that made them want to kill Lolo. Or perhaps something else. Something unknown to us. I felt a tingling sensation at the base of my neck and realized the necklace was heating up. It wanted to be reunited with its owner. I took the necklace off and placed it around Mama's neck where it belonged.

"Why did you give me your powers? You could have escaped from them if you kept it."

"I had to protect you. I didn't have enough time to explain to you about your past. I hoped that my powers would protect you."

"Lolo protected me. The night when Mirasol followed us to Alyssa's house. He protected us."

Mama sighed. "I didn't think your Lolo would come. He never came to look for me so I didn't want to rely on him. All I wanted was to protect you, no matter the cost."

I wanted to ask Mama what they did to her. I wanted to ask who tortured her. I wanted to know if I could still save Jason, if there was a chance he could be saved.

"You can ask me, mija. I will tell you the truth," Mama said. Did she know how I felt about Mirasol's son? How could she when she had never even seen us together until last night? But I forgot that Mama wasn't a normal human mother.

"Did he hurt you?" I asked, wanting to take the words back the moment they came out.

Mama shook her head and relief flooded over me. "He's not like her. Even during moments when he wanted to impress her, I could sense that he wasn't. It was Mirasol who did all the work. She wanted the satisfaction of punishing her enemy. But she never got anything out."

"How did you survive for so long?"

"You and your dad kept me going. You are both my source of strength. My source of real power. Mirasol underestimated the power of my love for you, my resolve to protect you. She never understood that. She doesn't have that capacity to love."

I felt sad for Jason, growing up in a family without love. I couldn't imagine having parents who couldn't show affection to their own child.

"He can't help who he is, mija. He was created for one purpose alone, to destroy Mirasol's enemies. But I saw the changes in him when he started falling for you."

"How do you know that?"

"Although I don't have my powers anymore, I am still an *engkanto*. I can smell you around him. I knew he was sent out to get closer to you. But he never expected to feel something for you. He showed me little acts of kindness without his mother knowing. He fed me more, gave me more water to drink, things that would be easy to hide from Mirasol. He is afraid of her. Deeply afraid. Even without my powers it was easy to sense that."

My heart ached after hearing this. A life without a loving mother. What would that be like? I knew he cared for me. But was it enough to make him go against his own mother? Do I risk the safety of my family just to find this out?

"I want to save him, Ma. But I don't know how."

She sighed, squeezing my hands. "I know, mija. But . . . no one knows if he can be saved. Or how to do it if it was possible. He is the creature that my kind has been fearing for a very long time. Even if we save him, everyone in Engkantasia will want him dead."

There was nothing to say. She was right. I already knew this. But I wanted to have some hope. Letting us go last night was proof he could control what he was. Maybe he just needed someone to help him, motivate him to be good. But could I help him change a lifetime of indoctrination?

"Let's go have breakfast downstairs," I said, changing the topic. "I'm hungry."

We walked together, holding on to each other for support. I saw more scars on Mama's legs and her back as she moved slowly to the kitchen. I gritted my teeth to stop myself from saying anything.

The conversation stopped when they saw us. Dad came to Mama's side, taking her to her favorite chair in the dining room, the one with the extra cushion. He had already made brunch for us—bacon, eggs, mushrooms, and toast. A feast fit for Mama's homecoming.

No one talked as we dug into our plates. The clan leaders were scattered around the room, looking at us. Lolo's stare was transfixed on Mama. It was like being in a fishbowl. Finally, I couldn't stand the silence any longer.

"Where are Mark and Alyssa?" I asked Dad.

"They went home last night. They're probably still at school but they promised to drop by later."

"What did you say to the principal about my absence?"

"Well, that part wasn't hard. I told them the truth. That your mother is back and that we'd like to take some time together. You won't be going back to school until next week."

I felt glad not to have to go to school but also disappointed that I wouldn't have the chance to see Jason again until then. I knew I was being absolutely juvenile, thinking about Jason when everything was still up in the air. But I couldn't help it.

Lolo cleared his throat. "When you're finished, we need to discuss some things about last night. It seems that Mirasol has managed to make the dark clans cooperate. We may be facing more trouble than we anticipated."

We finished breakfast and headed to the living room. I sat between Dad and Mama. I was still afraid to take my eyes off her. I felt like she would disappear on me again if I blinked. Dad probably felt the same way. We gathered around Lolo as he told us what happened last night.

"As I feared, the *manananggal* has gathered the dark leaders to help eliminate us. We fought them last night and the only reason we made it out in time is because they did not anticipate one of Mark's contraptions."

A smile tugged on my face, knowing that my friends helped save the all-powerful leaders of Engkantasia. I never even heard Lolo mention Mark's name before. This was definitely a first. I made a mental note to let Mark know when I saw him next.

"As far as I can tell, they have four of the dark clans with them. I don't know how she has managed to keep them in line but this only means more danger for us. They have never been able to cooperate with each other and this is the first time it's happened."

"What kind of creatures are they, Lolo?" I asked. It was bad enough I had to fight Mirasol and Jason without four others to worry about, too.

Lolo waved his hand in the air to show me the creatures from last night. It still fascinated me how he could create a movie screen out of literally thin air.

"This is Yanuk, the leader of the *tiyanak* clan. You're already familiar with how feral they can be. Segunda is the queen of the *sigbin* clan," Lolo continued. She looked like a hornless goat with shorter hind legs, batlike wings, and a tail sharp enough to split things into two.

"Her mouth is designed not only to rip flesh. She also has a long tongue to suck blood. It is easy to tell when the *sigbin* is nearby as it smells like decaying carcass. A single spit from a *sigbin* can turn anyone's insides into goo."

All of them smelled like decaying something though. Even Jason.

"Nonok, the king of the Nuno sa Punso, is always eerily calm. He is guarded and suspicious. Humans sometimes mistake him for a dwarf because he looks like one. He sits on top of a mound of soil, invisible to humans, and if someone makes the mistake of kicking his 'home', he finds great pleasure in punishing them. Swollen feet, limbs, genitals and body parts, and vomiting of blood. They are capable of more horrendous punishments than that.

"Finally, this is Kurnula, the queen of the *wakwak* clan. Like the *manananggal*, the *wakwak* also has red eyes. The *manananggal* and *wakwak* clans are closely related, but there is a hatred between the clans that go back hundreds of years. Although similar in many ways, the *wakwak* can never turn into a beautiful human form. It is cursed to remain in it monstrous shape—with huge batlike wings, sharp talons, and a body covered in fine fur that could almost pass as human if not for the hideous head."

I sat there, staring at the images, afraid to say anything. The creatures I had been fascinated about all my life had turned into reality. I now understood why Mama never wanted me to read about her world. They were not just products of someone's imagination. They were real. And they had been hunting us through the years. What confidence I had over last night's successful rescue slowly started to fade.

I felt Mama's hand holding mine tightly. I thought she was just as scared of letting go of my hand as I was with hers. This was what she had been trying to protect me from. All the secrecy, the lying, hiding my identity all these years. It was because of this. What little anger I felt for her for lying to me quickly dissipated and was replaced with fear. Fear for my parents, my life, my friends' lives. It was becoming clear that I had dragged them into something much bigger than I originally thought.

Before I could ask Lolo about the plan, the doorbell rang. Everyone held their breath. We rarely have visitors but today was the worst time to have one. Lolo rushed the clan leaders into the garage as Dad walked to the door. He waited for a couple of seconds before opening it. My heart raced as I saw two cops standing outside.

"Hello officers, can I help you with something?" Dad asked, his voice an octave higher.

"Mr. Harris?" the tall officer asked.

"Yes, that's me."

"We got a phone call from your daughter's school. They said your wife has been found. We would like to have a word with her, if you don't mind," the shorter officer said.

"My wife is very tired. She needs to rest. If you can come back another time . . ."

"No, hun, that's fine," Mama cut in before Dad could close the door. I gave her a quizzical look. I didn't know what story they could tell the authorities but it definitely couldn't be the one that involved the *manananggal*.

Mama smiled to the officers and led them into the living room. They sat across Mama while Dad sat next to her on the couch. I stood at the back, listening to the conversation. Dad was as clueless as I was about Mama's plans. He was fidgeting with his hands, as nervous as I was.

"First of all, we're relieved to know you're okay, Mrs. Harris. It's very rare to find a missing person in such good health after disappearing for quite some time."

"Thank you," Mama said, still as graceful under pressure as ever.

"Can you tell us what happened to you? Start with the night you disappeared."

"It's all a blur. I remember getting out of bed late to take out the trash because I forgot to earlier that evening. I must have slipped on something and lost consciousness. When I woke up, I was somewhere else totally unfamiliar, and I couldn't remember anything except that I fell and hit my head. I just kept walking, begging for food, finding shelter where I can."

"For three years? Why didn't you go to the police for help?" the shorter officer asked, raising an eyebrow.

"I was too scared. I didn't know who I was. I didn't know if I was a fugitive, an illegal immigrant. So I wandered around, surviving on anything I can find. Until around two weeks ago when I started remembering things. Just fragments at first, flashes of images of my life."

"How did you get back here? How did you find your way?" the taller officer asked, immersed in my mother's fake story. I must admit I was quite impressed with how easily she weaved the lies together. She had had years of experience hiding the truth from everyone around her.

"I walked, hitched a ride, asked around for directions. I remember the location of our old house so I went there. That's where Karina found me yesterday afternoon, standing in front of our old house."

Did she see that in my head? My dreams of finding her standing in front of our old house, wondering why there were strangers living there?

"Yes," I chimed in, catching my mother's story. "I sometimes walk past our old house, just in case she comes back." I wasn't really lying. It had only been lately that I hadn't dropped by the old house because of the training sessions.

The other officer, the shorter one, still needed some convincing. "What about all your scars? How did you get them?"

Mama covered her face with her hand, holding back what sounded like a sniff. When she looked up, her eyes were teary. Her acting ability fascinated me. I almost believed she really was in distress. She focused her attention on the officer, almost mesmerizing him.

"Things didn't go smoothly all the time. I got into dangerous situations and had to fight my way out," she wiped away a tear then stared at the shorter officer. "Have you ever lived in the wild on your own? Not knowing anyone, not knowing who you are, not knowing where you come from? It takes something from you. Sometimes, you question if you're still even human."

That worked. The shorter officer swallowed and fidgeted with his notes, obviously uncomfortable being placed on the spot. The taller officer stood and nudged the other one.

"Thank you so much for your time, Mrs. Harris. Again, we're glad you're home safely. If there's anything else you want to tell us, please don't hesitate to give me a call," he said, handing Mama his card.

When they left, Mama turned around with a smile. "What?" she asked.

"I'm not sure if I should be proud or be scared of you," Dad said, finally speaking again. He'd been so quiet during the officers' visit. We finally realized just how good Mama was at hiding the truth.

She took his hand and mine, holding on to us as she spoke carefully. "The things I lied about in the past, it wasn't to hurt you. It was to protect you. My life here in the human world is only worth living because I have both of you. I would do anything to protect this family. Anything."

We hugged her as tightly as we possibly could. We believed her and understood why she did what she did. After what we had seen, we knew it was the only way. I wished we could go back to before Engkantasia, the innocence of not knowing the things we had to face, the things we had to do.

The clan leaders and Lolo walked back in the house. Lolo asked Mama to talk with him privately. I wanted to listen to what they were saying but I knew Mama needed this time with Lolo. It was the first time they had actually spoken to each other since Mama ran away from Engkantasia.

I used this time to clean myself up and change into something other than my pajamas. It was a good thing the sleeves hid the wound from the police officers. I didn't know how I would have been able to explain it to them. The pain was still there, throbbing and constant, but I could ignore it now. I put on fresh clothes and looked in the mirror. I felt naked without Mama's necklace but I knew it was back to where it truly belonged.

I heard Mark's and Alyssa's voices downstairs and rushed to see them. Mark had already set his laptop on the dining table surrounded by everyone else.

"What's going on? Why aren't you at school?"

"Your mother's back. We used that as an excuse to cut some classes today and it worked well," Mark smiled.

"We're looking at the footage from last night and this morning, to see if there's anything that can help us," Alyssa said. "How are you feeling?"

"Okay. It's not too bad," I said, taking a seat beside Mark. He showed us last night's fight from two angles. A shudder went through me, seeing the creatures Lolo was fighting with the clan leaders. They were vicious and relentless.

"We watched this several times last night, hoping we can pick something up," Alyssa started.

"And? Did you find anything?" I asked. Alyssa looked at me, hesitating for a bit.

"They mean business. See how they are all targeting the heads and throats?"

I nodded.

"They don't fight to maim, they fight to kill. I think they're making sure none of you guys ever go back to Engkantasia."

They wanted to take over everything. Not just the throne, but all the clans as well. And if they succeeded, it wouldn't stop there. They would definitely target the human world next.

"We are powerful in our own world, but here, we are quite vulnerable. We don't have the resources we need to strengthen ourselves," Pili said. "We can't consume flesh like they can. We need longer to recuperate in this world. And they know that."

Everyone fell quiet. How would we defeat enemies that were much stronger than us? Would we even have a chance to win this thing? I looked at Lolo, trying to read his mind. The situation had escalated and he knew that. The original plan was supposed to be just to train me, find Mama, and defeat the *manananggal*. Instead it had turned into a full-scale battle. One that would require more from me. I just hope I could deliver whatever it was they expected from me.

"I want to discuss matters with the adults and the clan leaders, if you don't mind," Lolo said. "I suggest you use this time to create more of those things we used last night," he looked at Mark.

Alyssa and Mark followed me to my bedroom, taking all their things with them. They looked tired but still seemed to be excited about things. Before I could ask Alyssa anything, she answered the question in my head.

"He wasn't there. I don't know if anyone noticed though because the whole school is buzzing with news of your mother coming back."

"What did you tell people?"

"The same as Mark. That we haven't seen you yet, we don't know the story and that's it."

I looked at Mark but his brows were furrowed, looking intently at his screen.

"What is it?" I asked. I sat next to him and looked at the loop he'd been playing since he got in the room. It was a footage of me confronting Jason last night when he slashed my arm.

"He didn't want to kill you," Mark said. A part of me already knew that, but it made me feel better knowing Mark agreed. "The other creatures were aiming for throats, heads, and hearts. There was nothing stopping Jason from doing the same to you but he didn't. He went for your arm instead."

"It doesn't matter," I said. "He can't stay in this world being what he is. And if he gets deported to Engkantasia, every clan and his dog will try to kill him."

"So you're just going to let him die?" Alyssa asked, surprised at my resignation.

"His life is beyond my control. I need to focus on what I can do. Right now, he's on his own."

No one said anything for a while. They knew this was a hard decision for me to make but what could I do? What could anyone do?

I changed the topic and told Mark about Lolo's mention of his UV bomb and how it saved them all last night. A big smile spread across his face. He took out his notepad from the backpack and showed it to us.

"I've been working on a new concept, similar to the one you place on your wrist. This one attaches to weapons—a stick, a sword, anything you can use to fight. You activate it and it just sends out UV rays constantly while you're fighting. It won't be enough to kill them but it'll be enough to distract and burn them, inflicting extra pain."

"How are you able to afford all this, Mark? Tell me it's not something illegal," I asked. He was far from financially stable which was why he was juggling two jobs. I wouldn't be able to take it if he got caught doing something illegal because of my problems.

"It's not illegal. There are other means of trade on the Internet that doesn't require money. Trust me, okay?" he smiled. I could only hope he was telling the truth.

Alyssa looked at her watch. "I need to go to training. Text me if you need to talk," she gave me a hug and rushed off. Mark left as well, to finish the new gadgets he conceptualized. I watched my friends leave and a pain shot through my chest. I was already missing them.

Chapter Twenty

June 2015
Channel 12 Breaking News

Three years after disappearing from her home in San Jose, Filipino migrant Marie Harris has finally returned.

At the moment, it is not clear what happened to Harris. Authorities are still conducting investigations, interviewing all members of Harris' family. However, according to our sources, Harris sustained several injuries when she returned.

This has been one of the most baffling cases the authorities have faced because of the lack of evidence as to Harris's whereabouts. In the three years of investigation, no clues were ever found. Harris's husband was a suspect at one point but the authorities have now cleared him of any charges.

I felt his presence before I saw him. Skulking in the dark like the monster that he was.

He was outside the house, waiting for me to come out. Every fiber of my being was rushing me to meet him, but logic dictated I should wake the elders. I could sense my Jason, but his *manananggal* side was there as well, hibernating with one eye open.

I walked as quietly as I could down the stairs, trying not to wake anyone up. I looked around the room. It was dark and I couldn't sense anyone. I reached for the door knob and gasped when I saw Serra standing in front of me. I looked at her, not saying a word, begging her to let me through.

She nodded but stayed outside to watch me talk to Jason. I was grateful that she was watching over me but also giving us enough space to talk.

I walked slowly, bracing myself for a possible attack. The closer I was to him, the more I felt it. The darkness was covering him like a fog. It was the same thing I felt when I sensed the *manananggal* outside Alyssa's window that night. Instead of being afraid, my heart broke into a million tiny pieces.

I didn't even notice the tears streaming down my face as I walked across the road. Nothing else mattered. All I wanted to do was hold him, hear him say that he truly loved me, and that I wasn't just a target. I stood in front of him, close enough to see the black veins coursing through his arms.

"You're not even trying to hide your real self anymore. So was everything just a plot to get to me? I was so naïve to fall for it so easily," I said, trying to sound brave, even if inside I was crumbling to pieces.

He just stood there staring at me. I couldn't read the expression on his face. I wanted to believe that maybe he did have some feelings for me. He let us go. Didn't that count for something?

"Why are you here? Did they send you to kill me? What are you waiting for then? I'm alone. No one is here to protect me."

More silence.

"Say something!" I said, slapping his face. He felt like solid marble, so unlike the gentle guy who made me feel protected. He caught my hand and held it to his face.

"I love you, Karina."

"What?" I couldn't breathe. His words took me by surprise. I searched his face to see if he was mocking me, but all I saw was his pain.

"I've never met anyone like you. A part of me is screaming to rip you to pieces, but there is also a part of me that wants to protect you from everything. I've never felt like this before."

I pulled my hand away from his face and stepped back. I wanted to cover my ears so I couldn't hear his lies but I couldn't stop myself from listening.

"All my life I've been trained and prepared for this moment. To have the chance to kill you and be rid of your clan. I have my orders. I know what needs to be done. But I'm having a hard time following my mother's commands."

"It was your mother that night, wasn't it? The one I saw flying back to your house wounded and bleeding," I asked even if I already knew the answer. Somehow I knew he wanted to tell me everything even if we were on the opposite sides of the war.

"Yes, that was her. She knows you have asked for the other clans' help and she is doing the same. The leaders of the dark clans are preparing to attack."

"Why are you telling me this?"

"Because I want to let you know that I don't want to do this. That I have fallen for you. But I can't change what I am. When I transform, I don't know if I can stop myself from hurting you, from killing those who are close to you."

I wanted to stop crying but the tears kept coming. "So you tell me you love me but you will still kill my family? How can that be love?"

"Karina, I'm sorry. I am so sorry. This is who I am. I can't change that," he pleaded.

My chest felt heavy, like my organs had been replaced with jagged rocks.

"You can't possibly understand what it's like to grow up not feeling any love from the one person who is supposed to love me unconditionally. When I was with your mother, I felt her love for you every time Mother questioned her. I felt how protective she was of you. I never had that. I never knew love. Not until I met you."

"I don't know how to help you," I whispered to him, closing the gap between us. I reached for his hand and he closed his own around mine.

"You can't help me. No one can help me, Karina. This is all I've known. This is all I am."

"No, that's not true." I pressed my face to his hand. The black veins disappeared. His hands were warm, gentle on my face. "I saw you last night. You could have killed me but you didn't. You stopped yourself."

"It took all my willpower to stop myself. I almost killed you," he said, looking at my bandaged arm.

"Jason, no . . . " I started to say but he cut me off.

"Listen, Karina, there's not much time. We are going to attack. I don't know when but tell your family to be ready."

"We? Are you joining them? Are you coming to kill us, too?" How could he be the enemy? How could he still go with them?

"My place is with them," he looked down, unable to look me in the eyes.

"That's not true. It doesn't have to be this way," I said, putting my hand on his chest, feeling the beat of his heart.

"No?" he said, pulling back. "Can you really tell me that your family, your clan leaders won't kill me if I join you? Can you guarantee that they will not execute me? Will they let us be together?"

I said nothing because there was truth in his words. He was a threat. He would always be a threat to the humans and to Engkantasia.

"It's your mother. It's not you. She made you into this. It's her fault," I said. If it wasn't for her, he could have turned out differently.

I felt his body stiffen as he pulled away. "It's not her fault," he said evenly, containing his anger. I knew I hit a nerve. No matter how bad Mirasol was, she was still the only family he knew.

"Ask your grandfather about my mother. Ask him what he did to her. What they all did to her. You can't just blame her for all of this," he said, his eyes reflecting my pain.

"I'm sorry," I told him, touching his face. I haven't been told the whole story. Yet, again. I wondered if Lolo would be honest enough to tell me what they did to make Mirasol hate them so much.

I felt Jason's arms around me, his heart beating fast. He smelled of citrus again, like that first day at school.

"I can protect you better if I stay with my mother and the dark clans," he whispered. "I'm sorry. For everything."

I knew what he was saying. It didn't matter what choice he made. In the end, he was still everyone's enemy. He was my enemy. He didn't come here to appease me. He came to say goodbye. He knew the next time we see each other would be when they attacked.

Jason kissed me, tenderly at first, then more urgent. I pulled him closer to me, trying to stop the pain that was eating me inside. I let my emotions flow freely as I touched his face. I felt his pain, too. I felt the love, the anger, the resentment, the hopelessness. He was resigned to the fact that only his death would make things right for me.

He pulled away and then was gone.

I sat on the ground on the side of the road, sobbing. I felt like my chest was on fire and something was eating my stomach. I had never felt so much pain in my life.

A peaceful presence engulfed me. I looked up to see Serra, extending her hand to help me up. We walked back to the house in silence and sat together in the living room for a long time.

"I understand why this hurts. But remember that this has never happened before. Not to you, not to him, not to us, not to anyone in Engkantasia. Who is the authority on love? Who says that enemies have to be enemies? Who says that a dark creature cannot fall in love?"

"But he can kill us all. How can I just ignore that?"

"He doesn't want to kill you or your family. But when he transforms, he loses his humanity. They become monsters, relying on instincts, with only one goal in mind—to win no matter what. It's not his fault he is like this. Remember that he is a product of decades of actions by his mother who wants nothing but to destroy us. He didn't ask for this."

"What am I supposed to do? I'm in love with a monster."

"I don't know. I really don't know. But I am certain that when the time comes, you will know the right thing to do," Serra said, hugging me.

I went to bed more troubled than ever. I hardly slept, and when I did, it was filled with dreams of Jason turning into a *manananggal* and eating my entire family while I wept on the floor, covered in their blood.

194

Chapter Twenty-One

San Francisco Tribune, June 2015
Missing Migrant Found: Amnesia Cause of Disappearance

It has been three years since new migrant Marie Harris disappeared from her home without a trace. While her sudden return has brought overwhelming joy to her family, police are questioning where she's been since she went missing.

Authorities are saying that Harris "sleep walked" the night she disappeared and "had an accident that caused her amnesia." Being new to the country, Harris lived like a nomad, moving from town to town and survived on small jobs.

The police interviewed Harris where she confirmed that her memory started returning only weeks before her return. However, since she is not familiar with the country, it took her a while to realize where she lived.

According to official reports, Harris has several old injuries all over her body. Although Harris can't remember what accident caused her amnesia, doctors are saying her old injuries are consistent with major trauma. The family has refused media interviews but has released a statement.

When I woke up, Mama was watching me sleep. She smiled as she tucked my hair behind my ear. She looked a lot better than yesterday. The dark circles under her eyes were fading and her skin was going back to its normal glow, like she was never tortured for three years. I sat up, still staring at her, almost doubting that she was actually here.

"Bad dreams?" she asked, touching my hand.

I nodded. I was afraid to say anything that might seem like a lie. I wondered if she could read my thoughts and feelings like Serra could.

"Jason?"

I nodded again. She could read my mind. But I didn't want to talk about him. There was nothing I could do. I had to focus on what I have to do to prepare for the attack. By now, Serra would have already told everyone about the plan against us.

"I know you're training today, but I'm hoping we can talk before you go. I'm sure you have a lot of questions for me."

She was right. I did have a thousand questions to ask her. But I didn't know where to start. Why did she run away? Why did she lie to us? Why did she decide to stay in the human world? Does she miss her old life? I decided to start with the most immediate ones.

"What happens after we close the veil?"

"Everyone goes back to their proper places, their proper realms. The *engkanto* will finally stop using the humans as playthings or food. Order will resume."

"Lolo told me about how I can't come back once I take over the throne."

Mama looked alarmed, like she wasn't expecting this at all.

"You're not going to Engkantasia, Karina. I won't allow it."

"But who will take over the throne? Lolo said it has to be from our bloodline, it has to be . . . " Then it hit me. I wasn't going because she was taking my place. Mama was going to go back with Lolo. She was going to disappear again. She was going to leave us again.

"There are creatures in Engkantasia who are not willing to be ruled by a half-being. The only good choice for both worlds is if I leave this one and take over my rightful place in Engkantasia. I'll have to marry an *engkanto* and forsake my own human marriage, which isn't considered a marriage in my people's eyes anyway. I'll have to produce an heir that is a purely untainted *engkanto*. That's my destiny and I have to accept it," she said, a tear rolling down her cheek.

What she said made sense. From a logical perspective, the original *engkanto* was the best person for the job. Except that she was my mother. My mother who I only found again two nights ago. I couldn't let her do this. I couldn't let her leave Dad again. It would crush him. I didn't know if he would be able to make it if Mama disappeared again.

"I'm going to talk to your Lolo about this," Mama said. "I want you to come with me."

I nodded. Maybe he could convince her not to do it. Maybe I could convince her to change her mind. I put on my training clothes and walked downstairs with Mama to find Lolo. We found him in the garden staring at a picture of me as a child. Mama sat down next to him.

"I didn't want this on you and your family," he said without looking at us. "As much as I want you back in our world, I also don't want to take you away from the life you've made for yourself. I understand why you want to stay. I understand why you left. But there is a greater need to fulfill, and sometimes we have to sacrifice ourselves for the greater good."

I had never seen my Lolo so defeated. He had always been so royal and stern, the epitome of a king. I looked at him and saw a human side that was not there before.

"I'm going home with you, Father. I'm taking my rightful place on the throne. I, too, understand why you had to do this. I can't let Karina do this. Her life is here. Mine is there with you," Mama said.

He looked at Mama, stunned by her words.

"Are you sure about this? You can never come back. You can never see your family again," he said, looking at us with tired eyes.

"I know but I've lived my life here. I've experienced so much and I can't let Karina pay for my mistakes. If I go with you now, we can immediately organize our army and force the dark clans to go back to our world."

He didn't say anything for a long time. I started to wonder whether he heard what Mama said.

"I'll call for a meeting with the leaders," he finally said. Lolo took Mama's hand and kissed it. "I'm so sorry, mija. I just wanted you to know that even though you ran away all those years ago, I've always been proud of you. You're the only one in our family who had the courage to find her own path. I hope you know how much I love you."

They hugged for the first time since Mama ran away. My heart melted and ached at the same time for what was about to come. There was always a downside no matter which decision we made. After getting her back, I didn't know how I would be able to let her go again.

Mama stood up to leave but I stayed with Lolo. I needed to know Mirasol's story. I didn't know what good it would do to my situation but I couldn't shake the pain in Jason's eyes.

"Lolo, tell me about Mirasol. Who is she? Do you know her?"

He hesitated, looking away before answering. "I've told you the *manananggal* and *Engkanto* have been enemies since the days of creation. Everyone in Engkantasia knows that. Both sides keep to themselves. We've always kept an eye out for the *manananggal*'s offsprings in the human world. It was no different when Mirasol was born.

"Arman, my right-hand man, was assigned to watch over her. Unlike other guardians in the past, he never judged the Manananggals. He watched Mirasol, making sure she did not become a threat to the kingdom. What I did not expect was for him to fall in love with her. I was confident that was never going to happen. It has never happened in the past. But Arman saw the kindness in Mirasol and he asked to see her in the human world."

Kindness? It was difficult for me to understand how such a monster could ever be kind. As if reading my mind, Lolo continued.

"Mirasol may have been born a monster but there was a point when she didn't want that curse. She fought it. She avoided killing humans. She tried to curb her hunger. But in the end, it was too much for her to fight on her own. For a while, she only fed on criminals but even then she still didn't feel right about killing a human being. Arman knew that about her."

Lolo showed me Mirasol's past, the first time she met Arman. An open field with the moon high in the sky. Her dress was covered in blood. The *engkanto*, Arman, was behind her.

"What do you want from me?" she asked him.

"Nothing. My name is Arman and I'm . . . "

"An engkanto, I know. And I presume you know what I am then? Why haven't you attacked me yet? Isn't that what an engkanto does?"

"Not all of us jump to conclusions. I know what you are but you're not from Engkantasia. In fact, you've never lived there, have you?"

"No, I was born in the human world because your good king banished my mother. I have no intention of going back there anyway. This world is my smorgasbord," she said, spitting her words.

"That's a shame. You probably would have liked it."

"I highly doubt it. From what I heard, the engkanto hunts creatures like us just to eliminate our clan once and for all. That doesn't sound to me like a very friendly place."

"Did your mother tell you that?"

She nodded, but looked uncertain.

"What your mother probably omitted was that the engkanto only retaliates when being attacked. We do our best to keep the peace among the clans. We leave the dark clans to do their own business on their side of the world. As long as they don't attack, everything is fine."

She said nothing, but her face softened.

"If your kingdom is so noble, why are creatures like me not allowed to go across? My mother's sins are not mine and it wasn't *my choice to be born in this world. Maita's descendants shouldn't be punished."*

"I thought you didn't want to go back?"

"I don't but I would like to have the freedom to choose," she replied sharply.

"Good point. I'll ask the King myself and let you know what he says."

"Did he really ask you, Lolo?" I asked as the image stopped.

He sighed and nodded.

"What did you tell him? Why couldn't Mirasol go back to Engkantasia?"

"I understood her point. However, the rules have been placed there for hundreds of years for a reason. Changing them or breaking them will end in chaos," Lolo said.

"Doesn't that sound like you're just washing your hands?" I asked, not wanting to anger Lolo but also confused as to why they just watched Mirasol deteriorate instead of find a way to help her out.

"Engkantasia is a different world, Karina. It is hard to explain our ways to you when you've never even seen it before," he said.

I tried to understand their ways but I didn't agree with a lot of it. "What happened to Mirasol and Arman?"

Lolo unfroze the images and I saw Arman again, with Mirasol in the human world. They looked like a normal couple in the beginning of a relationship, watching movies, dining together, laughing.

"He visited Mirasol often, even without permission from me or the council. He would sneak during times when he knew we were not watching the human world. And because he was tasked to watch Mirasol, he knew we wouldn't be watching them. It took a while before anyone found out."

There was a goodness in Mirasol and one *engkanto* saw it. He did something about it. He didn't just sit down and watched like everyone else. How did it end up so bad then?

"Arman never claimed to know how one would cope with such a curse. He never detested Mirasol for what she is. He accepted her, truly and fully. This scared us all. It scared me the most."

Lolo's pain was painted on his face, a heaviness from deep within. I could see that Arman was more than just Lolo's apprentice. He loved him like his own son. Digging all this up must be hard on him. Still, I needed to know everything.

"Months after disappearing from Engkantasia, Arman asked Mirasol to marry him. He gave her his healing ring, one forged with a rock from Engkantasia. It speeds up the healing process of whoever wears it and it is passed on by our ancestors within the family. It caused a great debate in the kingdom. I had to do something."

"What's so bad about them getting married?" I asked.

"The union would have bonded them. It meant they could be together here or in Engkantasia if they wanted to. Even I would not have been able to separate them. Although he was uncertain about our reaction, Arman returned to ask me for my blessing. The royal council was angry at what he did. They asked for his immediate exile or a more severe form of punishment. I spoke to him in private and he begged for my mercy."

Lolo paused, running his hand over his head, subtly wiping a tear away. I pretended not to notice it.

"I understood him. I knew he wasn't a traitor. I knew his intentions were pure. But my hands were tied. In the council's eyes, he betrayed the clan by running away to the human world and uniting with the enemy. He was exiled to the human world, stripped of his powers, never allowed to return to Engkantasia ever again, even if he ended the relationship. He never got to say goodbye to his family. The execution of his punishment was swift."

I felt my insides being crushed. At the same time, a seething anger ticked silently for Engkantasia's council. I was angry with Lolo, too. But I could see he had been punishing himself over the years for the decision he made a long time ago.

"Wasn't that a good thing for them though?" I said, hoping for a happy ending although I knew there wasn't one. "I mean, if he was exiled that meant they would be together in the human world."

Lolo nodded. "I hoped for the same thing. I wanted him exiled rather than imprisoned or killed. At least then he would have a chance of happiness. But it was too much for him to bear. All his life he had only known Engkantasia to be his home. It was where his family and friends lived and suddenly, he couldn't see any of them anymore."

"What did you do?"

"I watched him. That was all that I could do. I watched as he got worse. The healing ring helped heal him physically, but it couldn't lift his spirit. He deteriorated. He barely ate or slept. Until one day, Mirasol found him sitting on a chair, not breathing, cheeks covered in streaks of dried tears. It angered Mirasol. She blamed us. She blamed me for what happened to him."

I sat there quietly, unable to comfort Lolo. My anger boiled inside me slowly. The *engkanto* did this to their own kind even after Arman gave years of loyal service to the throne. They cast him aside like he was nothing. They broke his heart all because of their own fears and antiquated laws. In the end, all Lolo could do was watch.

Chapter Twenty-Two

Harris Family Statement

We would like to thank those who supported our efforts to look for Marie, even when everyone else had given up hope of finding her alive.

We are very happy to finally have her back with us and we request for some privacy at this very sensitive time in our lives.

We want to thank the Filipino-American community for their continued support. Now, our family is finally complete.

Lolo and the clan leaders decided against leaving this world immediately. They wanted me to finish my training to make sure I would be able to control my abilities after they had left. We spent the rest of the week training from morning till nightfall. Mark and Alyssa visited every day after school, bringing me schoolwork. Alyssa joined me with the fight sessions, learning from each other. Mark gave up trying to learn how to fight. Instead, he focused on perfecting the gadgets. We were always on alert, watching the videos we planted at Jason's house for any signs of attack.

I focused on everything on my plate, kept myself busy. But every item, every movement, every photo reminded me of Jason. I didn't hear from him after that night. I didn't know if the dark clans found out, if his mother punished or tortured him. I knew he was alive. I could feel it. In a way, I looked forward to their attack. At least I would see him again.

On my last day of training, I decided to go to school to pick up the contents of my locker. I didn't know why I was expecting to be treated differently now that Mama was back, but I was disappointed to find that the students at school still gave me a wide berth. I took out my things and waited for my friends outside.

Although I knew it was dangerous, I told my parents I would be walking home from school with Alyssa and Mark. Serra and the rest of the clan leaders set up checkpoints to ensure I got home safely but they kept their distance. We stopped by McDonalds for some ice cream cones and fries. By the time we headed for home, the sun was already setting, drowning the horizon with hues of orange and red.

We didn't talk much on the way home. I told them of Mama's decision to take on the throne. I mentioned the catch, too—that she could never come back. Already Engkantasia's scouts had been deployed to search for others that needed to be pulled back into their realm. Only the dark clans were left, including Mirasol. And Jason.

I shook my head, trying to stop myself from thinking about him. Mark and Alyssa were uncomfortable with what we were doing. There was an underlying fear with our afternoon out. So very unlike the carefree nights we used to have. They never left my side at school. They had both been carrying salt and ash in their bags after searching information on how to defeat our enemies.

According to some old folks, putting ash on the lower half of a *manananggal* would stop her from reconnecting with her body. It wouldn't kill her but when the sun rose and she was still disconnected, she would burn and die.

As for the salt, Google said if anything from Engkantasia ingested food with salt, it could never return to its world. If it were in its world and it ate something with salt, it would die.

But how would you convince a vicious monster to eat salty food? Throw salt and vinegar chips into its jagged mouth? Plus, how would you find the lower half of a *manananggal*? By the time you found it, the *manananggal* would have probably beaten you to it. It was futile, but it gave them a bit of confidence so I didn't say anything about it.

I was about to make some lame joke to lighten up the mood when I felt the familiar jolt. My senses told me there was danger nearby. I didn't know how many. All I knew was that I was suddenly very much aware of the threat. I looked up to see the Kapre king on alert. We were close to his post and he also sensed something was coming.

Before I could decide what to do next, I heard a woosh of something big aimed at our heads. I yanked Alyssa and Mark down on the ground with me just in time to see a huge goat-like creature coming toward us. It was either its tail or tongue that almost hit us.

"Get up, hurry!" I pulled my friends up and pushed them in the direction of my house, running through back roads. The sun had already set, leaving a strange blue hue in the sky. I turned around to see Kamudo behind us. I heard the thumping of large hooves behind Kamudo. From the sky there was a sound of large wings and a loud cry that sounded like a screeching birdcall.

Then I saw it. An ugly flying bat that looked like a *manananggal* except for its whole body. A sharp pain sliced my shoulder. The creature's talons ripped through my flesh. I fell on the ground, blood soaking my clothes. I had to get up, save my friends. I turned around. It was coming back to finish me off. Its long tongue whipped out, hitting Alyssa on the face. She screamed in pain and fell to the ground.

"No!" I swerved, raising my hands, aiming at the creature. A flash of light came out of my hands, hitting the monster in the chest, hurling it across the sky. I felt Kamudo's huge hands lifting the three of us, jumping from tree to tree until we reached my house. We fell on to each other, huddling together as the monster goat ran toward us. It hit the protective wall Lolo put up and screamed as its flesh burned. The creature whimpered away, snarling at us before disappearing into the darkness.

"Karina, are you okay?" Mama said, dashing out of the house.

"I'm fine, Mama, it's just a scratch. Help Alyssa first."

Kamudo picked up Alyssa and we walked inside the house, gathering in the living room. Mama closed the curtains and turned off the lights, protecting us from prying eyes in case they were still out there watching. The clan leaders gathered around us, healing our wounds. I looked over to Mark to make sure he was okay.

"Only scratches and bruises, don't worry," he said, managing a nervous smile.

Lolo sat down on the floor next to me, looking very concerned.

"What happened, Kamudo?" he asked the Kapre King.

"The attack was planned. It wasn't intended to kill her. They wanted to know how powerful she is and if she's a threat to them," Kamudo replied in his deep voice.

"Do you know who it was?" asked Serra.

"It was Segunda and Kurnula."

"They were the ones we caught on camera that night we saved your mother, weren't they?" Mark said. He had finally stopped shaking.

I nodded.

Lolo turned to my mother and asked her to take Mark and Alyssa to the kitchen.

"No, I'm staying here," Mark's raised voice was a surprise to everyone. He had been the most Zen one since all of the chaos started but after the attack I couldn't blame his outburst. "It's our lives, too. We almost died out there. I know you said they didn't target to kill Karina, but what about us? It seemed like they were fine making us collateral damage."

He was right. They wanted to see my reaction when they targeted Alyssa and I didn't hesitate to strike back. The attacks on my friends would have been fatal had I not intervened. Lolo stood to face everyone.

"The leaders of the dark clan will be attacking, probably tonight. We need to get ready. If anyone wants to leave, do so now." No one moved.

"Are all the dark clans friends or something?" Alyssa said, holding my hand.

"They were never friends and they will never be friends, but they know the threat and I assume they'll fight for the throne once the dust has settled," Serra said.

"I fear that there may be more dire news, your highness," Gulat remarked, approaching the group."

"What else have you heard?" Mama asked Gulat.

"I've heard from my sources that they are preparing to attack the palace. They've banded together in Engkantasia, waiting for the signal from their leaders in the human world. Once the word is out that we've been defeated, they will attack and take over the kingdom."

Pili, who had been silent for a while, approached Lolo. "Some elements from the light and dark clans have been looking into the human world, trying to assess the situation."

"And?" Lolo asked.

Pili sighed and looked at Mama. "The scariest rumor is that the male *manananggal*'s power is more developed than we initially thought. So much so that even the leaders of the dark clans fear him."

He was definitely alive. I didn't know whether to be scared or be proud of Jason. If they won, he'd certainly be chosen as king of Engkantasia. In a way, I didn't feel too bad about that happening. I felt the good in him, even when he was in monster form. But then again, how much control does his mother have over him?

"Father, we have to do this tonight. We know where they are. We're ready to do this. We need to finish this now before anything else happens," Mama pleaded with Lolo.

"You're right. We know where they are and we have the advantage of not being vulnerable in the sun. We leave close to dawn and attack them just when they're getting ready to rest," I said, feeling a great desire to pummel something to the ground.

"You're staying here with Alyssa and Mark," Mama said to me.

"No! It's either I come with you guys or I go on my own."

"We're not staying either," Alyssa said, wincing a bit from her wound. I admired my friends' resolve to help even if it meant the possibility of death. I understood why they wanted to help. This was their world, too. If we lose, they lose.

Mama hugged me, tears in her eyes. This was ripping our family apart and I was going to make sure I caused as much pain to our enemies as I could.

Lolo faced the group. He seemed so much more regal tonight.

"I know you all want to be part of this but I need you to listen and understand what is about to happen. These creatures are murderers. They will not hesitate to kill you when they get the chance. But they have vulnerabilities as well. Karina is right, the sun is our best weapon. We move in close to dawn and attack then. Serra will be able to sense where they are when we're close to their hideout. Her telepathic capability will show us where to go."

"I want you to create a circle of defence and aid each other in the fight. You five will take on the leaders of the dark clan," he said to the clan leaders. "Serra and Yukoy, there is a body of water near the house. Take them there and fight close to your source of strength. Karina, Marie, and I will take on Jason and his mother," Lolo said.

"What about me? I can't just sit here and do thing," Dad said.

"Patrick, I know you want to help your family but you need to be safe so they don't worry about you. This house is protected. Stay here with Karina's friends and make sure they are out of harm's way," he said. Before Mark and Alyssa could protest, Lolo turned to them.

"Your strength is in your minds. Use your technology to help us win this," he told them. Mark nodded, although Alyssa looked unconvinced.

"Take this as well," Lolo said, handing Dad a ring with a black rock. "This is a healing rock that my people use to heal humans afflicted with illnesses from Engkantasia. You will need this to heal us when we return. None of us will have the strength to use it by the end of the fight, so it's up to you."

Dad took the ring and shook Lolo's hand. That was the closest thing to affection that they had shown each other since Lolo came to our world. Maybe things were improving in a way.

"Prepare yourselves. We are leaving in a couple of hours. Gulat, send word to Engkantasia. Make sure they're prepared for whatever is coming," Lolo said before retiring to the garage. "Karina, come. We have much to do."

I followed Lolo to the garage with Mark and Alyssa. The last couple of weeks had been a blur of intense training, combining physical fights while channeling my abilities, summoning elements of the earth and using them as weapons in the fastest time possible. My powers had intensified in such a short span of time. Lolo said it was because of my emotions, although he was also not sure because he had never trained anyone like me before. He revealed that initially he thought my powers wouldn't be as strong since I wasn't a full *engkanto*, but it confused him when he realized how much I could do. I hoped it was enough to defeat them.

"How are you doing?" Lolo asked, interrupting my thoughts.

"I don't know."

I watched Mark and Alyssa going through the case of gadgets we stashed in the garage.

"You don't have to face him, Karina. I can handle this myself," Lolo said.

"You need my help and I need to do this. I can't keep denying that he is what he is. How do I defeat both of them? I don't know how powerful they are, especially together."

"I'm giving you a different task for tonight's attack. And I need you to remember my instructions clearly. This is crucial," Lolo sounded even more serious than before.

I nodded.

"The most certain way to kill a *manananggal* is by destroying its lower half. It's very hard to find and it's usually guarded by her minions. Your mother and I will be facing Jason and his mother. I need you to find her lower half and destroy it."

"How do I find it? How do I destroy it?"

"Humans always have a hard time finding the lower half of a *manananggal* because they don't have our power," Lolo said. "You have that now. You will be able to sense where it is and all you have to do is use your powers and burn it. Their lower half is not powerful like their torsos. It remains in human form and can be destroyed like you would a human. By burning it, you ensure it can never be reformed."

Lolo opened one of the drawers in the garage, taking out a thin branch-like stick engraved with signs I did not understand. Lolo gave it to me and it glowed in my hand.

"I made this from an old tree in Engkantasia. It was a gift I made to give to your mother before she left our world. But I think you'll need it more."

I took the piece of wood in my hand, feeling no weight at all. I felt a bit like Hermione from *Harry Potter* and although I was scared, I almost smiled at the thought.

"What does it do, Lolo?"

"It's a weapon that only works when used by our bloodline. You can transform it into any weapon you want, a sword, a spear, a bow, and arrow."

"Any weapon? What about a machine gun or nunchuck, or ninja stars?"

"I don't know what those things are so I'm unsure if it can be done. Just to be safe, you might want to stick to the weapons we've been using for training. Shall we try it?"

We spent the next two hours practicing with the stick from Engkantasia. It was an amazing creation. It turned into whatever weapon I needed, even a battleaxe. When I didn't need it anymore, it shrank back into an ordinary stick.

We all sat together around the fireplace after we finished with the training. Lolo said we needed to rest before we went out. I laid my head on Mama's lap while she stroked my hair like she used to when I was a little girl. It felt like my last moment with Mama.

211

Chapter Twenty-Three

MAMA'S DIY
ENGKANTASIA BOOK

Nuno sa Punso

The nuno sa punso is a goblin who lives underground and within lumps of soil. It can give humans who step on its shelter good luck or bad luck. Strange and sudden illnesses that befall humans are sometimes attributed by the superstitious to a nuno, and most of the time they are right. The nuno's spit is deadly to humans. It can use it to defend themselves.

The nuno can curse trespassers. People who arrogantly destroy the nuno's home and disrespect it become victims of curses. The curse can have the following symptoms:

Extreme body pain in focused areas of the body
Vomiting blood or puss
Urinating black liquid
Excessive hair growth on the back

I woke up on the couch with a blanket over me. Dad, Mark, and Alyssa were sleeping on the floor. Mama was sitting near the fireplace, staring at the dying embers. The silence in the house was eerie. I didn't feel secure being here even with the clan leaders watching over us. Somehow it felt wrong to

K.M. LEVIS

be just sitting around and waiting. I stood up to go outside for some fresh air.

"Mama, do you want to come out with me for a bit?"

"Sure, hun."

We stood outside watching the moon, our arms around each other. I remembered the time we used to do this when I was a kid. Mama didn't like parks and camping areas but to make up for it, we'd take our camping gear outside the house and slept under the stars in our backyard. It was so much fun that it became a family tradition. We'd build a campfire, roast marshmallows, and cook camp food. Mama made sure I didn't miss out on the experience because of her.

"I'll miss you, Ma."

"I'll miss you, too, baby, so much more than you will ever know. I'm so sorry for all this. I never meant for all of it to escalate this far. Had I known . . ."

"You wouldn't have done it?"

"I don't know. Because not running away would mean I would never have met your father, and I wouldn't have had you. And I can't *not* have you. You are my greatest achievement."

I hugged Mama like I had never hugged her before, because after that night I was never going to see her again. It was at that moment when I felt something in my chest, a tugging, a connection with my mother I never had before. I looked at her as she changed from my mother to her true *engkanto* form. Her skin flattened out the scars, removing the traces of three years of torture, evening out the creases around her eyes. Every strand of hair filled out, full and shiny, so black in the glimmer of the moonlight. I had never seen my mother so beautiful in my entire life. Mama looked regal and powerful.

"Mama, you look stunning," I gasped.

"I haven't changed in this form in a very long time. I guess your love just drew it out of me. I am so proud of you, Karina. No matter what happens tonight, remember that I will always love you."

213

I held Mama's hand and let my own feelings travel through her. It probably intensified our powers because suddenly my spider senses tingled. Mama felt it, too, and we both focused on where the danger was coming from. There was something closing in on us fast. We ran inside to where the others were waiting. The ground shook beneath us. Something was digging its way up. It was fast and powerful but we didn't know where it was going to end up.

"Get yourselves ready, we're being attacked. Patrick, take the kids to the garage. Karina, go with your father," Lolo instructed us. I grabbed Alyssa and Mark and ran to the garage, taking the stick out of my pocket. I slammed the door shut and took out several weapons from the cupboards that we had been using for practice. Dad took the sword, Alyssa the spear, and Mark opted for a smaller sword. It was a good thing we put our UV gadgets earlier on. We wouldn't have had the time to sort it out.

It was so ridiculous to think that only a couple of months ago, these same people had relatively peaceful lives. The image of us holding weapons we only saw in movies, hoping to save our lives and the human world, was utterly surreal. Ridiculous was an understatement.

Inside the house it sounded like all hell had broken loose. There were screams I had never heard before and howls of creatures not from this world. Serra's powers connected us so that Lolo could give us instructions without having to speak. They were drawing the enemies away from the garage. Everyone was moving out into the backyard. I hoped that Lolo's force field limited the sounds that escaped to our neighbors.

He was warning us that within moments, no one would be able to get out of the shield to ensure the fight didn't spill to our neighbors. Poor Mrs. Lindum would probably have a heart attack if she saw one of the creatures crawl onto her front yard.

"Dad, take Alyssa and Mark with you and get in the car. Drive away before the force field fully closes."

"No, I'm not leaving you here."

"Dad, please. We are putting my friends in danger. Lolo will be sealing us in and they won't be able to get out. I need you to do this for me. Please."

I knew he didn't want to leave me in the middle of the fight, but I also knew that he cared about my friends and that I was right about this. He took me in his arms and kissed my forehead.

"I love you. I have my cell phone with me, okay? Call me."

I nodded.

"I love you, too, daddy," I said before giving Alyssa and Mark a hug. They rushed to the front yard to get in Dad's car, but before they could reach it, Dad hit an invisible wall and slumped to the ground. They were locked in. It was too late.

I screamed for them to come back to the garage. I could protect them if they were inside. They ran toward me, helping Dad on his feet. Before they could reach the garage door, something emerged from the ground, like the undead, poking its claws out of the earth. I had never seen anything so hideous in my entire life. There was nothing left of the Jason I knew.

Then I heard it, the growl of a *manananggal*. His beautiful mother was equally as scary.

"It's good to finally see you face to face, King Magatu," Mirasol said. "So noble, so royal, but also so very useless. Where were you when your most loyal servant needed you? Tell me, did you defend Arman when he needed your help? You killed him. You killed your most loyal servant! You are not a noble King. You are weak and spineless!"

Lolo stared at Mirasol, unable to talk. I could feel his pain, the guilt he'd been carrying all these years. He blamed himself for Arman's death.

"I loved him like my own son. But the kingdom's rules are there for a reason. He knew the rules, he knew what was going to happen if he broke them. I am sorry he died away from his family. I did all I could to help him."

"Liar! You are the king! You could have done more! I will take from you what you took from me!"

Mirasol's long sharp tongue sliced through the air, aiming for my head. I moved out of the way in time but I saw blood coming out from a huge gash on my arm.

"Run, Karina, get away from here!" Mama screamed.

I pushed Alyssa, Dad, and Mark into the garage as I scampered after them. I turned to see Mama and Lolo aiming for Mirasol, throwing her up onto the force field and burning her flesh. I was grateful the shield only hurt the dark clans and not humans. She screamed in pain as she dropped from the sky. I heard the thumping of clawed feet behind me. It was Jason coming for his kill. Unlike his mother, Jason's body was fully formed. He had the hind legs of a horse but with sharp talons.

I heard Lolo in my head saying we needed to take the fight somewhere deserted. Keeping the force field sealed was draining him quickly. We had to take them somewhere far away. I thought of the old cemetery a couple of blocks from the local university. It was the perfect place for a fight in the middle of the night. Lolo saw the place in my head and prepared everyone.

In the blink of an eye, everyone found themselves in the middle of the graveyard.

The enemies were surprised by the unexpected teleportation and we took advantage of their confusion. The *kapre* pounded the *sigbin* to the ground, dropping a giant rock on it. Serra deafened the *wakwak* with her sonic wave, rendering it temporarily immobile. A *tiyanak* jumped onto Serra and bit her shoulder, stopping her mid-scream. But Yokoy came to her aid, stabbing the little critter in the chest. The *wakwak* jumped on the chance and slashed Serra with its sharp talons, sending the mermaid leader flying. I remembered the pond near the entrance of the cemetery and told Serra and Yokoy to make their way there.

I saw Gulat and Kamudo fighting the *nuno* and *sigbin* back to back. It was hard to get a hand on the *nuno* with it constantly disappearing in and out of the ground. Its spit burned Kamudo's leg, sending the big guy toppling down on some tombstones. Pili's powers enabled him to shield the ground so that the *nuno* couldn't dig down anymore. The two little men took on each other, jumping around so fast it was hard to follow their fight.

It was not looking like we were going to win. Mama and Lolo were barely hitting Mirasol and Jason who were honed in years of training. Lolo was still weak from the teleport and the enemies knew this. Mirasol had prepared for this moment far more than we have. She was convinced she was doing the right thing, avenging her love. She'd been driven by hatred and anger all these years and she was not about to let all her hard work amount to nothing. She managed to convince her only son that killing us all was the only thing that mattered, even if Jason had no reason to hate us.

Mirasol swiped her long tongue and grabbed Mama by the neck, choking her. Lolo zapped her wings on fire and she came crashing to the ground, releasing Mama's neck. I saw Mark setting up the UV lights, forming a circle around him, Alyssa, and my dad. They were fending off attacks, helping the other clan leaders with their own enemies. Mark turned on the UV lights, sending the creatures screaming away from them. Dad took several UV grenades from his fanny pack and threw some toward Serra and Yokoy. The grenades blasted the night with UV rays, burning the dark clans.

I sensed what Lolo intended to do next. He wanted to see inside Mirasol's head to find a way to defeat her. Mama heard this and pushed Mirasol back toward him. He held the back of Mirasol's head and entered her mind, showing all of us the memories in her head. We felt her pain, her love, her confusion, her anger. I was not used to this ability and my head throbbed in pain. I dropped to the ground, holding my head in agony. I didn't even notice the tears. I saw Mirasol. I felt her. So alone. She had been through so much. Her hate overwhelmed me.

But finally we also knew her secret.

Jason was Arman's son—not half-human like he was made to believe. He was half-*engkanto*, the son of one of the best and most loyal of the *engkanto*. He was half-light and half-dark. All his life he had been trained to transform into a weapon, a monster, a killing machine. He probably didn't know that he had other skills. That if he chose to, he could transform into something other than a killer.

I felt a searing pain on my back and turned to see Jason's claws dripping with my blood. I let my instincts kick in and fought back, sending him flying across the graveyard. He stood up quickly, and with one leap, landed beside me, slicing my chest with his talons. I fell back, blood dripping from my clothes. It was hard to breathe. The pain in my chest burned. Lolo saw Jason closing in on me and released a bolt of lightning on him, sending him flying away from me. I tried to get up, looking at how the others were doing.

Serra and Yukoy had managed to kill the *tiyanak* and were helping Gulat with the *wakwak*, tearing its limbs one by one. Kamudo and Pili were back to back, fighting the *sigbin* and the *nuno* together. Every single one of them was badly hurt, but they continued fighting the leaders of the dark clans.

Lolo instructed everyone to form the defensive circle to protect each other. I ran toward them to join the circle but a claw grabbed me from behind.

It was Jason squeezing my neck, digging his claws into my skin. I fumbled to find the stick in my pocket and turned it into a sword. I stabbed Jason hard on the arm. He let out a shriek, letting go of my neck. I slumped on the ground, coughing to catch my breath. Jason was trying to get up, and he started walking toward me, eyes blazing red with anger.

Instead of going to the circle with my mother and grandfather, I walked toward him. I heard Mama scream for me to join them, but I ignored her. I knew how I could reach Jason. He had to know the truth.

I stopped before reaching him and summoned huge roots from underground, wrapping around Jason's entire body. He fought the plant, slashing the roots with his arms and tongue. I made more vines and roots come out to hold him down. He struggled to claw out of the thick vines but I wrapped them tighter around his body. I moved toward him, close enough so he could see my face.

"Jason, listen to me. I know you're in there. I need you to know that you're not half-human. You are half-*engkanto*." He bared his jagged teeth, snarling at me, letting out an inhuman growl.

"Jason, please, listen to me. If you really cared for me, listen to me now. Turn back. Turn back into Jason and look into my eyes."

He growled and sneered, struggling even harder to get away. He swiped his long tongue and almost sliced my arm off. I pulled out another root to bind his snout together and forced him to look at me.

"Jason, you know me. I am Karina, remember? Remember what you said to me? You said you loved me, you said you don't want to hurt me. I saw the good in you, Jason. I believe there is some good in you."

I moved closer to him, ignoring Mama's protests in my head. I ignored the sound of fighting behind me, the wails of pain as dark clashed into light. It was like approaching a rabid animal. The clan leaders were trying to contain Mirasol and the others, pushing them as far away from me as possible. I didn't have much time. I needed Jason to sense me fast.

I looked at the sharp claws on Jason's monstrous arms, so different from the protective hand that caressed my cheeks. I reached out to touch his arm. He stared at me. His eyes were red, so different from Jason's blue hues. I gripped his arm and whispered to him, channeling everything in my heart so he felt it, too.

"Kill her, Jason, kill her now!" Mirasol screamed as she struggled to free herself from Lolo.

I focused on Jason and the thoughts and feelings I wanted him to have. I thought of the images I saw in Mirasol's head. I made him see her mother's smile, her mother's happiness, real and pure. I made him see his father and the love he shared with Mirasol. I thought of the love I felt for him, the memories we shared together. I showed him how I saw him when I was with him. "I love you," my head screamed.

"This is how I feel about you even after I've seen you like this. I know you're in there. I know you are. Fight it, Jason, come back to me. We are the same. We are both half-*engkanto*. Find your way back to me," I whispered to him, using everything I had to reach Jason.

He didn't transform back into Jason but he stopped struggling. His eyes registered a small recognition of who I was. I let the vines shrink back to release him. He fell to the ground then stood, towering over me. I stepped back, my heart pounding in my chest. I was scared but also hopeful that he somehow saw everything in my head. That he understood.

"Karina," he said, not in Jason's voice but still comforting.

I smiled at him and placed my hand in his, the huge claw of a *manananggal*. The sound of his voice startled the others. They all stopped fighting to stare at us, wondering what was going on. Mirasol wailed in anger and flew toward me in a blur. Jason pushed me behind him and blocked his mother, sending her crashing onto tombstones meters away.

"Mother, no!" Jason growled as he leaped toward Mirasol.

"Enough, Mother. You lied to me. You said I was made for this. That I can never be good because we are made to destroy. I am your son. I am not your pawn. She's done nothing to deserve this. I've done nothing to deserve this."

Mirasol recovered and hovered over Jason, swaying unsteadily in the air with half a wing missing. She screeched a deafening scream.

"Everything I've done I did to make sure you take over the throne in Engkantasia. This is all for you, Jason. Don't believe her. She is using her powers to manipulate your thoughts."

"This has never been for me. All of this has always been about you. I never wanted to live in Engkantasia. You never asked me what I wanted to do. You've only pushed what you wanted me to do with my life."

She flew down, pushing her face close to Jason's, hissing her words. The other dark clans slowly moved away, hiding themselves in the dark.

"You believe her over me? I nurtured you. I hunted for you. I taught you everything you know and you cast me aside for this little tramp?"

"Please, Mother, don't make me choose," Jason whispered.

I saw sadness in her eyes that vanished quickly, replaced by the familiar hatred and anger she held on to for years.

Mirasol growled and grabbed me from behind Jason. Her claws dug into my neck, making me gag. I gasped for air, trying to peel her off me, but she was too strong. I felt myself being pulled off the ground and my vision started to blur.

Before I could react, I heard Mirasol shriek in pain. I was falling fast, my body meeting the earth with a loud thud. Kamudo lifted me in his huge arms. I looked up to see Jason hanging off Mirasol's wing. She whirled around, slicing Jason's chest as he slashed her wing, sending Mirasol crashing on to a statue.

I staggered to where Jason fell. He had transformed back into his human form. The others gathered around us, forming a protective circle while our enemies stayed on their spot preparing to attack. Mirasol screamed at them as she struggled to get back up in the air.

"Kill them, kill them all!"

The leaders of the dark clans charged at us, coming out of the shadows as the fight resumed. I helped Jason to his feet. I hugged him and kissed him, letting go of all my fears.

"I love you," I said to him, burying myself in his arms.

"I love you," he whispered to me. Blood was dripping from the deep cuts on his chest. I saw Mirasol flying toward us in a mad zigzag, both claws aimed for my heart. Jason pushed me down and jumped to meet his mother's attack, sending them sliding on the ground across several tombstones. I ran toward them, screaming Jason's name. He was buried under a huge rock. His stomach had been ripped. There was dark blood everywhere.

One of his arms was in *manananggal* form, the one he used to fight off Mirasol. He was barely breathing. He was vulnerable in his human form, he knew that. Still, he risked his life to save mine.

Mirasol was a few meters away, transformed back into half her human form. She wasn't moving and there was a big hole in her chest. I looked at Jason's arm as it slowly transformed back into its human form. His hand opened. I saw his mother's still beating heart.

"I'm sorry, Mother. I'm so sorry. I didn't mean to. I'm sorry," Jason mumbled quietly, his eyes fluttering open, blood coming out of his mouth.

Jason gasped for air. More blood came out of his wounds. The leaders of the dark clans had run away after seeing Mirasol's dead body.

"Lolo, he's dying. Please do something! He can't die now. It's over. It's finally over."

"I can't, *mija*, I'm sorry. My powers cannot heal a *manananggal*."

"Try. For me, please try. He's half-*engkanto*, Lolo!"

I watched as Lolo tried to heal Jason, but nothing was happening. I remembered the healing stone. The one with Dad. It might work on Jason. Before I could call out, I saw Dad running toward us, the dark ring glinting in his hand.

Chapter Twenty-Four

Hey Diary,

This is it.

I'm not sure what to write down. I'm afraid to write down my thoughts. What if someone else reads this?

What is the right decision? What is the right thing to do?

Who knows the answers?

Is Mama's decision the right one?

My chest feels like someone is pulling out my heart. How long do I have to hurt like this?

I saw the familiar orange rays, swirling with red and yellow as the sun greeted us with another morning. Although I was exhausted beyond words, I couldn't sleep. So I stayed outside with everyone and watched the morning come.

I knew things were going to change for everyone. I sensed Lolo's confusion. What was once a clear line for him between right and wrong had blurred. He used to be so certain with what is black and what is white. Now he was questioning things more.

After the battle, Lolo sat down next to Mirasol's body. He took her hand into his and I felt his pain as he said goodbye.

"I'm so sorry," Lolo said, before he let her go.

I asked Lolo to let Jason bury all of Mirasol's remains under one of the giant trees in the graveyard. Although the others wanted to burn her body, I begged them for this one last favor.

Jason was going to be a tricky one to sort out for the royals. He was a new kind of *engkanto* who didn't fit in with the old laws of the kingdom, the laws they meticulously put in place so creatures like Jason never happened. I was apprehensive about what they would decide to do with him. I trusted that Lolo would see Jason as a victim of his mother's anger, honed in battle since the day he was born. Lolo believed he deserved a second chance. I knew that Lolo was doing this to make up for his role in Arman's death. But I knew others in Engkantasia would not see it that way.

I could sense Lolo's conflicted emotions about Mama's decision to take on the throne. He was torn between the needs of the kingdom and the happiness of his daughter. I hoped things would change in Engkantasia. They couldn't continue to bury their heads in the sand with the reality that their kind had spawned half-*engkanto* around the world. They couldn't ignore that half-creatures like me could become threats if we didn't help them discover their abilities and guide them to use it for good.

I heard my friends' quiet snoring, asleep on the grass. Mark's gadgets helped them survive the night. Even before the fight ended, Mark was already calculating the changes he needed to make to improve the weapons. I smiled as I watched them sleep.

Mama squeezed my hand. I put my head on her shoulder as she kissed the top of it.

"I am so proud of you," she whispered to me. "I used to sleep next to you when you were a baby because I was so afraid something would take you away from me. But after what you did, I feel a bit better about leaving, knowing that you can take care of yourself."

Dad came out and sat next to me. He took my hand, too, and I squeezed it tight.

"Thank you for saving him, Dad."

After the fight, Dad placed the ring on Jason's finger. I wasn't sure it was going to work, given the injuries he sustained from the attack. But I guess he wanted to live, to have a second chance.

He would have to go to Engkantasia, which scared me because there was a great chance other clans would try to kill him. I hoped I could convince them to let him stay in this world, where he would be safe. But I wasn't certain that was possible.

I felt his pain that night. I felt his desire to protect me from his mother. But I also knew that he didn't want to kill Mirasol. He just didn't have a choice at the moment. I would forever be grateful to him for saving my life. It was my turn to find a way to save his.

Chapter Twenty-Five

Rose Garden Private School Newsletter
From the Principal's Desk

As everyone knows, Karina Harris's mother has finally returned after going missing for three years. This is a wonderful time for Karina's family and we wish her all the best. Karina will not be attending term one next year to catch up on lost times with her family.

Understandably, the family is asking everyone to respect their privacy. To support this, I ask the students not to give interviews to the media. Let us respect the family's wishes.

"We're almost ready, hun," Mama called to me.

"Okay." I went through the family photos one last time.

"It's going to be okay. This is the right thing to do. You know I'll always be watching over you. Every now and then I'll check what you've been doing and send you a message. Just watch the trees and flowers out the back," Mama said, reaching for my hand.

"What about the other clan leaders out there? They ran away. We don't know where they are."

"Your Lolo's elite team have caught them over the week. The *nuno* was the hardest to find but they managed to catch it. They're already in prison as we speak."

"I still can't get over the images I saw in Mirasol's head, the plans she had for Jason after she takes over Engkantasia," I said, shuddering at the memory.

When Lolo read Mirasol's thoughts, we saw what she intended to do in Engkantasia. Mirasol figured out that in order to create male *manananggal*, the *manananggal* had to procreate with the *engkanto*. She was going to create her own army once she took over the throne and change the population in Engkantasia forever. She was going to use Jason as a stud, like a prized horse, making as many male *manananggal* as possible. She wanted to unleash her kind into Engkantasia and the human world, bearing an entire army with her as the queen. Jason was going to be her prince, following her orders until the day he died. Parenting at its worst.

"Ma, thank you for helping out with Jason's training. If you weren't going to Engkantasia, would you have continued helping him?" I could see the changes in Jason as we worked together to find his *engkanto* side. I was right. He wasn't all bad.

"Of course, mija. He is important to you and so he is important to me, too. Aside from that, I agree with what you're trying to do."

"I'm glad Lolo allowed Jason to stay in the human world. He will have a lot of explaining to do when he gets back."

"I know Jason's probably done a lot of damage to this world since the day he was born, but it's hard to totally blame him for everything when the only guidance he ever got was from Mirasol."

Mama held my hand and sensed my emotions. I looked into her eyes and saw sadness but also something else.

"I am proud of you, Mama. I know you'll be a great leader. I just know it," I told her.

"I've almost forgotten how strong your powers are now. One touch and you're suddenly a super empath. I don't think I was ever that good," she said, touching my cheek.

"I got it from you and Dad. I'll keep practicing too until I'm as good as Lolo."

I hugged Mama, letting the tears come as we said goodbye to each other.

"I won't be far from you, mija. Remember that."

"I love you, Mama."

"I love you, too, baby, always."

We walked together to the backyard, holding each other's hand. I was so afraid to let go. Outside, the mood shifted, like someone in the family had died. My heart was breaking into a million pieces. Dad looked like he hadn't slept in a year. Mark was looking so morose, comforting a crying Alyssa on his shoulder. We were outside with the clan leaders, Jason, Lolo, and Mama, looking at the portal slowly opening. Everyone said their goodbyes. Lolo gave me my healing ring in case I needed it in the future but I gave it to Dad instead. I wanted him to be safe.

I walked to Lolo and gave him a big hug. He hugged me back tightly. I wanted to think that I softened him up a bit. I was connected to him now. We would be forever bound by what we went through.

"Lolo, you are the best King for Engkantasia. Don't ever doubt yourself. Follow your gut even if everyone else thinks you're nuts. You've seen this world. You've experienced it yourself. If you feel you need to make changes, then make the changes."

"You are a very wise young woman," he said, kissing my forehead.

"I know," I smiled.

I hugged each of the clan leaders, thanking them for their help as they stepped into the portal one by one. I squeezed Lolo's hand as he entered into his kingdom.

I walked toward Dad and pulled him closer to Mama. I knew how painful things had been for them and it broke my heart to see them so miserable. I had always known what I needed to do. It probably wouldn't make sense to a lot of people. It didn't even make sense to me, but I was following my gut. I was trusting what I felt in my heart was the right thing to do.

"Dad, Mama, I want you to know you guys are the best parents in the world. I am what I am now because of you. I could never have asked for better parents, even if one of you isn't from this world."

Tears were blurring my vision as we hugged each other tightly. I kissed my parents and said goodbye.

"Goodbye?" Dad asked, puzzled.

I left letters for everyone I needed to say goodbye to—Jason, Alyssa, Mark, my parents. I hoped they would understand. I hoped they would be able to forgive me.

"I hope you understand why I have to do this," I said as I pushed Mama away from the portal and stepped in.

"No!" Mama screamed, trying to reach out to me.

"Karina!" I heard my friends scream, my mother crying as the portal closed.

Jason didn't say anything. I saw everything in his eyes—the shock, the love, the understanding of what needed to be done.

I heard their voices echoing further and further away as the portal disappeared. I turned around to find the clan leaders and Lolo staring at me. The portal had been sealed completely. No one in and no one out. Mama was supposed to be here, which meant there would be no more *engkanto* in the human world. But I guess I tricked them. I tricked them all. I knew I was in trouble and I only just got there.

I had always been certain that I didn't want Mama and Dad to be miserable. They deserved to be happy. Besides, wasn't this the best way to avoid homework for the rest of my life?

In the letter, I asked Mama to help Jason with his training. I knew they would help him. Mama was an *engkanto* princess. She would make the best trainer for him. I knew I would soon see the consequences of my impulsive action but if I kept busy with learning about this new world, I might just avoid a full nervous breakdown.

Epilogue

Jason

I had been visiting mother's grave frequently, bringing her flowers and talking to her. Was I trying to ask for forgiveness? Yes and no. I never meant to kill her. I wanted to stop her from hurting Karina. I wanted her to stop everything. It was the *manananggal*'s instinct that took over. I never meant to kill her. Never.

A part of me still hoped that in the end she was grateful I did what I did, that somehow I released her from the anger and hatred that took control of her life.

Mother did know how to love. I saw her life in my head when Karina showed me Mother's past. In her many decades as a *manananggal*, she fell in love twice. To me, that showed she was different from her mother and great-grandmother. But having no one there to support her and teach her how to love made it hard for her to move away from the dark side. I truly believe Mother loved me. In her own way, I knew she loved me.

It had been weeks since her death. I still remembered feeling her beating heart in my hand, fading away slowly. Even though Mother and I had the strangest relationship, I still felt like I had lost a limb after she died. Was that how a child would normally feel when their parent passed away?

My stepfather was inconsolable. He worshipped my mother since the day he met her. He buried himself in more work, traveling all over the world even more than he did before. I told him Mama ran away. That she said goodbye to me before she left, and never returned. It would be better this way. It was better to keep him in the dark about everything. He would send financial support, more than I needed to live on. Probably overcompensating for not being around. I didn't mind. It gave me a chance to change myself and discover my *engkanto* side. It also helped me get to know Karina's family even more, and experience what a loving family felt like.

I didn't know how long I'd continue visiting her. Our "conversations" in the cemetery were probably the only moments in my life when I had been totally honest with Mother about how I felt about the world, about who I was, and about her. I told her about the latest skills I had discovered and about what being half an *engkanto* meant.

I was still fighting the urges to kill and destroy. Every time I tried to converse with nature, it would take more effort for me not to use it to eliminate something. There had been several misses—like accidentally killing the mouse I was supposed to be communicating with. Because aside from the urge to destroy, there was also the urge to eat all living creatures. I didn't know if Mother would have been proud of what I was learning now. Maybe she'd be furious I was trying to stop my "natural" instincts.

I knew she was dead. I saw her die. But I still couldn't get myself to talk to her about Karina. It was a betrayal I couldn't let go. I hope she'd forgive me. I hope she'd understand.

I took the flowers out of the car and decided to refresh the wilting ones using my new skills, although I was not sure if Mother will appreciate that. Maybe she would. Maybe it would remind her of my real father.

No one knew where Mother was buried so I was really the only one who came to see her. I gave my stepdad one of mother's necklaces and told him she wanted him to have it. It was a lie, of course. She never really thought of him as anything else but a source of money. He'd never know we buried Mother under the big tree in this old cemetery.

I walked toward the old tree when I felt it. Another presence nearby. It was not human or *engkanto*. It was something else. Something dark and sinister. I looked around to see if anyone else was there. A shadow flickered through my vision. A woman with long dark hair standing over Mother's grave. Who was she? I couldn't see her face but I was close enough to smell her. She smelled like Mother, a musk of earth and grass, but with a stronger trace of iron. Blood? Was she a *manananggal*?

My instincts were telling me this woman was dangerous. I changed my arm into claws, as slowly and as quietly as I could so I would not be detected. But the woman sensed my transformation and turned around quickly, looking straight at me. I gasped at the face staring back at me.

The woman looked so much like Mother, the familiar nose and lips, the eyes filled with pride and hate. She was beautiful even with the creases around her eyes and mouth, and the scars that never quite healed right. She could easily be my mother in a couple of years if she was still alive. Her clothes were torn around the edges, fraying and tattered. Her dirty old rags and bare feet were a striking contrast to her creamy skin and silky hair.

"Who are you? What are you doing here?" I called out as I started running toward her. She looked at my claws and instantly turned around. She ran away from me, her steps steady on uneven ground. I ran after her but she was much quicker than I expected. She jumped the fence in one effortless move and disappeared in the bushes.

I followed her tracks, sniffing her scent but I lost her when I reached the train line. Did she jump on the train while it was passing by at full speed? That wasn't humanly possible but a *manananggal* could do it easily.

I walked back to Mother's grave to see if the old woman left anything behind. I knelt down and saw her footprints. There was nothing else there, nothing to indicate what she was or who she was. Nothing else but a smell on the soil, a very delicious familiar scent.

Blood. I gathered some soil from the ground and sniff it, inhaling the sweet aroma of the sustenance I once enjoyed so fully. Definitely blood. Had someone been pouring blood on my mother's grave?

I touched the ground where Mother was buried. It was probably unwise of us not to burn her corpse but I couldn't bear watching her burn. Ripping her heart out of her chest was painful enough. Burning her would have driven me mad with sorrow.

There was something stirring underneath me. Was there something else buried under there? There was definitely movement. Although it was not as strong, I could tell something was squirming, and it was something big.

And then I heard it. The faintest of heartbeats. I moved away. Impossible. How could there be a heartbeat under the ground? Mother could not possibly be alive.

I remembered something that night I was hurt. Karina's father brought a ring with him and placed it on my finger. King Magatu said it was a healing ring forged from the rocks of Engkantasia. The ring could heal anything. But could it bring someone back from the dead? It looked very similar to the ring Mother owned.

I remembered Mother's special ring, the one that looked so ordinary it could pass as a worthless trinket. She wore it on her finger all the time and never took it off. I was never even allowed to touch it. But I never noticed if she also wore it when she hunted at night. Surely the ring would not fit her hand when she transformed into a Manananggal? But if it was from Engkantasia, it could probably change itself to suit the owner's hand. Was Mother wearing it the night we attacked the *engkanto*? Could the ring repair the mangled body of a *manananggal*? A chill ran through my body. I couldn't leave without knowing what was under the ground.

I looked around to see if there were people in the cemetery. Thankfully, it was empty. The sun was already starting to set. Nightfall meant I would be cloaked in darkness. I sat on the ground waiting for the orange and reds of the horizon to fade.

I couldn't be seen digging with *mananangaal* arms, especially since I didn't really know what I was going to find under there. Was it a full moon tonight? I hoped not because if it was Mother coming back from the dead, I didn't want to be her food.

Finally, darkness fell. I rolled my sleeves up and transformed both of my arms into claws allowing me to dig Mother's grave faster. I got on my knees, focusing on getting the soil out of the way. Was I hearing my own heartbeat or was the heartbeat under the ground getting faster and faster? I felt the stirring again. This time it was much stronger. I stoped and moved back as the ground started to shift. Whatever it was that was coming out, it was determined to escape. I felt its desperation, its panic.

My heart was pounding in my chest, I could hear it ringing in my ears. My breath came in ragged gasps, every single vein in my body was tingling, screaming at me to run from the danger. But there was something familiar about the creature emerging from the ground. I knew the scent, the thoughts, the feelings. I knew even before I saw her come out of the grave.

"Mother?"

She turned around and adjusted her head so it was facing the right way.

"Hello, son. Would you like to give your mother a hug?"

Acknowledgments

This is my first ever traditionally published novel so there are a lot of people to thank. I have been working on this novel for around five years—not all five years straight since I do have a day job, a daughter, and a husband.

But I digress.

Thank you to Justin, my hubby who sees what I want to do and supports it, and Inara, my little girl who is fascinated and proud that I write books, even if it's not for her age group.

Thank you to my family, in the Philippines and in Australia. They do not seem to be surprised every time I tell them something new that I want to do.

Thank you to the SR7D, The Midnight Society, KGB, and friends from around the world who are my personal cheerleaders and PR people.

Thank you to my beta readers—Roanne Monte, Michelle Baltazar, Kristene Hekmi, Kat Mayo, Abby Lumsdaine, Claire Dy, Anastasia Tellis, Alexandra Eleftheriou, and Lisa Pennell. Your inputs have helped. A lot.

Thank you to Kriscia and Kitinn, my Sydney sisters, the first people I told my concept to while eating at a restaurant with belly dancers.

Thank you to Allison Tait, a clever and amazing author who always answers my questions even when she's on holiday.

Thank you to Anna Katrina Gutierrez, a brilliant editor who helped me reshape the manuscript with gentle guiding hands.

Thank you to Marrow Jerry Cabodel for the illustrations. Your artistic skills are beyond exceptional.

And a big thank you to the people at Anvil Publishing for giving me this amazing opportunity. You never forget your first.

QUESTIONS FOR CLASSROOM AND BOOK CLUB DISCUSSIONS

1. What was your experience while reading the book? Did the story capture you?

2. Which character do you find most interesting? Why?

3. What do you think about the concept of taking Filipino mythological creatures overseas?

4. What can you say about Karina's struggle? Do you think she made the right choice in the end?

5. Compare and contrast Karina and Jason. How are they similar? How are they different?

6. If you were Karina, which one will you choose—leave your world permanently to rule a kingdom you don't understand, or stay in your world and let Engkantasia fall? Why?

7. Based on Karina's state at the end of the book, how do you think she'll fare in Book Two?